# THE BRIDE WORE CONSTANT WHITE

## WHITE

### MYSTERIOUS DEVICES · BOOK ONE

SHELLEY ADINA

CH

Cover art by Jenny Zemanek at Seedlings Online.

Edited by Moonshell Books, Inc.

The Bride Wore Constant White / Shelley Adina—1st ed.

ISBN 978-1-939087-78-2

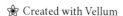 Created with Vellum

**Book 1 of the Mysterious Devices series of clockwork cozies set in the Magnificent Devices world!**

*A bride in search of safety. Young ladies in search of their father. A man in search of self-respect. But in the Wild West, you always find more than you're looking for...*

Margrethe Amelia Linden (Daisy to her friends) is a young woman of gentle upbringing, some talent as a watercolorist, and firm opinions that often get her into trouble. Determined to find her missing father, in the summer of 1895 she sets out for the last place he was seen: the Wild West. It's a rude shock when her younger sister stows away on the airship—such behavior no doubt the result of her unsuitable friendship with Maggie Polgarth and the Carrick House set.

On the journey, friendship blooms between Daisy and Miss Emma Makepeace, who is traveling to the Texican Territories as a mail-order bride. When Emma begs the girls to delay their search by a day or two in order to stand with her at the altar, Daisy is delighted to accept.

But the wedding day dawns on a dreadful discovery. Within hours the Texican Rangers have their man—but even in her grief, Daisy is convinced he cannot have killed her friend. She must right this terrible mistake before he hangs ... and before the real culprit realizes that two very observant young ladies are not going to allow him to get away with murder ...

> "Shelley Adina adds murder to her steampunk world for a mysteriously delicious brew! You'll love watching her intrepid heroine (and unexpected friends) bring justice to the Wild West while pursuing a quest of her own."
>
> —Victoria Thompson, bestselling author of *Murder in the Bowery*

Visit Shelley's website, www.shelleyadina.com, where you can sign up for her newsletter and be the first to know of new releases and special promotions. You'll also receive a free short story set in the Magnificent Devices world just for subscribing!

*For Paul and Renee and the fanchickens*
*who refused to let it be over*
*and with gratitude to*
*Victoria Thompson and Nancy Weatherley*

# PRAISE FOR SHELLEY ADINA

"I loved *The Bride Wore Constant White*. Shelley Adina has brilliantly combined steampunk with the 'clockwork cozy' in this series in which a young painter solves mysteries. Best of all, the novels feature familiar characters I love from her bestselling Magnificent Devices series. I can't wait for the next book!"

— NANCY WARREN, USA TODAY BESTSELLING AUTHOR

"This is the first in a series of well-reviewed books set in the steampunk world. For those who like the melding of Victorian culture with the fantastic fantasy of reality-bending science fiction, this one will be right up their alley."

— READERS' REALM, ON LADY OF DEVICES

"An immensely fun book in an immensely fun series with some excellent anti-sexist messages, a wonderful main character (one of my favourites in the genre) and a great sense of Victorian style and language that's both fun and beautiful to read."

— FANGS FOR THE FANTASY, ON MAGNIFICENT DEVICES

# THE BRIDE WORE CONSTANT WHITE

# CHAPTER 1

JULY 1895

*J*t is a truth universally acknowledged that a young woman of average looks, some talent, and no fortune must be in want of a husband, the latter to be foisted upon her at the earliest opportunity lest she become an embarrassment to her family. This had been depressingly borne in upon Miss Margrethe Amelia Linden, known to her family and her limited number of intimate friends as Daisy, well before the occasion of her twenty-first birthday.

"Certainly you cannot go to a ball, escorted or not," said her Aunt Jane. "You are not out of mourning for your dear mother. It would not be suitable. I am surprised that you have even brought it up, Daisy."

Daisy took a breath in order to defend herself, but her aunt forestalled her with a raised salad fork.

"No, I will invite a very few to lunch—including one or two suitable young men. Now that you have come into my sister's little bit of money, you will be slightly more attractive to a discerning person than, perhaps, you might have been before. Mr. Fetherstonehaugh, now. He still cherishes hopes of you, despite your appalling treatment of him. I insist on your considering him seriously. His father owns a manufactory of steambuses in Yorkshire, and he is the only boy in a family of five."

"I do not wish to be attractive to any of the gentlemen of our acquaintance, Aunt." *Particularly not to him.* "They lack gumption. To say nothing of chins."

This had earned her an expression meant to be crushing, but which only succeeded in making Aunt Jane look as though her lunch had not agreed with her.

"Your uncle and I wish to see you safely settled, dear," she said with admirable restraint.

Aunt Jane prided herself on her restraint under provocation. She had become rather more proud of it in the nearly two years since her sister had brought her two daughters to live under her roof, and then passed on to her heavenly reward herself. When one's sister's husband was known to have gone missing in foreign parts, one was also subject to impertinent remarks. Therefore, her restraint had reached heroic proportions.

"When you have been married fifty years, like our beloved Queen, you will know that a chin or lack thereof is hardly a consideration in a good husband—while a successful manufactory certainly is."

Daisy was not sure if Aunt Jane had meant to insult the prince, who from all accounts was still quite an attractive man. It was true that she could no more imagine Her Majesty without her beloved Albert than the sun without a moon. They had a scandalous number of children—nine!—and still the newspapers had reported that they had danced until dawn at Lord and Lady Dunsmuir's ball in London earlier in the week. Her Majesty was said to be prodigiously fond of dancing—between that and childbirth, she must be quite the athlete.

Daisy had never danced until dawn in her life, and doing so seemed as unlikely as having children.

Especially now.

For as of ten days ago, she was no longer a genteel spinster of Margaret's Buildings, Bath, but a woman of twenty-one years and independent means, having procured not only a letter of credit from her bank, but a ticket from Bath to London, and subsequently, passage aboard the packet to Paris, where she had boarded the transatlantic airship *Persephone* bound for New York.

"My goodness, you're so brave," breathed Emma Make-peace, her breakfast companion in the grand airship's dining saloon this morning, the third of their crossing. She had been listening with rapt attention, her spoonful of coddled egg halting in its fatal journey. "But at what point did you realize you were not alone?"

Daisy glanced at her younger sister, Frederica, who wisely did not lift her own attention from her plate, but continued to shovel in poached eggs, potatoes, and sliced ham glazed in orange sauce as though this were her last meal.

"As we were sailing over the Channel. At that point, my sister deemed it safe to reveal herself, since there would be no danger of my sending her back to our aunt and uncle." She gave a sigh. "We are committed to this adventure together, I am afraid."

"I certainly am," Freddie ventured. "I used all my savings

for the tickets, including what I could beg from Maggie Polgarth."

"Who is that?" Miss Makepeace asked, resuming her own breakfast with a delicate appetite. "One of your school friends?"

Freddie nodded. "Maggie and her cousin Elizabeth Seacombe are the wards of Lady Claire Malvern, of Carrick House in Belgravia."

"Oh, I have met Lady Claire. Isn't she lovely? What an unexpected pleasure it is to meet people acquainted with her."

While Daisy recovered from her own surprise at a reliable third party knowing people she had half believed to be imaginary, Freddie went on.

"With Lady Claire's encouragement, both Maggie and Lizzie own shares in the railroads *and* the Zeppelin Airship Works, though they are only eighteen—my own age. But that is beside the point." Another glance at Daisy, who had been caught by the deep golden color of the marmalade in her spoon.

If she were to paint a still life at this very moment, she would use lemon yellow, with a bit of burnt umber, and some scarlet lake—just a little—for the bits of orange peel embedded deep within.

"The point?" Miss Makepeace inquired, and Daisy came back to herself under their joint regard. It was up to her to redirect the course of the conversation.

"The point is that, having had some number of astonishing adventures—I have my doubts about the veracity of some of them—Miss Polgarth was all too forthcoming in her encouragement of my sister's desertion of her responsibilities to school and family."

"You deserted yours, too," Freddie pointed out. "Poor Mr. Fetherstonehaugh. He is not likely to recover his heart very soon."

"Oh dear." Miss Makepeace was one of those fortunate individuals who would never have to settle for the chinless and suitable of this world. For she was a young woman of considerable looks and some means, despite the absence of anyone resembling a chaperone or a lady's maid. Perhaps that individual kept herself to her cabin. Her clothes were not showy, but so beautiful they made Daisy ache inside—the pleats perfection, the colors becoming, the lace handmade. Clearly her time in Paris before boarding *Persephone* had been well spent in purchasing these delights.

Miss Makepeace had been blessed with hair the shade of melted caramel and what people called an "English skin." Daisy, being as English as anyone, had one too by default, but hers didn't have the perfect shades of a rose petal. Nor did her own blue eyes possess that deep tint verging on violet. At least Daisy's hair could be depended on—reddish-brown in some lights and with enough wave in it to make it easy to put up— unlike poor Freddie, who had inherited Mama's lawless dark curls. No one would be clamoring at the door to paint Daisy, but Miss Makepeace—oh, she was a horse of a different color.

She absolutely must persuade her to sit for a portrait in watercolors.

But talk of poor Mr. Fetherstonehaugh had brought the ghost of a smile to their companion's face, so Daisy thought it prudent not to abandon the subject of gentlemen just yet, despite its uncomfortable nature. They had been in the air for three days, and after the second day, had found one another convivial enough company that they had begun looking for each other at meals, and spending the afternoons together embroidering or (in Daisy's case) sketching. The lavish interiors of *Persephone* fairly begged to be painted in her travel journal. In all that time Daisy had not seen Miss Makepeace smile. Not a real one. But now, one had nearly trembled into life, and she would use Mr. Fetherstonehaugh ruthlessly if it meant coaxing it into full bloom.

"Have you ever been to Bath, Miss Makepeace?" she asked, spreading marmalade on the toast.

"Only once, when I was a girl," she said. "Papa's business keeps him in London and New York nearly exclusively, and after Mama passed away, I did not have a companion with whom to go to such places. I remember it being very beautiful," she said wistfully. "And at the bottom of the Royal Crescent is a gravel walk. I wondered if it could be the very one where Captain Wentworth and Anne Elliot walked after all was made plain between them."

Frederica, being of a literal turn of mind, blinked at her. "They were not real, Miss Makepeace."

The English skin colored a little. "I know. But it was a pretty fancy, for the time it took me to walk down the hill to the gate."

"Poor Mr. Fetherstonehaugh," Daisy said on a sigh. "He attempted to quote Jane Austen to me while we were dancing in the parlor of one of my aunt's acquaintance three weeks ago."

"That sounds most promising in a man," Miss Makepeace said.

"But it was the first sentences of *Pride and Prejudice*, Miss Makepeace." She leaned in. "And they were said in reference *to himself*."

To her delight, the smile she had been angling for blossomed into life. "Dear me. Miss Austen would be appalled."

"My sentiments exactly. And when he turned up on my aunt's doorstep the next morning proposing himself as the companion of my future life, I took my example from Elizabeth Bennet on the occasion of *her* first proposal. I fear the allusion was lost on him, however." She frowned. "He called me a heartless flirt."

Miss Makepeace covered her mouth with her napkin and Daisy could swear it was to muffle a giggle. "You are no such thing," she said when she could speak again. "I should say it was a near escape."

"Our aunt would not agree," Freddie put in. "She and my uncle have very strong feelings about indigent relations and their burden upon the pocketbook."

"Granted, it is not their fault their pocketbook is slender," Daisy conceded. "But that is no reason to push us on every gentleman who stops to smell the roses nodding over the wall."

"How do you come to be aboard *Persephone?*" Freddie asked their companion shyly.

She was not yet out, so had not had many opportunities to go about in company. Add to this a nearly paralyzing shyness —for reasons both sisters kept secret, and despite the misleading behavior of her hair—and it still astonished Daisy that she had had the gumption to follow her all the way to London with nothing but her second-best hat and a valise containing three changes of clothes, her diary, and a canvas driving coat against bad weather.

Now it was Miss Makepeace who leaned in, the lace

covering her fine bosom barely missing the marmalade on her own toast. "Can you keep a secret?"

"Oh, yes," Freddie said eagerly.

Which was quite true. Among other things, she had concealed from everyone—except perhaps that deplorable Maggie Polgarth—her plans to run away and accompany Daisy on her mission.

"I am what is known as a mail-order bride." Miss Makepeace sat back to enjoy the effect of this confidence on her companions.

"A what?" Freddie said after a moment, when no clarification seemed to be forthcoming.

"There is no such thing," Daisy said a little flatly. Well, it was better than sitting and gaping like a flounder.

"There I must contradict you." Miss Makepeace aligned her knife and fork in the middle of her plate, and the waiter, seeing this signal, whisked it away. "In the guise of a literary club, I have been meeting these last six months in London with a group of young ladies determined to make their own fortunes. An agency assisted us in finding the best matches of ability and temperament in places as far-flung as the Canadas and the Louisiana Territory."

"There are agencies for this sort of thing?" Daisy managed under the shock of this fresh information. It was lucky that Aunt Jane was as ignorant of these facts as Daisy herself had been until this moment, or heaven knew where Daisy might have been shipped off to by now.

And what was a young woman like Miss Makepeace, with every blessing of breeding and beauty, doing applying as a mail-order bride? It defied understanding.

Miss Makepeace nodded. "I have been writing to Mr. Bjorn Hansen, of Georgetown, for some months, and am convinced that he will make me a good husband." She touched the exceedingly modest diamond upon the fourth finger of her left hand. "He sent this in his last letter, and I sent my acceptance by return airship."

"My goodness," Freddie breathed. "I have never met a mail-order bride. I thought they only existed in the flickers— you know, like *Posted to Paradise*." She and Daisy had stood in the queue outside the nickelodeon on Milsom Street for half an hour to see that one, much to their aunt's disgust. But it had been so romantic!

"We are quite real, I assure you." Two dimples dented Miss Makepeace's cheeks. "My suit and veil are in my trunk. I will meet Mr. Hansen in person for the first time when I alight in Georgetown, and we will be married two days later in the First Presbyterian Church on Taos Street. It is all arranged."

"Where is Georgetown, exactly?" Daisy asked.

Not that it mattered—she and Frederica were bound for Santa Fe, on a quest that could not be postponed. Their father, Dr. Rudolph Linden, had been missing for nearly two years. Influenza had taken their mother last winter—hastened, Daisy was certain, by the anxiety and depression she had suffered after his mysterious disappearance. Now that she had reached her majority, Daisy was determined to take up the search where her mother had left off. And this time, if love and determination meant anything, she and Freddie would find him.

"It is in the northern reaches of the Texican Territories, in the mountains," Miss Makepeace explained in answer to her question. "From Denver, it is merely an hour west by train. It is said to be one of the loveliest towns in the territory—and certainly one of the richest. Silver, you know. It is surrounded by mines on every side, and has a bustling economy, I am told."

A young man who had been passing on the way to his table now hesitated next to theirs. "I do beg your pardon. Forgive me for intruding, but are you speaking of Georgetown?"

If Aunt Jane had been sitting opposite, Daisy had no doubt there would have been either the cut direct—or an invitation to breakfast if she thought the young man might be good husband material. But they were en route for a continent where one might stop and strike up a conversation without having to be formally introduced by a mutual acquaintance—or to give one's family antecedents back four generations.

"We are, sir. Do you know it?"

His square, honest face broke into a smile, and Daisy noted with interest the quality of the velvet lapels on his coat, and the fashionable leaf-brown color of his trousers—not the dull brown of earth, but the warmer tones of the forest in autumn.

"I am bound there as well. Please allow me to introduce myself. My name is Hugh Meriwether-Astor, originally from Philadelphia. I have recently bought a share in the Pelican mine."

"And are you going out to inspect your investment, or have you been there before?" Miss Makepeace asked.

"This is my first visit. I'm afraid I have an ulterior motive—that of escaping the bad temper of certain members of my family, who are not quite so conservative in their business dealings. I should like to get my hands dirty, and do a little excavating myself if I can, before I go back to law school. And you?"

As the eldest, and practically a married woman, Miss Makepeace made the introductions. Daisy noted that she did not vouchsafe any personal details of their voyage, she supposed because she had no personal observations of her future home to offer him. They parted with promises of seeing one another at the card tables after dinner, and the young man continued to his table by the viewing port.

"What a nice person," Frederica ventured. "He does not seem much older than you, Daisy, and yet he owns part of a mine. His family must be rather well off."

"If my facts are in order, he is closely connected to the Meriwether-Astor Manufacturing Works in Philadelphia," Miss Makepeace said in a low tone. Heaven forbid the young man should know they were discussing him. "Surely even in Bath you will have read in the papers about his cousin, Gloria Meriwether-Astor, who owns the company."

"It's a difficult name to miss," Daisy said. "Wasn't she the one who singlehandedly stopped a war in the Wild West and returned home in triumph with none other than a railroad baron's long-lost heir for a husband?"

Honestly, while it might have been quite true, it did sound like one of the sensational plots beloved of the flickers.

"I am sure it wasn't singlehandedly," Miss Makepeace said. "But I will say that the union of two such industrial fortunes made headlines in the Fifteen Colonies, and London and Zurich as well. It was all any of my father's cronies talked of at dinner for weeks."

"My friend Maggie knows her," Freddie said most unexpectedly. "Gloria, I mean. Mrs. Stanford Fremont."

"Nonsense," Daisy said. Honestly, she was becoming very tired of these references. "Another of that girl's absurd fabrications."

"It isn't!" Freddie drew back, affronted, and refused to speak for the rest of their meal.

There were some misfortunes for which one could only be thankful.

# CHAPTER 2

FRIDAY, JULY 26, 1895

*8:25 a.m.*
*Somewhere over the Atlantic*

*D*aisy's character did not allow her to indulge in wheedling and cajoling in order to get her way—such humiliating behavior—but in convincing Miss Makepeace to sit for a portrait she came very close to it.

Finally, Miss Makepeace agreed. "On the condition, mind you, that no one but yourself sees it," she told Daisy with an expression the latter could not quite read. It wasn't fear, exactly. That would be silly. But there was a certain amount of anxiety that could be put down to admirable feminine modesty.

"Certainly not," Daisy assured her. "It will remain in my sketchbook with the other memories of our voyage. And if I may importune you further—I hope you will honor me with your address before we part. I should like very much to correspond with you." She flushed, a little awkwardly. "I do not

13

have so many friends, you see, that I can afford to wave farewell to a new one without feeling the loss."

Now it was Miss Makepeace's turn to color under the compliment. "I was just thinking the same thing, and did not know how to ask. If we are to correspond, then you must call me Emma."

"And you must call me Daisy."

They shook on it, smiling, and before they landed in New York, the portrait was well on its way, aided by the relaxation and good cheer of friendship. However, when they transferred to a sleek blue and silver airship called *Swan* that looked as though it might have been military at one time, their sittings must perforce be interrupted by moving luggage and settling into new cabins. *Swan* was nowhere near as luxurious as *Persephone*, and could only take four passengers, the fourth being Mr. Hugh Meriwether-Astor. But the fare for passage was certainly reasonable, and Mr. Meriwether-Astor had recommended it.

"I am acquainted with the captain, you see." They had been looking at the lift schedules for the various ships bound for Denver and doing arithmetic in their heads as to distance times luggage weight times passage price. "We did not begin well, and she likely has no very high opinion of me, but Lady Hollys's skill as an aeronaut is very highly regarded in certain circles."

"*Swan* is captained by Lady Hollys?" Frederica had repeated in surprise. "Why, my friend Maggie Polgarth is an intimate friend of hers. Can it be the same lady?"

"You are a friend of Miss Polgarth?" It was Mr. Meriwether-Astor's turn to look surprised. *Staggered* would be a more accurate word. "How is it possible that this has not come up in our conversations?"

"I do not know. But until recently, she and I were class-mates," Freddie told him. "After we matriculated, she went on to university in Munich to study genetics, while I came home to—" She hesitated. "Bath. Until I decided to accompany my sister here. Daisy, this settles it."

Daisy was torn between glaring at the complicated sched-ules and responding to her sister's appeal.

Freddie's tone became urgent. "We must fly on *Swan* with Lady Hollys. And then perhaps you will not be so quick to judge someone else's adventures when they are corroborated by a woman of her standing. I read in the papers that because of her, Prince Albert changed the Admiralty's rules about female captains flying in the Royal Aeronautic Corps."

"I hardly see why that should matter to you," Daisy said, with some annoyance. Arithmetic always made her cross.

"It may matter if I choose some aspect of aeronautics for my career."

"For heaven's sake, Freddie—there is as much chance of that as of my being accepted to the Acadème de Beaux Arts in Paris. We have other matters to attend to now."

"But—"

Thank goodness Mr. Meriwether-Astor stepped in at this juncture with a remark about *Swan*'s speed and capacity, as posted on the lift schedule. It was less the captain that decided Daisy, and more the price of the fare, but now, as the land-scape scrolled away beneath them, she did not regret being inveigled into her choice. She had three days in which to finish her portrait of Emma—one day faster than the next fastest ship could have transported them to Denver. And though she would not have that time with her new friend, at least the search for Papa could begin a day sooner.

The sittings took place in Emma's cabin, which, while every bit as cramped as that of Daisy and Freddie, at least had the benefit of a larger viewing port that let in the light in a most satisfying way. Daisy had finished Emma's face and coiffure, which left only her shoulders and a hint of her clothes to paint.

"I wish you could paint me in my wedding suit," Emma said wistfully. "Your talent flatters me most unnecessarily, but I cannot help wishing I might change the terms of our agreement and give the portrait to Mr. Hansen for a wedding present. At the moment, I have only myself to give, you see."

"I am sure he would much rather have the original than a mere representation," Daisy said loyally.

"I hesitate to put on the entire ensemble, anyway. I feel as though I should be tempting fate."

Daisy lifted her head. "May I see it? The bodice, at least? For if you hung it on the closet door, I could see its details and simply add them in—you see how there is merely the idea of your torso so far." She turned her sketchbook to show her.

Emma's eyes sparkled. "You can do that?"

"Certainly. Call it … artistic license."

For only the second time during the voyage, Emma laughed. Then she opened her trunk, which was one of the expensive ones with wheels, designed to rest on one end and open out into a traveling closet. Swathed in a linen bag was her wedding suit. She left the rich camel-colored skirt and the short jacket trimmed in cream soutache upon the double hanger and gently lifted the lace bodice from its shroud to hang it on the closet door.

"Oh, how lovely," Daisy said on a sigh. She adored pretty things and simply couldn't afford them. "The lace and tucking all down the inset front—the flutter of lace on the sleeves—oh, I shall have just enough time to paint it before we moor!"

"I am at your disposal tomorrow," Emma told her. "But for now, we must dress for dinner. And you know how Sir Ian is about punctuality."

Since the number of their passengers was small, the captain, her husband, and the crew dined with them at the main table as though they were all family, rather than moving from table to table with each meal, as the officers had on *Persephone* with its fifty passengers. As Daisy packed up her brushes and cloths, returned to her own cabin, and gently laid her sketching journal open on the desk to dry, she realized that she was looking forward to dinner.

At home, she never did.

Between plans to marry her off and painful references to her mother and father, Daisy had come to regard meals as an ordeal that had to be got through so that one did not fall down in a faint from lack of nourishment. She had forgotten that they could be congenial affairs with lively conversation and amiable company.

On this occasion the menu consisted of roast beef with Yorkshire pudding, and instead of the usual root vegetables boiled to within an inch of their lives, it was served with a kind of pickled salad that Daisy found delicious, carrots glazed in butter and brown sugar, and rich, shining gravy.

Jake McTavish, a whipcord-thin and rather frightening individual who was the ship's navigator, succumbed to the flavors with a sigh. "Captain, can I just say again that hiring on young Charlie was inspired?"

Lady Hollys smiled at him with such affection that Daisy understood their friendship—for such it was, since no ordinary crew member would speak to a woman of her rank in such a manner—to be of long standing. "You say that every time he dishes up roast beef for us. But I understand why."

"Why?" Frederica asked before Daisy knew what she was about.

"Freddie!" she whispered. "That is clearly personal."

"Perhaps," Jake said, having somehow heard her, "but I am happy to answer. We had a very difficult childhood, you see. My half-brother and I lived as street sparrows in London for many years, eating what we could beg or steal. On cold winter nights, shivering together in warehouses or squats, some people might dream of castles and titles. But we would dream of roast beef and Yorkshire pudding. Charlie might only be fourteen, but he is no stranger to the street either. When you meet Lady Claire and Dr. Malvern, everything about your life tends to change."

Lady Claire Malvern. Here was that name again. The woman whose wedding reception at Hatley House the Queen had personally attended. In Bath, Daisy had read of it in the society pages with wonder.

"Did they take you in?" she asked.

Jake grinned a feral grin that hinted the street sparrow might not be as far from the surface as people thought. "We took the Lady in, more like," he said. "You've heard of the Arabian Bubble riots?"

"Oh, yes." Many of London's rich and not so rich had invested in the combustion engine several years before, and when the venture had failed—everyone knew that steam was the power that ran the world; what had they been thinking?—there had been riots in the streets.

"Her father, Viscount St. Ives, was one of the principal architects of the scheme," Sir Ian put in. "Sadly, he took his own life. The house was attacked and Lady Claire was forced to flee and find her own way. She was only seventeen at the time."

"Best thing that ever happened, though none of us thought so at first," Jake went on. "She gained control of the South Bank gangs and eventually we all became proper businessmen. And ladies," he added with a glance at the captain.

"I met her in the Territories." Lady Hollys took up the tale. "Air pirates captured the Dunsmuirs' ship, and in rescuing themselves, Claire and the family rescued me." She exchanged a smile of tender humor with Sir Ian. "Some rescues take longer than others, mind you."

Daisy had a feeling she was not talking about air pirates any more.

"Anyway, a meal like this is a tradition among us now," Lady Hollys went on. "We remember what was, and count our blessings." She squeezed her husband's hand. Daisy did not know what to expect of a baronet—cousin to one of the most powerful lords in England—at such displays of affection. But when he leaned in and kissed his wife, she blushed for both of them.

This would certainly never happen in Bath.

Perhaps that was why she was in the air, heading for the Wild West. Because what happened in Bath was no longer enough for her. Perhaps she ought to stop behaving like Aunt Jane, who had blushed for Daisy herself on many less emotional occasions, and begin counting her own blessings.

A longing that she had never felt before bloomed in her heart, the way pigment blooms on paper when it is too wet—spreading and forming its own shape regardless of the orderly lines of the sketch beneath. A longing for this kind of love, right here in the dining saloon. So unafraid of the opinions of others. So confident in its own rightness.

A glance showed her that Emma Makepeace was similarly affected, though with much more likelihood of actually achieving such a happy state. At least she was engaged to be married. Daisy was as far from it as *Swan* was above the surface of the earth. Some ancient knowledge deep within told her that the Fetherstonehaughs of this world were not capable of holding a woman in the regard with which Sir Ian held his wife.

By George, if she were ever to join her fortunes with a man, she would settle for nothing less.

"What brings you to the Wild West, three young ladies traveling alone?" Sir Ian asked.

"They are not alone," Mr. Meriwether-Astor pointed out. "I am accompanying them as far as Denver, at least. There I believe our paths will diverge, and Miss Makepeace has graciously allowed me to escort her on to Georgetown."

"Georgetown," Lady Hollys repeated. "Never been there, but I understand it's become quite the place since silver was discovered."

"So I understand. After the events of last January in which you and I were involved, I bought a share in the Pelican mine. I hope to improve my situation by spending the summer learning the ins and outs of a mining operation. One never knows when such knowledge might come in handy."

"The silver certainly might," Jake remarked.

"And you, Miss Makepeace?" Sir Ian said. "Do you have family there?"

She blushed, dropping her gaze to her plate. Daisy took pity on her. "She will," she said. "Miss Makepeace is traveling there to be married."

"Are you now," Lady Hollys exclaimed, pleased as only a woman happily married can be. "Why, our very best wishes to you. Ian, we must break out a bottle of champagne. This calls for a toast."

He went astern into the galley, and returned a moment later with a young man in a white apron and a bottle of champagne. With a pop of the cork, everyone's glass was filled, except for that of Emma, who declined.

"I never take spirits," she whispered. "But you are all so very kind."

They toasted her health—even the cook, who must be Charlie—and then they toasted him and his fine roast beef.

Daisy and Freddie, who had never had the opportunity to take spirits in their aunt's house, found the champagne quite the most delightful thing they had ever experienced. One glass was enough to make a person feel as though her head itself were filled with bubbles and bobbing gaily along the ceiling.

"When will the wedding be?" Lady Hollys asked, her blue eyes bright with interest.

"Two days after I arrive," Emma said shyly. "Which would be Friday, the second of August. How I wish you all might come!"

"That would be a very great honor," Sir Ian said with some gravity. "But I am afraid we are bound for Edmonton, that great city they call the Northern Light, for a similar occasion in my wife's family."

"My mother is getting married," the captain explained. "It's an occasion worth traversing half the world for, believe me."

"But that is not to say that the rest of us may not attend," said Mr. Meriwether-Astor to Emma with a smile.

"Yes—Daisy—I wonder if you might—" Emma began. Then she shook her head. "But I cannot ask it of you. I know you have an errand that cannot wait."

"Ask me what, dear?" Daisy said, tilting her head to look into Emma's eyes. "If it is in my power, I hope you know I will be happy to help."

Emma lifted her chin. "I suppose you can only decline, which is what I might expect in any case. I—I have no one to stand up with me, you see, save one of the mail-order brides who preceded me to Georgetown. But ours is a more congenial relationship, so I wonder if you and Freddie might—might be my bridesmaids? I would be so honored—but—your father—"

Freddie clutched Daisy's hand under the damask tablecloth. "Oh, Daisy, mightn't we?"

"Freddie, you know we are bound for Santa Fe," she said in a low tone. "I would like nothing more, but—"

"Papa has been missing for two years," Freddie reminded her in a whisper that could be heard all around the table. "I am sure that our search could begin on Monday instead of Friday with no difference to his current circumstances, whatever they are."

"Freddie!" She had never suspected her sister capable of saying such a thing. Her stomach churned, her heart pulled two ways. They had come so far to begin their search, given up so much. But oh, how badly she wanted to share such a lovely occasion with their friend!

"Your father is missing?" Lady Hollys asked, her gaze now filled with concern. "I know it is no business of ours, but we hear news from all over the continent, and have connections in many places. Perhaps we might have heard something that can be of use to you."

"I do not see how," Daisy said miserably. The last thing she wanted was to disappoint Emma ... yet ... perhaps if she were a little less reticent, Emma would understand. "Two years ago our family was in the Texican Territories, bound for Victoria in the Canadas. My father, Dr. Rudolph Linden, RSE, had been offered a position in the new university there, as dean of engineering."

"Most prestigious," Sir Ian murmured.

Daisy nodded. "So we thought, also. He had been teaching in Edinburgh, but with such a prospect for his career, he did not feel he could refuse. And it was an adventure. The Queen, you see, takes a special interest in the capital named for her, and there is a symphony, and several playhouses, and good society to be found there rivaling even that of your Northern Light."

"To say nothing of the gold," Jake put in.

"Quite so." One could not deny that supplying the gold miners in the north had made the city—and Her Majesty— rich. "We had stopped at a train siding somewhere west of Santa Fe to take on water, when we were set upon by a host of riders all in black."

Lady Hollys and Sir Ian straightened in alarm. Jake leaned in on one elbow. "Californios?"

"We found out later that it must have been. Once we

regained consciousness, it was to find that every man on the train had vanished, leaving the few females of the company in the naked desert to live or die as God willed."

"How dreadful," Emma whispered, pale with horror. "What did you do?"

"We flagged down the next eastbound freight and begged assistance," Daisy said. "My mother stayed nearly until the onset of winter searching fruitlessly for my father, to no avail. We ran out of funds and were forced to return to England, but she never stopped writing—to the Rangers, to the railroad offices, even to the Texican delegate in the crossroads city of Reno. No trace of him was ever found, and when the influenza swept through Bath last winter, she had no strength and no hope left with which to fight it." Daisy's mouth trembled, and Freddie took her hand, holding it tightly. "She died never knowing if our father was alive or dead."

Lady Hollys covered her mouth with her hand, her eyes full of—not sympathy, as one might have expected—but a dawning realization.

"I am so sorry," Sir Ian said. "What a terrible loss." He glanced at his wife. "Alice? A thought has just occurred to me. But surely—"

"It has occurred to me, too. What are the odds?" The captain's gaze locked with that of Daisy. "Your father—he was a man of considerable height? About the size of Sir Ian, but heavier?"

Daisy nodded. What a peculiar question at such a moment!

"And he spoke with a Prussian accent?" Sir Ian asked.

"Yes. He was born in Dresden and educated in Munich and Edinburgh."

"Dark hair going gray at the temples, and a scar across the back of his right hand?" Lady Hollys persisted.

Daisy felt the blood drain out of her face, and her skin went cold. "He was wounded in a duel as a young man. What do you know of my father? For he is the very man you describe."

"Great Caesar's ghost," Jake said. "Captain—you're not talking about Dutch, the man who was in the Californio gaol all those months, locked up with our friend Evan Douglas and the Viceroy's half-sister?"

*Gaol!* Daisy did not know who the other people were, but it did not matter. *Papa in gaol?*

"The man we said good-bye to in Reno in the spring," Sir Ian said.

"In April, to be exact," Lady Hollys said. "The last we saw of him, he was walking away into the dusk wearing one of the military greatcoats from this very ship."

"Walking … away? Not in gaol, then?" Daisy's heart was beating practically out of her chest and she could barely breathe.

"Yes." Lady Hollys's gaze moved from Daisy to Freddie. "He was heading off on foot to look for you."

# CHAPTER 3

## WEDNESDAY, JULY 31, 1895

*Approaching Denver, the Texican Territories*

*D*aisy gazed into her paintbox, but it was difficult to distinguish the colors when her tears blurred them together. Emma had postponed the sitting this morning because she was feeling indisposed, but if she had not, Daisy might have. Waves of happiness fought with troughs of complete despair. Add a sleepless night and the effects of the champagne into the mix, and she swung from one to the other with sickening effect.

But the portrait must be finished today no matter how momentous the news from last night. She must put aside her own emotions and finish what she had promised to do.

She had taken Emma a cup of tea and fetched the bridal bodice from her room. Now it hung on her own closet door while she painted it into Emma's portrait. She was glad she did not have to go into company. She wasn't fit to see anyone. Except Freddie, who sat upon the bed writing in her diary.

Painting would help. It always did. And this was so much lovelier and more challenging than teacups.

Constant White was the name of the pigment she was using for the blouse with its tucks and lace. The narrow shadows under the delicate filigree she had picked out with a touch of Payne's Gray and even Prussian Blue and a little Imperial Purple. Many watercolorists simply left the paper empty to indicate white, but Daisy's teacher—a spinster whose prodigious talent had gone unsung except among her admiring students—believed that if one wanted a rich white, one did not leave it up to the vagaries of the manufacturers of pressed paper. Instead of negative space, Constant White would reflect the beauty of the garment as a complement to and frame for its wearer's face.

By the time she had completed the shoulders with the triangular point of lace over the puffed sleeves, and a discreet portion of the tucked and lacy bust, Daisy had begun to recover. Her use of Prussian Blue had recalled the later events of last night, when Lady Hollys had taken her and Frederica back into the crew's quarters and shown them a coat similar to the one Papa had worn as he had faded into the desert twilight at the Reno airfield.

"Prussian Blue," she said now, into the silence of the cabin. "This *was* a military airship."

Freddie lifted her head and her pen ceased its scratching. "The color of that coat, you mean? I have just been writing about it. I wonder if he is still wearing it?"

"I wondered that myself. It is a distinctive color. Oh, Freddie," she said on a sigh. "Despite my efforts to distract myself, a decision still lies before us."

"It is no decision at all. You know my feelings on the subject."

"Yes. You wish us to postpone our search long enough to see Emma married."

"I have never been a bridesmaid, and neither have you. If you have any affection for her, you will support her and so will I."

"Our combined lack of experience is hardly relevant, dear."

"So you would embrace her at the foot of the gangway in Denver, wish her well, and choose a southbound airship with complete peace of mind?"

"I have no idea where to start. Santa Fe was our original destination, to pick up where Mama's efforts left off. Now, with this new information, would it not be sensible to go west to Reno, the last place Papa was seen?"

"But that was months ago," Freddie objected. "Even if he was on foot, Papa is a man of considerable resources. Lady Hollys said he was determined to search for us, so would he not retrace his steps to the place he last saw us—Santa Fe?"

That made two tick marks in the Santa Fe column.

But Freddie was not finished. "How can you leave Emma friendless as she begins her married life? Or deny me a chance to be a bridesmaid? You are always telling me I must widen my life experience, and now when I have the opportunity, you deny us both."

Daisy put down the tiny rigger brush with which she had been painting shadows, and clasped her stained hands on the rag covering her lap. "I only tell you that because Papa used to say it to us. Think of it, Freddie! As of four months ago, he was alive! That is more than I ever hoped for—a gift of incalculable value. If only Mama could have heard that news, too. If only we had not taken that train that fateful day …"

"If only Papa had not accepted the position …"

Her clasped hands tightened. "No, we must stop. Mama trod that hopeless road with all its signs reading *If Only*, and look where it took her. We cannot afford to do that. Papa is alive, and looking for us as well. We have every reason to rejoice. We will all be together again."

Freddie looked up at her from under her lashes. "I pray so. And meanwhile, the person opposite me, who has so few friends she can count them on one hand, now has one who has asked her to perform an office that only she can do. Will you really refuse her?"

Freddie could be so persistent. And so right. Daisy really didn't think she could refuse.

Naturally, Freddie saw it in her face. "You are not going to!" she crowed. "Oh, I am so glad. Now we will begin our search with a glow of happiness instead of loss."

"We must still face the loss. We must still say good-bye."

"But it will be tempered with goodwill and good memories, not regret." Freddie leaned over and kissed her, then looked down. "Is it finished?"

Daisy gazed at the portrait. "It is. If I do anything more, I will spoil it from too much fussing. But I will not give it to her yet. Mr. Meriwether-Astor says there is a daguerreotype studio in Georgetown. They may have a frame, and Emma will have something more substantial than a piece of paper to give her new husband on her wedding day."

She left the portrait to dry, and washed her brushes at the basin. The ship was too small to have its own steward, but a young midshipman named Benny delivered hot water each morning. She hoped he would not object to this use of the remainder.

"What do you think of Mr. Meriwether-Astor?" Freddie asked in such a casual tone that Daisy looked at her sharply. She was eighteen—a very impressionable age. So impressionable that in her own admiration for him, Mr. Meriwether-Astor's similar admiration for her friend Maggie might not have registered altogether.

"I think he is a most pleasant gentleman. I will be glad of his company if we are to go to Georgetown."

"He has a high regard for Maggie." Freddie glanced up. "Unlike some."

So Freddie had observed his partiality, then. Daisy hoped that would cool things down, since any tender feelings could not be reciprocated.

"I am revising my opinions of your Miss Polgarth," she said steadily, removing the false sleeves that protected those of her tucked linen waist from splatters of paint. "With the additional accounts of Mr. Meriwether-Astor and Lady Hollys, I may even owe her an apology, should I ever meet her."

Freddie's smile held satisfaction. "That is one thing I appreciate about you, Daisy. Many things drive me to distraction, but at least you are gracious when you're in the wrong."

"Thank you so much," she said dryly. "Now do pack up your things. I must go check on Miss Makepeace. We are to moor at four o'clock, and if she is not well she may need assistance."

Emma, it turned out, had recovered from her indisposition, and was overcome with embarrassment at having caused Daisy any trouble. The three of them took luncheon together, and then between packing and preparations for landing, and watching the landing itself from the viewing ports, the afternoon quite disappeared.

"Goodness," Daisy breathed. "Look at the mountains. I have never seen anything like them."

"I have seen the Alps, but they look altogether different," Emma agreed. "There is the mooring mast rolling out to meet us. We shall be on the ground in a moment."

While Mr. Meriwether-Astor arranged for themselves, Emma's trunk, and the valises to be transported from the airfield to Union Station some distance away, Daisy and Freddie took their leave of *Swan* and her crew.

"I can never thank you enough for telling me of my father," she said to Lady Hollys, who looked anything but aristocratic in canvas pants, a flight jacket, and boots, with airmen's goggles sitting on top of blond curls as unruly as Freddie's. "We have determined to begin our search in Santa Fe after the wedding. Even on foot, it is likely that he would make for the last place he saw us."

Lady Hollys hugged her. "I believe you are right. We must stay in touch. Here are the call numbers for *Swan*. Send a pigeon when you find him. Or if there is any help we can give you." She gave Daisy a card on which the magnetic code that guided the mechanical pigeons had been scribbled in pencil. "But where may we reach you?"

Daisy thought for a moment. "The Texican Ranger detachment in Santa Fe, I suppose."

Lady Hollys hesitated for the briefest second, as though the thought of the Rangers was somehow disturbing. "Not the post office?"

"Oh, of course." Daisy shook her head at herself. "How silly of me. Of course there is a post office in the capital of the Territories, isn't there?"

"At least it isn't a sack on the back of a wandering friar, as we've seen in some places," Sir Ian remarked, shaking her hand. "Good luck to you. I hope you find your father. Our acquaintance was brief, but he seemed a fine and honorable man. We will keep our ears and eyes open for news of him, as well, and notify you immediately."

Daisy's throat closed with so much gratitude she could barely muster a reply. It had been a very long time since anyone had spoken of Papa as a real and living being. The words were like raindrops falling on parched ground.

And then they were being chivvied on to a steambus, which took them to the train, which left an hour later, bearing them west at a pace that made the mountains seem to rear up out of the plains with unexpected speed.

"How beautiful it is!" Freddie was pressed to the window as they wound between the peaks. "When will we get there? Where is the town?"

No sooner were the words out of her mouth than the train emerged onto a trestle so high and spindly that it seemed as though its trembling length could never support a single human being, much less a fully loaded steam train and its coaches. Freddie squeaked and gripped the bench on which she sat, frozen into immobility by terror. Daisy couldn't have spoken if she tried—not until the train made its way across the deep notch of the valley, curved around, and pulled into the station with great billows of steam and an ear-splitting whistle.

"Whether this is Georgetown or not," Emma said, her

voice trembling, "I am getting off this train. I do not think I can cross that trestle again."

Mr. Meriwether-Astor was already gathering up his coat, and handed her reticule to her with a bow. "It is indeed, Miss Makepeace. And if this is to be your home, you may never want to leave it again in truth. I have never seen such scenery —and I have traveled around the world."

Once again he proved his worth as an escort and a gentleman, securing them passage on a peculiar vehicle that seemed to be an old-fashioned freight wagon tacked on to the rear of a steambus. But since the station was some two miles up the side of a mountain from the town, Daisy was not about to complain about its looks, as long as it functioned.

"Mr. Hansen is not here?" Daisy inquired quietly as the equipage rattled down the hill. "I had hoped to meet him when we got off the train."

"I sent a note telling him our arrival time while we were waiting in Denver, but perhaps it was not delivered in time. I did not think to send a pigeon from *Swan*." Emma's chagrin showed on her face. "So I will depend on our other arrangements—he has engaged rooms at the Hotel de Paris, and we are to have dinner there this evening."

"Oh, that is much better," Daisy said encouragingly. "You will have a chance to refresh yourself and change, so that upon your first meeting you will look your very best. I am so glad you are feeling better."

"I am, too," Emma said. "Oh my." Her voice dropped to a whisper. "Look at that woman on the steps of that establishment to our left. She is wearing only a corset! And those two men in the caps and goggles—they seem to be fighting over her!"

Daisy barely had time to avert Freddie's gaze with a ruse. It appeared that the section of town devoted to drink and bad behavior was here at the bottom of the hill. Once they rattled across the bridge over a wide, fast-flowing creek, the character of the place changed. Here were tall buildings with elegant cornices, painted in the most fashionable colors. Here were restaurants and business establishments, a hostelry, even a tearoom. The streets themselves were busy with horse-drawn wagons, people on horseback, and very occasionally a steam landau or bus, clearly inventions that had not come into such common use as they enjoyed already in England and Europe. People wearing everything from day dresses and suits to the goggles and caps of men who must be miners crowded the boardwalks, raised, Daisy supposed, because the packed dirt streets would become a morass of mud should it rain or snow.

The steam wagon climbed a rise and pulled up in front of an elegant high building. "Hotel de Paris," he said, pronouncing it as it was written, not as Daisy had heard the word said at home by her mother—*Paree*.

"Goodness, what is that?" Emma pointed up the hill, where an enormous tower dominated the view, connected by lines to a smaller building. From here, a block away, they could hear a sustained, crackling buzz over a subterranean rumble.

"That's Mr. Nicola Tesla's power plant," the driver said, and spat tobacco out of the door, narrowly missing the man rolling a barrel down a ramp under the hotel. "Entire town runs on hydro-electricks thanks to him, from street lamps to cooking stoves. No coal furnaces and woodstoves for George-town, no sir."

"Goodness." Daisy accepted Mr. Meriwether-Astor's hand

and climbed down. "In England, electricks are only strong enough for street lights and the illumination of houses. I can't imagine anything more powerful running on them."

"Won't see none of that silly yellow stuff here," the driver said, swinging down Emma's trunk. "The light the Tesla plant produces is like being out in the sun, even at midnight."

Daisy soon experienced the strange, harsh light for herself, as they were shown into a room that, they were assured by the young man at the reception desk, "was for female travelers only."

"I should hope so," Emma murmured as she directed her trunk to be set down by the porter. Unlike the cabins on an airship, which allowed considerable privacy, the room contained no fewer than four beds of different sizes. She and Freddie were to share one, and Emma had the narrow single to herself. Two other beds were empty, but the desk clerk told them they had been reserved as well.

Married couples might stay in a private room, and traveling gentlemen had their own. It was an efficient system, apparently, and the rooms were warm from steam heat. This was most welcome, as the air in the mountains was decidedly cool. However, one would be employing all the means one could to maintain one's privacy.

An hour later, washed, dressed, and her hair freshly arranged, Emma smoothed her skirts with trembling hands. "I am inexpressibly glad that you are with me," she said to Daisy and Frederica, likewise washed and dressed in ensembles more appropriate to dinner than travel. "Shall we go down?"

"Mr. Meriwether-Astor suggested that we take a table near you, so that you would have friends close by. I hope you do not consider that officious?"

"By no means. It is a relief," Emma assured her. "If I run out of conversation, I can turn to you for help."

Daisy could not imagine that happening. Not to a woman as accomplished as Emma. Not when their future would give her and her fiancé endless things to talk about.

They proceeded down the staircase to the dining room, which might have come straight from the boulevards of Paris, so well appointed was it. The tables were covered in snowy linen and polished silver, with the addition of a flower in a bud vase on every table where a lady sat. The owner of the hotel, a Monsieur Louis Dupuy, ushered Emma, Daisy, and Freddie in the direction of a table where Mr. Meriwether-Astor was already seated. Both he and the gentleman at the table next to him rose as the ladies approached.

"Miss Makepeace," Monsieur Dupuy said grandly, "I am honored to present to you Mr. Bjorn Hansen, a most respected citizen and a personal friend of mine. Please allow me to welcome you to our fair town and offer my very best wishes for your future happiness."

Emma sank into a curtsey, and as she introduced Daisy and Freddie, Daisy examined Mr. Hansen with interest. It was impossible, of course, to judge a man's character on first seeing him, but if his gobsmacked expression was any indication, Emma had described herself in her letters with far too much modesty. He appeared to be in his late thirties, with thick blond hair and the ruddy complexion of a fair-skinned man who spent the greater part of his days in the sun. His carpenter's hands engulfed Emma's, but he held hers with the gentle care of a man cradling a hummingbird or a butterfly.

"Will you be seated?" he asked shyly, and held the chair for her as she settled into it with the grace of a queen.

Daisy and Freddie likewise took seats opposite Mr. Meriwether-Astor, who took pains to keep the conversation lively so that the couple at the next table might have a semblance of privacy. Daisy could not remember having had such a meal before. Truly, with the hotel's elegant service and dishes such as oysters and pheasant, Georgetown was no frontier outpost. If she did not look outside at the street, she could have imagined herself in one of the best establishments in Paris. Not that she had ever had a chance to do much more than gawk at Paris before they boarded *Persephone*, but still. When they found Papa, perhaps they might come back here and introduce him to Mr. and Mrs. Hansen, and they could have a celebratory dinner in this very hotel.

After dessert, Mr. Hansen cleared his throat and his gaze included the occupants of the table beside him. "I hope you will honor me by coming to my home for coffee. For I confess I am so anxious to show Miss Makepeace her future home that I cannot wait another moment. The addition of her friends would make the occasion complete."

How could anyone resist such an invitation? Daisy accepted with alacrity, and soon the little party was walking along Rose Street under the light of a half moon, the mountains rearing up on either side of the town and cupping a river of stars between them. At Rose and Eighth Streets, Mr. Hansen opened a gate set in a low picket fence and stood aside as they filed up the flagged walk to a cottage so new that Daisy could still smell fresh paint.

"Welcome to your future home, my—my dear," he said, as though this were the first time such words had crossed his lips.

Smiling, Emma took his proffered hand, mounted the two

steps to the little porch, and entered the snug little cottage first, as its future mistress.

"I built it myself," Mr. Hansen told them, removing his hat and hanging it on a peg just inside the door. "At that time, of course, I had not much notion of a woman living here. All I could think of was getting it dried in before winter, and after that, being able to show prospective customers my work."

"I am sure you have more work than you know what to do with, in that case," Mr. Meriwether-Astor remarked, gazing about him. "The floor is solid oak, and the wainscoting and plasterwork show such attention to detail as a man might be proud to show to anyone."

"Thank you, sir." Mr. Hansen's fair skin flushed with pleasure. "If you will excuse me, I will put the coffee on."

Emma went with him to render assistance, her soft voice providing a counterpoint to his deeper one.

Daisy looked about her with satisfaction underlain with a kind of longing. How wonderful it would be to live in such a snug little home! For every room showed care in its construction, and while the furnishings were spare and the house was free of the clutter and frippery so common in homes Daisy had visited in Bath, it was still comfortable. She would not be surprised if Mr. Hansen had built the sofa and chairs himself, and ordered the blue-and-yellow striped cushions and linen drapes from Denver.

When at last they made their farewells, promising to return the next day to prepare the house for the wedding reception, Daisy walked beside Emma, their feet ringing hollow on the raised boardwalk.

"And what do you think of your correspondent now?" she

asked, under cover of Mr. Meriwether-Astor pointing out the home of the owner of the Pelican mine to Freddie.

Emma smiled a very feminine smile. "I think he is the kindest of men—and certainly one of the most talented I have ever met. When he said he had a home for me, I confess I pictured a log cabin on the side of a mountain, with a crooked stovepipe and a five-mile drive to town."

"Very much like the house in *Posted to Paradise*, am I correct?"

Emma laughed—and Daisy realized that the sound had changed. It no longer held a note of caution, of tension, but instead was free and filled with true happiness. "You are quite correct. And I am so relieved that I will not be required to bring in supplies on a mule, as our intrepid heroine did, but can grow my own vegetables and buy what I need at the general store within a few minutes' walk."

"And Mr. Hansen himself?" Daisy asked. "What is your opinion of him?"

Emma walked on a few steps before answering. "I had some idea of his character because of our correspondence. But his kindness this evening has me much farther along in the kind of affection a wife ought to feel for her husband." A sly glance at Daisy—almost a twinkle. "You need not fear that I shall be like Charlotte Lucas, preferring to know nothing of her husband as they entered the marriage state. On the contrary, I am as satisfied as a bride can be."

Daisy took her arm and squeezed it. "Then I am as satisfied as a maid of honor can be. I cannot wait for Friday."

## CHAPTER 4

### THURSDAY, AUGUST 1, 1895

*7:30 a.m.*

*Georgetown*

*I*n the morning, however, all their industrious plans came to nothing when Emma made a dash for the lavatory and Daisy heard the faint sounds of retching. When she returned, Daisy was up and dressed, and on the point of going downstairs for a cup of restorative tea.

"Oysters," Emma croaked, and rolled into bed with an arm clutched across her belly. "Never again."

"Oh dear." Daisy drew up the comforter and tucked it around Emma's chin. "I'll get you some tea. It seemed to help last time."

A gray head tied up in curling rags poked out from under the comforter on the far side of the room and the black eyes of one of the travelers who had come in on the late train peered at them. "Breeding, is she?" the woman said. "Tea and soda crackers. Best thing."

Daisy drew herself up, affronted nearly to speechlessness on Emma's behalf. "Certainly not. We both had oysters for the first time last night in the restaurant, and they do not agree with either of us."

"Suit yourself." The woman turned over and went back to sleep.

Honestly. The nerve of some people—speaking when they hadn't been introduced, and so insultingly, too!

When by eight o'clock Emma did not seem to be improving despite the tea, Daisy went down to the front desk to inquire after a doctor. The nice young man gave her an address nearby and even drew a map on a slip of paper.

She could have sent a boy, she supposed, as she put on her hat and slipped the strings of her reticule over her wrist. But she did not want to risk the kind of impertinence they had already suffered this morning. It was better to go herself, and explain the situation properly.

Like her own physician in Bath, the Georgetown doctor ran his practice from his home, but the man at the desk had said to inquire at the surgery around the side. As she rounded the corner of the house, the door of the surgery was flung open, bounced off the wall, and a young man propelled out of it by main force. Luckily, he got his feet under him before he measured his length on the lawn, but the wooden case he carried was not so fortunate. It landed in the flowerbed and crushed several plants.

"I'll have none of your sort here!" An older man in a greenish-brown tweed suit and gold spectacles stood at the top of the steps shaking his fist. "Damned snake-oil salesmen, duping people and endangering their health for the sake of the almighty gold piece. I know your kind."

He went in and slammed the door behind him. The glass in the four-light pane rattled—Daisy could hear it from where she stood on the neatly flagged path, transfixed.

The young man ran both hands through his hair—it stood rather on end, as though this happened quite a lot—and finally caught sight of Daisy. "Good morning," he said. "I'm sorry you had to witness that."

She edged past him on the path, quite certain that one was not supposed to speak to people who had just been thrown out of the house. On the other hand, despite the fact that he wore the decorative and protective boots common among the Texicans, he was favoring his left ankle.

"Are you all right?" she said at last, opting for civility over propriety.

He shook his ankle like a cat with one wet foot. "I'll be fine. Just knocked it on the step. Excuse me while I examine my case—I hope nothing inside is broken."

While he was occupied, she hurried up the steps and into the surgery, which was bright with Mr. Tesla's electrics, and made even more so by whitewashed walls and gleaming brass upon the door leading into the back. With the addition of the sun peeping over the ridge behind the house, she almost needed to squint against the light. Four people sat on chairs in the waiting room, and a lady about the same age as the doctor presided over a desk.

"Do you have an appointment?" she inquired as Daisy crossed the room.

"No—I am here on behalf of a friend, who is indisposed this morning. I wondered if the doctor might have something to settle an upset stomach."

"He has many things for many purposes. What has upset

your friend?" The lady's eyes were kind, but she did not appear inclined to let Daisy speak to the doctor, either.

"Oysters."

"Ah. They were bad?"

"Certainly not. They were served last night at the Hotel de Paris, and I had some as well."

"Then it cannot be the oysters, can it? Has this happened before?"

"Yes, four times since we met on the twenty-fourth of July."

"Four, you say? In nine days?"

"Yes." Why was she smiling?

"Then you must advise your friend to take a cup of tea and eat sparingly of soda crackers. Flat ginger ale will also help. They will be able to provide all three at the hotel."

That was what that nasty woman in the curling rags had said, too. But nothing on earth would force Daisy to mention how the woman had prefaced her remarks.

"I would like my friend to come in to see the doctor, please. She might have a complaint of the stomach. Or something more serious." Terrible memories of her mother's last days assailed Daisy, and she swallowed. "She might have the influenza, and must be treated at once."

"I can just about guarantee that she does not have the influenza, if she was eating at the Hotel de Paris last night," the woman said, her expression still filled with amusement. How dreadfully unsympathetic she was, for someone in the business of healing.

Being stonewalled was making Daisy cross. "How can you know that? You are not a doctor. I insist upon my friend being given an appointment."

"We are full for today." The woman's face closed like a shutter.

Daisy realized a moment too late that her concern—and probably her annoyance—had made her rude.

"Come back tomorrow."

"I cannot—she is being mar—"

"We have no openings until then. Good day to you, miss." She rose and called a name. A woman with two children clinging to her skirts crossed the room and all three were admitted to the inner sanctum.

Blast and bother and all manner of nuisance! Daisy stalked out the door berating herself for not controlling her tongue. Now poor Emma would have to come in herself after her wedding, and that was a fine beginning to a honeymoon.

Halfway along the path, she realized that the young man with the wooden case had not yet gone, and in fact was kneeling in the grass, carefully checking glass vials filled with various kinds of liquids in slender velvet beds. He looked up as she crossed behind him.

"That was quick. No room at the inn?"

"No satisfaction of any kind," she said bitterly. "It seems my friend will simply have to suffer."

"What's the matter with her?" His accents were similar to those of Hugh Meriwether-Astor, which meant he hailed from the Fifteen Colonies. His voice was musical and pleasing.

Oh, what was the harm? Daisy described the symptoms and when she finished, the young man thought for a moment. His face seemed to be a study in triangles, even in repose. His eyebrows quirked up to a point in the middle, and his chin was an angle inverted in the other direction. His nose, though straight and well formed, was as triangular as noses tended to be, and his lower lip dipped in a long angle that was aesthetically attractive, and would be challenging to paint.

"What did they say in there?" he asked at last. "You didn't see Dr. Pascoe, did you?"

"No, I didn't get past the Gorgon at the threshold. She suggested tea and soda crackers, with flat ginger ale. What nonsense. If my friend has the influenza, that will not help in the least."

He gazed at her for a moment. Opened his mouth. Changed his mind, and instead said, "I have something that might."

"You?" *A snake-oil salesman?* The words hung unspoken but loud and clear in the morning air.

Oh, she knew all about snake-oil salesmen—those traveling confidence men who charged enormous sums for what was essentially dyed alcohol in those delicate glass vials. In *Posted to Paradise*, they had gone from town to town defrauding innocent people and raising their hopes, only to have them dashed when their loved ones died in heartbreaking bedside scenes.

"I'm not what he called me," the young man said, clearly perceiving the train of her thoughts. "Truly. I sell herbal medicines. There is not a single drop of snake venom to be had in any of these cures. Consequently, they actually work." He patted the vials, brushed off his trousers, and rose, a hand extended. "William Barnicott, at your service."

Daisy stepped back, declining both his hand and his acquaintance. "If you will excuse me."

"No, please, I beg of you." He reached into his box and plucked out a vial containing a dark green liquid. "This is a tincture of lady's mantle and lemon balm, concocted for just the symptoms you describe. If she takes ten drops in a glass of water twice a day, her symptoms will fade—or at least be reduced enough that she will not suffer such discomfort."

Daisy stared at the vial as though it was indeed full of snake venom. Hunter Green would make that color, mixed with Lamp Black. "No, thank you."

To her dismay, he caught her hand and pressed the vial into it. "It's not poison, I promise you. I am staying behind the tavern on Argentine Street. I will call in the morning, and if she is not feeling even a little better, you may call me a liar and have me arrested for peddling. But I'll wager you will not."

He was so sincere—but then, the best confidence men always were. But despite her distrust, something in his brown eyes, some honest concern, made her fingers close around the vial instead of flinging it down in the grass.

"I will call tomorrow," he said again.

"Early," she said stiffly. "We are staying at the Hotel de Paris. She is being married at eleven."

He nodded in acknowledgment. "And one more thing—be sure the two of you drink at least six glasses of water daily while you are in the mountains. Otherwise you will succumb to the headaches and nausea of altitude sickness."

If poor Emma had not been suffering from the same for some time now, Daisy might have thought this a good diagnosis, and been grateful for such a simple cure. "Thank you. I will remember."

He bowed, then returned to his case. He pressed a button on one side, and tiny brass filigree harnesses slid out to enclose each vial in its slot. Then the lid snapped shut automatically. No wonder none had broken on landing in the garden. They were well protected.

As though they were valuable. Actually functional, as he had said.

Frowning, Daisy pushed the vial into her reticule and got herself out of the garden. She had dallied too long and kept poor Emma waiting.

EMMA WAS FEELING SO MUCH BETTER after taking the tincture that Daisy was almost sorry to have declined the snake-oil salesman's acquaintance. Almost. For really, her friend's symptoms tended to lessen when she was distracted and busy with the events of the day—and today would be eventful, to say the least.

Mr. Hansen's house had to be cleaned from top to bottom, and while he seemed to be a good housekeeper for a bachelor, it took all three young ladies most of the afternoon to meet Emma's exacting standards. When they were finished, Daisy sent Freddie out to pick wildflowers to put in canning jars on the table (Mr. Hansen having not one vase to his name) while she snatched a few minutes to walk into town, find the daguerreotype studio, and purchase a frame for the portrait. Once her watercolor was carefully inserted, the proprietor wrapped it in tissue paper and tied it with silk ribbon.

The bridal party had been invited to dinner at the home of a Mrs. Davis, who had been one of the first mail-order brides to find husband and home through the same agency as Emma. Her situation did not seem to be quite so pleasant, though Daisy would never dream of saying so. The house was tall, narrow, and dark, without the pretty covered porch or the interior details that made the cottage on Rose Street so delightful.

Mr. Davis was a manager at one of the mines and had come up through the ranks. He spat tobacco into a brass spittoon placed conveniently close to the head of the table. Every time he did it, Daisy had to force herself not to look to see if he'd missed. Or if he had, to think about the state of the floors.

But Mrs. Davis was a good cook, and had lovely manners, and was clearly delighted that she had made a match between her friend and Mr. Hansen, though it had taken place over thousands of miles.

"And now you will be close enough to me that we can take tea together," she said happily as she cut the groom's cake for dessert.

"I won't have you gadding about," Mr. Davis said, frowning into his coffee. "Sends a bad message to the men if I can't manage my wife."

"I do not think a woman needs to be managed in that way," Mr. Hansen said. "Everyone needs a friend, and Miss Makepeace is no gadder."

"Hardly." Emma smiled at him. "Though I shall wish to make acquaintances and find good society. I feel rich in the possession of such friends already."

This compliment to his wife seemed to mollify Mr. Davis somewhat, and he accepted a second piece of cake agreeably, joking that he had best not have a third, or he would not be able to button his waistcoat, which would never do if he was to be among the witnesses in church tomorrow.

While Emma stayed a little later to visit with Mrs. Davis

and talk over old times, Daisy and Frederica declined any escort and walked back to the hotel together in the moonlight. But a block from the hotel, Daisy was forced to reconsider the wisdom of such a walk. For out of an alley between two buildings not fifteen feet ahead came three men who were clearly drunk.

Miners. Their goggles were slung around their necks, their hats were missing, and under the whiskey fumes that wafted toward them, Daisy could smell sweat and the earth.

"Lookit, boys! Ladies in the night," slurred one.

"Ladies *of* the night," his companion corrected him. "Hey, ladies, care for company? I got a pocket full of silver."

"Off the sidewalk, Freddie—hurry," Daisy whispered.

As the men careened closer, their boots beating a disjointed tattoo on the boardwalk, Freddie jumped the two feet into the street, Daisy a heartbeat behind her. For some reason this produced raucous laughter, and the men leaped down after them. Daisy picked up her skirts and ran toward the lights of the hotel.

"Daisy, wait!" Freddie panted behind her. "It was too much for them. Look."

The miners had misjudged their leaps and lay in the street tangled together, no doubt attempting to figure out which way was up.

"Come along." Daisy took a high step back up on the boardwalk and held out a hand to her sister. "Remind me never to walk at night again. It is certainly not Bath, is it?"

After they reached the warm safety of their room and settled themselves down in the routine of preparing for bed, Daisy could not help a groan as she stretched out under the quilts.

"Our aunt made sure we could keep house," she whispered out of consideration for the curling-rag women, who were rolled up and snoring on the other side of the room. "But it has been a long time since I was on hands and knees scrubbing a kitchen floor, to say nothing of leaping on and off boardwalks."

"I hope it will be a long time before we do either again," Freddie whispered back. "I broke two nails on the plaster medallions in Mr. Hansen's ceiling."

"Consider it a wedding gift." Daisy yawned. Really, she wanted to wait up for Emma, but she must close her eyes.

Just for a moment.

# CHAPTER 5

## FRIDAY, AUGUST 2, 1895

*7:00 a.m.*

*Georgetown*

*D*aisy woke to the bustle of the curling-rag ladies getting their bags through the door to catch the first train, and looked at the other bed closest to see if Emma was awake, too, on this her wedding day.

But the bed was empty, as neatly made as it had been when they had come in last night.

"Freddie!" She poked her sister, who moaned and snuggled more deeply into the feather pillow. "Freddie, wake up! Emma is to be married in four hours. She has already gone down, and is probably saving us a table for breakfast."

The immediate prospect of food had its usual effect on Freddie. She rolled out and dressed in the skirt and plain waist she had worn yesterday. They would dress properly after breakfast, when there was no risk of an errant bit of egg dropping down the front of one's only good waist.

When they entered the dining room, however, Emma was nowhere in sight. Daisy recognized several patrons from dinner the night before, but a number of newcomers filled the tables as well. These included six very prosperous looking gentlemen who seemed to be having a meeting that involved the morning newspapers and much waving of coffee spoons.

One of them wore a brocade waistcoat of such an unusual purple that she found herself staring. Actually it was closer to plum. One would have to use French Ultramarine and a cool yellow, certainly, but add one of the bluer reds as well. Or would a warm red produce such—

With a blink, she realized that the man was staring at her, too, only with considerably greater rudeness. His flat gaze swept her from head to foot, and when it returned to her bosom, one corner of his lip lifted in contempt.

With a sharply indrawn breath, Daisy turned her back upon him and attempted to listen to what Freddie was saying.

"... can she have breakfasted already, and gone to Mr. Hansen's without us?" Freddie sounded as though rising so early was the height of lunacy. "She came in very late. She leaned over me, as though to see if I was awake, but I wasn't ... not enough to speak, at least."

Daisy had slept too heavily after her labors of the day before, and remembered nothing. She hustled her sister to a table on the opposite side of the room from the businessmen, hopefully forestalling any further impertinence. She and Freddie helped themselves at the sideboard.

"I thought Emma was to take her things over, but her case is still in the closet."

"Maybe she is picking flowers for her bouquet," Freddie suggested, downing oatmeal covered in raisins, chopped apples, and brown sugar at a furious rate. "I found larkspur and lupine in a meadow by the creek. And any number of brown-eyed Susans. I wonder if she likes those?"

"I do not know. In any case, Mr. Hansen made arrangements with a florist in Denver to supply roses and orange blossom for a nosegay. Someone will already have fetched them from the train. You and I are each to carry a single rose from it, since he did not know she was to have attendants until she arrived."

"She'll turn up," Freddie said. "I hope she'll have a moment to do my hair the way she does hers. That pompadour style is so pretty."

"It is far too old for you," Daisy said firmly. "A crown of braids such as Lady Hollys wears will be more suitable for a girl who is not yet out."

If Daisy thought her sister would be pleased to emulate Lady Hollys, whom she so admired, she was disappointed. A pleat of rebellion formed between Freddie's brows. "If I must look like one of Mr. Waterhouse's old paintings instead of Mr. Gibson's, then I shall find some flowers to put in it."

There were moments in which one pressed one's advantage, and moments when one accepted victory and retired with grace. "That would be very pretty, dearest."

After breakfast, Daisy collected Emma's valise, which she would not need this morning. The antelope-colored wedding suit with its short jacket and lacy bodice hung waiting in the closet, and Freddie opted to wait at the hotel, too, in case Emma returned and could be persuaded to help her with her hair. When Daisy arrived at the house on Rose Street with the valise, it was to find Mr. Hansen pacing circles in the little parlor, his hands clutching as though each was restraining the other.

"Why, Mr. Hansen," Daisy exclaimed as she set down the valise near the door. "Whatever is the matter? Did the flowers not come? Where is Emma?"

He stared at her for a moment. "She is not with you?"

"No. When we woke, she had already gone down. I thought she would have come over here—though it is said to be bad luck for the bride to see the groom before the wedding."

"That is not the custom in the Norse Kingdom. We were to breakfast together in the private parlor at the hotel before she went up to dress. But I waited for an hour and she did not come."

A private breakfast? This was news to Daisy. "You mean you have not seen her at all?"

"No."

"Could she have gone to meet the train? To fetch the flowers?"

Wordlessly, he indicated the jar full of roses, orange blossoms, and lilies on the simple marble mantel. A length of ribbon lay next to it, and a pair of scissors, all clearly waiting for Emma to make up her nosegay.

"Well, this makes no sense at all," Daisy said, completely at a loss. "I shall return to—"

A sharp knock at the door cut her off.

Mr. Hansen stepped past her to open it, revealing the tweedy form of Dr. Pascoe on the porch. "Bjorn, I apologize for the early call. May I come in?"

"I have already said we may play Cowboy Poker here next week, whether I am a married man or not."

But the doctor did not smile at his attempt at a joke. He spotted Daisy standing next to the valise. "Miss?"

"Dr. Pascoe, may I introduce Miss Daisy Linden, the maid of honor at the wedding today. She is a friend of my bride-to-be."

"Ah. The wedding." The doctor shook Daisy's hand quite as though he had something else on his mind.

It struck Daisy that perhaps *this* was where Emma had gone this morning, instead of to breakfast. In a moment, the utter logic of it flooded her with conviction. And his solemn face confirmed it—Emma *did* have the influenza, and the doctor had come himself to break it to Mr. Hansen that his bride-to-be was very ill.

"Is Miss Makepeace with you?" Daisy burst out. "She has not been feeling well, and I came to your surgery yesterday to see if I might obtain medicine for her, but—" *Your wife ran me off.* "I was not successful."

The doctor looked startled. "Yes, she is with me, but not—not—oh dear—"

With a sigh of relief, Daisy turned to Mr. Hansen, laying a hand upon his arm. "There, you see? She has not waited for either of us to take her to see Dr. Pascoe, but has seen to herself like a woman of sense."

"Miss, er, Linden, is it? Please excuse me while I speak to Mr. Hansen privately."

She recognized once more the man who had shaken his fist at the snake-oil salesman and tossed him out the door, with the added detail of a distinct shade of puce flushing his cheeks. Goodness. Was the doctor a drinker? Or merely flushed with emotion?

"If it is about Emma, she may stay, Royce," Mr. Hansen

said, his brows lowering in concern. "We both have been concerned for her. Is Emma all right?"

The doctor sighed. "Perhaps you will want to sit down."

Wordlessly, they did so. *It is the influenza. I knew it! It must be much farther along than even I suspected because she concealed it so heroically. How much longer does she have to live? Oh, poor Emma, to have come so far, with so much hope! Well, they must still be married today. Even a few days filled with happiness is better than—*

"Do you know where your fiancée was last evening?" the doctor asked.

Mr. Hansen seemed taken aback. "Why, of course. She was with me, and Miss Linden and her sister, at the home of Eveline and Patrick Davis. While Patrick and I have had our differences, Eveline is an old friend of hers from London."

"Was she with you the whole evening?"

"For most of it. When I prepared to leave, she said she and Mrs. Davis had a year to catch up on, and she would stay a few minutes more. Mr. Davis would see her to the hotel."

"What time was this?"

Daisy judged it time to step in. "My sister and I left at ten by the mantel clock, and Miss Makepeace was still there, with Mr. Hansen."

"Then how much later did you leave, Bjorn?"

"Not long. Not more than a quarter of an hour. Please, Royce, you must tell me what is going on. Why these strange questions if Emma is with you?"

"Her body is at the surgery," the doctor said heavily. "But her soul has gone to be with its Creator. My friend, I am deeply sorry, but I must inform you that sometime last night Miss Makepeace met with mortal misadventure."

Mr. Hansen stared, his face flushing and then turning gray. "Misadventure. I do not know this word. She is—what?"

"Georgetown is a safe place, for the most part, but now and again the miners can turn rough. I suspect that she was mistaken for a—a desert flower, somewhere between the house of Mr. Davis and her lodgings at ...?" He glanced at Daisy.

"We are staying at the Hotel de Paris." Daisy's reply was as wooden as Mr. Hansen's expression of horror. Her face felt cold. Her lips did not move easily. Her heart ached, as though it had been struck by an unkind fist.

"A distance of little more than three blocks. She was found before dawn by one of the engineers going to Mr. Tesla's plant, who notified the Texican Rangers. The lieutenant in charge of the detachment here fetched me, and we brought her to the surgery, where she lies now." He rose, and extended a hand to Mr. Hansen, whose entire body had begun to tremble. "Please. It pains me to ask you this, Bjorn, but would you come with me to identify her?"

It seemed to take a long time for the question to register. "She is dead?" Mr. Hansen said in a wondering voice, as though he could not believe his friend the doctor would be so cruel as to play such a joke upon him. "My Emma? We will not be married today?"

"I am afraid not, my friend," the doctor said, his ruddy face paling now with sympathy. "My deepest condolences upon this dreadful loss."

"It cannot be Emma," Daisy said suddenly. Defiantly, and with certainty. "It is some other unfortunate woman. Mr. Davis would not let her walk back through the streets at night, alone. Besides, my sister saw her when she returned to the hotel, bending over her to see if she was awake."

Dr. Pascoe drew himself up. "Several people, including Lieutenant Ross, also saw her at dinner Wednesday evening with Mr. Hansen, at the hotel. The lieutenant has no doubt it is she, though his identification cannot be official, of course."

"But you have never met her, have you? And the lieutenant may have seen her at a distance. There were several ladies of similar age in the dining room Wednesday evening, including my sister. I tell you, Doctor, the woman in your surgery is not Emma. She came safely back to the hotel last night."

Doubt flickered over the doctor's face. Doubt, and dislike. He did not like her contradicting him in the midst of such a solemn errand.

But Emma and Mr. Hansen deserved such a contradiction. Because in it lay hope.

"Come, Miss Linden." Mr. Hansen collected himself with an effort. "We will go to the surgery together. And on the way, I will pray that you are right."

They had a silent walk, despite the trilling of birds and the voices of the town's inhabitants as they began their day unaware that a life had been taken from among them. The little party entered the surgery, where the doctor's wife looked Daisy over with swift recognition. But she said not a word, only opened the door to a room in the rear that, while brightly lit, was unheated and made of stone, unlike the house and surgery, which were snugly constructed of wood and plaster.

"Miss Linden, you will remain with my wife, if you please."

Daisy did not please in the least. She had only seen deceased persons in the dignified environs of funeral services at church, but that did not signify. This unfortunate lady was not Emma, so there was no danger of her being overcome. She ignored the doctor and stepped forward at Mr. Hansen's side. The former could not help a harrumph of irritation, but the hand that drew back the sheet was gentle.

The shock felt as though the earth had suddenly moved, and Daisy swayed to maintain her balance. Mr. Hansen made a sound, and she clutched at his arm, half in sympathy and half to keep herself standing upright.

Emma Makepeace lay as though carved of marble, her lips softly folded upon the secret of the disaster that had befallen her. Her hair was disheveled, perhaps from the attack, or perhaps simply from being carried between two men to the doctor's house. The skin of her throat and shoulders was pale as an unlit candle, except for a bruise just below her collarbone, brutal to the affectionate eye as a blow.

Indigo. Mixed with Ochre and Burnt Orange, it would create that blue with mottled gray shadows. At one corner of her mouth, a thread of Scarlet Lake had dried.

Daisy tore her gaze from the dreadful, pitiful sight. The blouse and skirt Emma had worn to the Davises' dinner lay folded on a chair, her kid boots neatly on the floor under it. A pile of undergarments lay on top of the blouse, oddly folded.

"Miss Linden, what I have to say is not for a young lady's ears. Please go with my wife."

A tremor passed through Mr. Hansen's body, bent over as though someone had punched him in the stomach. "Please do so, Miss Linden," he whispered. "You have been subjected to enough today in the name of friendship."

"How can this be possible?" Daisy's voice seemed to be an

octave above its normal tone. "My sister saw her, safely in our room."

"Clearly she did not stay there," the doctor said. "Please. My wife will get you a cup of tea." He took Daisy's arm and pulled her out of the chilly room, handing her over to Mrs. Pascoe like a piece of luggage.

Outside in the waiting room, Daisy refused the tea. She would not be able to swallow it. As it was, her breakfast was in such a state of agitation it was all she could do to sit still and control her body's rejection of food, since it could not reject the truth.

When Mr. Hansen came out looking like a haggard apparition, she took his arm wordlessly and guided him along the path and out to the street, half afraid he would collapse.

"Did you know?" he croaked as they walked, as slowly as a funeral cortege, back along Rose Street toward his cottage.

"Know what, sir?"

"Doubtless the bruise below her throat occurred as she tried to defend herself, or as she fell. There were marks upon her belly." The dreadful words fell from his lips as though he had forgotten he might be speaking to someone with delicate sensibilities. "As though her murderer meant to punish her, kicking her when she was down."

"How could I have known such a thing?" Tears welled in her eyes. "I cannot bear to think of it."

His head tilted back, tears leaking from the corners of his eyes as he gazed up at an uncaring blue sky. "How can I grieve her now? It seems I did not know her at all."

What was he talking about? "You knew her heart, through her letters. She could not wait to be your wife. She told me herself that she was well on her way to loving you. How can you not grieve her? I don't understand what you mean." Daisy's throat closed, and the tears welled up again. "She was so lovely, so blessed by nature—and yet, she only wanted to be worthy of you."

He made an ugly sound, halfway between a laugh and a sob, and dashed the tears from his cheeks. "I very much doubt that. Perhaps she thought I was a gullible fool, to be taken in again by a pretty face and a pair of beautiful eyes."

Again Daisy felt that sensation of the earth moving, as though she had been struck. But this time, she slackened her grip on his arm, drawing back a little in her confusion, in order to see his face. "Why would you say such a terrible thing?"

"Because, Miss Linden, the doctor showed all the signs to me, as I stood there bearing up under his pity. Three months —four months—how could I not have seen? And now everything I believed of her has been proven false, and I am left feeling the fool. So I will ask you again ... did you know that she was expecting another man's child?"

# CHAPTER 6

*10:15 a.m.*

*D*aisy could not later remember how she had returned to the Hotel de Paris, dazed and heartsick, yet she found herself somehow in her room, with Emma's valise in one hand and a cluster of unbound roses, lilies, and orange blossoms in the other.

Frederica stared at her. "Daisy, what on earth? We are supposed to be dressing. What has happened to you? Did you find Emma?"

She told her sister the events of the morning, succinctly, leaving out no detail. She sounded like one of the new speaking automatons that were all the rage in London and completely unknown here. She felt like a brass automaton, too—stiff and cold. But when Freddie exclaimed, "No! I cannot believe it!" it was all she could do not to fling the flowers at her and scream.

She could not breathe properly—as though her own

horror and dismay were choking her. "I told Mr. Hansen and the doctor that you had seen her, bending over you in the night." She struggled for calm. "They merely said she must have gone out again afterward. But that makes no sense. Why would she do that in the small hours of her wedding day? Why come in at all if there were some other errand? What errand could there possibly be in the middle of the night—she had just been with the only people she knew in Georgetown."

Freddie had gone very pale, and sat on the edge of their bed. Suddenly exhausted, Daisy thrust the flowers into the porcelain ewer and sank down beside her. The tears welled up and overcame her. It was a relief to let herself go, to mourn, to grieve not one life, but two.

Two! The curling-rag ladies had been right. How was it possible? How could she even think of her friend that way? And most mystifying of all, who was the third person in *that* invisible triangle?

When the storm showed signs of passing, Freddie took her sodden handkerchief from her and replaced it with her own. "Sister, I must tell you something."

After a moment she mastered herself, wiping her face with both palms. Weeping would not change the situation. Nothing would, now. The only thing that would balance the scales would be for the Texican Rangers to bring to justice the evil person who had done this, and how soon could that be accomplished?

Freddie hesitated, then said softly, "I know there are some things we never talk about, but now we must."

It took Daisy a moment to make the transition from the dreadful present to the merely peculiar past. "I do not see the relevance of ... those things ... to Emma's death."

"Bear with me. Remember how Mama always laughed about my imaginary friends?"

"We both know they were not imaginary, but Freddie, what does this have to do with—"

"Remember the little girl who died in Aunt Jane's house during the Civil War? I was very taken by her broad lace collar, which was so different from my practical serge school uniform."

"Freddie—" Daisy sighed. This was an old conversation. She had always believed her sister when she talked about the spirits who shared some of their houses, even when they were children. But whispered adult conversations that she was not supposed to hear had made her fearful. Had made her hush Freddie on the subject, lest she be discovered and taken away.

"Remember the house where we lived in Edinburgh? Remember how I would not sleep in my room, but always came to you?"

"You said there was a mean little boy."

"And so there was, though you would not allow me to speak of him. His ghost chilled the room so much that the fire kept going out."

"Mama thought it was because the upstairs maid was sloppy and did not lay one."

"Oh, the maid was not remiss in her duties. For all the good it did. And the day she saw him, too, was her last in our employ, remember?"

Daisy remembered all too well the maid's hysterics. She and Freddie had held hands tightly under cover of their skirts, and Mama had sighed at the prospect of finding another maid to train.

"Dearest, you know my feelings. We must not speak of such things. Even here, with the door closed. You know why."

Freddie nodded, sadly. "I do not want to be like that famous lady scientist in London, shut up in an insane asylum because she knew things other people did not."

"Papa would not have allowed that." But the words were spoken automatically. She had never been certain he would not be overruled, and so she had become skilled at hiding and even denying Freddie's gift. People grew out of childish things, anyway, and became rational beings. "Freddie, I am very tired, and distressed, and I must see the front desk about getting our luggage to the train. We have no reason now to stay any longer in Georgetown."

Freddie nodded. "We must pursue our original plan. It is odd—that was what she said to me."

"Who?"

"Miss Makepeace, of course, of whom we've been speaking. She bent over me just as the clock in the hall outside struck twelve thirty, and whispered, 'Father.' As though she knew we must be away on our search for him, and did not blame us for leaving."

A chill tingled down Daisy's arms. "She spoke to you? Did she say where she was going after—"

"Daisy, no. When I opened my eyes, I could see right through her to the bed beyond. She said 'Father' and vanished."

The chill spread to Daisy's heart. "The doctor estimated that she was set upon around that time. We left at ten ... Mr. Hansen before ten thirty ... and she and Mrs. Davis talked for more than an hour after that."

"It was not she, then, as I have been trying to convince

myself," Freddie whispered, her eyes wide with a comprehension that perhaps she had not allowed herself until now. "I saw a fetch, and thought it was the real woman."

*A fetch.* An apparition that sometimes appeared to loved ones at the moment of a person's death.

Daisy began to shiver in the warmth of the hotel room. "I told them she had come in," she said, trying to hide the chattering of her teeth. "The doctor and Mr. Hansen. If there is to be an investigation, we may have botched it, Freddie. For I certainly cannot take it back now, much less say that you saw a—" Her voice broke. "A fetch."

"You need not say anything," Freddie told her gently. "Clearly her dying thoughts were of us—that we should find Papa as quickly as possible. We must honor that, and leave as soon as we may."

"Yes. I suppose we will never know what happened. How Mr. Davis came to leave her alone. Who did this awful thing." What could two young ladies do in the case anyway? They had no information to offer the Rangers, and Dr. Pascoe already thought her an insufferable nuisance. Freddie was right. They must be about their business, take their grief with them, and leave Mr. Hansen to his own.

Would he think to tell the good reverend at the church that his services would no longer be needed for a wedding, but for a funeral? If he did not, Dr. Pascoe probably would. Would she and Freddie be welcome, or would it be better for them just to go?

Oh, dear. Maybe it *would* be better if they were out of town before Freddie had to explain why she was changing her story about seeing Emma at the hotel.

She rose and washed her face. "I shall be back in a few

minutes. I must arrange for a conveyance to take us to the train."

"What shall we do with Miss Makepeace's things? And her wedding suit?" Freddie's face crumpled as she gazed at the lovely suit, hanging abandoned in the closet. "Will Mr. Hansen not want them?"

"I think not." Daisy indicated the valise and the flowers. "He practically forced those upon me. If I knew her address in New York, I would send them to her family." She touched the traveling trunk. "The address card merely indicates the house on Rose Street."

"Which was her destination. Mr. Hansen will know her former address. He was writing to her, after all."

"When my courage returns, then, I will ask him."

But when she went down to the lobby to arrange for themselves and their luggage to be taken to the station, she found it all in an uproar, with people standing in little groups talking over one another. Four ladies, heads tilted together, handkerchiefs in hand. Two businessmen, one in a Derby hat and one in a bowler, solemnly shaking their heads and murmuring as one of the prosperous-looking gentlemen she had seen at breakfast joined them. With a blink, Daisy realized the man in the bowler hat was Hugh Meriwether-Astor.

Had the news of Emma's death spread so quickly? But these people did not know her. Why such public emotion, these murmurs of distress?

"What has happened?" she asked the clerk. "Has there been some disaster at the mines?"

"Not at the mines," the young man said, his pensive gaze moving from one group to another. "We just heard that a young lady was murdered this morning. We don't know who

—but I just had it from a reliable source that the Texican Rangers already have a suspect. They're on their way to apprehend him now."

Apprehend who? How could they possibly have found the guilty party so quickly?

A terrible foreboding came over Daisy. Since, unlike the clerk, the Rangers knew the young lady was Emma, who would they turn to first? Only three people in town knew her. Only one knew her intimately enough to be a reasonable suspect.

Daisy pushed out the door, hatless, coatless, and heedless of Hugh Meriwether-Astor's attempts to call her back. She leaped down from the boardwalk, picked up her skirts, and ran down Rose Street like a woman possessed.

# CHAPTER 7

*11:10 a.m.*

The wedding guests, who clearly had not been told about the bride's passing before they arrived for the ceremony, milled about in front of the First Presbyterian Church. Mr. Hansen stood on the steps, clearly doing his best to explain why there would be no wedding today. Daisy ran up, having not found him at his house, and pushed her way through the small crowd.

In morning coat and top hat, looking a little the worse for wear, Mr. Davis slid an arm around his friend's shoulders and raised his other hand to get the guests' attention. His wife sobbed into a handkerchief, surrounded by a small flock of women murmuring comfort in low voices while a pair of children clung to her skirts looking distressed and confused.

"Thank you for coming, friends. This is a terrible thing. Perhaps when Mr. Hansen has had time to recover from the shock, he will be able to receive your condolences, but for now, I'll ask for your understanding. Mrs. Davis and I will take him home."

"Stop, in the governor's name!"

With a gasp, Daisy turned to see no fewer than four Texican Rangers marching down the street. The one leading the way had three gold chevrons stitched on his sleeves, and every one of them carried a rifle at port arms.

"Lieutenant Ross," Mr. Davis said, inclining his head and descending the steps with Mr. Hansen. "What is the meaning of this?"

The rifles snapped upright as they halted in the church-yard. "We are here to arrest this man for the murder of Miss Emma Makepeace."

"No!" Daisy cried. The entire group broke out in a babel of disbelief and horror, and one lady fainted into the arms of her husband.

"On what grounds?" Mr. Hansen shook off his friend's arm and stood upright. "Lieutenant, you know me as well as any man here. I built a barn for you. Not a week ago your boys toasted me at the tavern and wished me joy of my marriage."

"A marriage that will never happen now," the lieutenant said most unnecessarily. "We have it from Dr. Pascoe that she was beaten, and there is only one man whose emotions would carry him away like that, especially upon receiving some *significant* news."

Mr. Hansen made a convulsive movement toward him. "One more word and you will have to arrest me for assaulting an officer of the law."

The crowd murmured, clearly trying to figure out what they were talking about. Daisy clenched her fists.

"I can and will arrest you for threatening one," the lieutenant said as three rifles snapped forward to point at him. "Bjorn Hansen, you will come with me and submit to a trial before the magistrate."

"This is ridiculous!" Mr. Hansen cried as two Rangers slung their rifles over their shoulders and grasped his arms. "I loved Emma. We were to be married this morning—can't you see these are the guests who have come?"

"Save it for the magistrate, Bjorn," the lieutenant said crisply. "I cannot trust you not to flee, so you will be incarcerated until he arrives."

"But that could be weeks!" Mr. Davis cried. "This is insane —he is no more guilty than I of such a dreadful crime. You've done no investigation. It is all supposition. This is an outrage!"

"Be careful what you say, Davis, or we will think we have a conspiracy on our hands." And with that, the lieutenant led his men out of the churchyard, dragging Mr. Hansen between them, the fourth one marching behind with his rifle pointed between the prisoner's shoulders.

"No!" Daisy shrieked again. "This is wrong! He didn't do it! He cared for her!"

But in the horrified cacophony of the crowd, no one paid her any attention.

Daisy knew to the bottom of her soul that they had the wrong man. No one could have walked beside her scant hours ago in such wrenching sorrow and made an act of it. Mr. Hansen's tears, his agony, had been real.

But someone was acting. And more than that, they were willing to let an innocent man go to the gallows while they walked away wiping the blood from their hands.

DAISY WAS NEVER QUITE sure what impulse made her whirl on Patrick Davis as the Rangers and their prisoner turned the corner in the direction of the detachment.

"Mr. Davis, may I have a word?"

For a moment, he stared at her as though he didn't recognize her. Then, "Miss Linden. You put up a brave fight."

"So did you, sir. For all the good it did."

"It grieves me that the Rangers have been so high-handed. It was never this way before Gavin Ross took command. What can I do for you?" He glanced at his wife and children in the midst of her friends. "I am needed elsewhere."

"Last night—please forgive me, sir, but I must know. When we left your house, you were to have seen her back to the hotel. How did Emma come to be alone on that street?"

His face seemed to set, as though she had accused him of something. Neglect, perhaps, or carelessness.

"Are you saying that this terrible mischance was my fault, miss?"

*Yes. Perhaps.* "Certainly not. But I would like to understand the circumstances, for they were not what any of us planned."

His face cleared a little, though sorrow and regret remained. "My wife and Emma were in the midst of their chin-wag when I was sent for by the night shift foreman at the mine. One of the support beams in the new section had collapsed and they feared the tunnel would not be far behind. It turned out to be safe upon inspection, mind you. We space the beams close together for just that reason. But as manager, it was my job to perform that inspection before the miners could go back in. I was there most of the night."

That would explain his pallor, which made his whiskers stand out even more, and the redness around his eyes. She had to admit that with so many witnesses at the mine, he would have found it difficult to slip away and ... and what? Do away with the girl who had just been a guest in his home?

No. She must look elsewhere for someone to blame.

"In my hurry to get up there, I am afraid I allowed myself to be persuaded by Emma that she could make a walk of three blocks alone without incident." His gaze returned to his wife, bleakly. "It will be my everlasting regret. I should have seen her to the hotel on my way. Believe me, no one is being harder upon my conscience than I am this morning."

"And your wife? Could she not have gone with her instead?"

The gaze he now turned upon her snapped with temper held on a short rein. "Do not overstep yourself, miss. For then who would be walking home alone, and even later at night?"

Presumably, as a member of the community for more than a year, Eveline would have had any number of doors to knock upon had she run into trouble.

Such as someone with a reason to kill her.

Had someone had a reason to kill Emma? How was that possible? She had been as harmless as a baby chick, and just as defenseless.

"Thank you for your forbearance with my questions, sir. I know that Mrs. Davis needs your strength now." Daisy stepped back and dipped a curtsey. "Good-bye."

"I don't expect we will see you again, then, Miss Linden."

An hour ago she would have agreed with him. But now, she only smiled sadly and turned away.

*Saturday, August 3, 1895*
*11:30 a.m.*

The Texican Ranger detachment was housed in a building adjacent to the fire hall, with its bell tower and steam-powered pumping engine. Next door, a large field housed a mooring mast, from which hovered a sleek blue airship bearing the crossed sabers and eagle that were also stenciled on the door of the building and worked into the pins on the collars of the Rangers.

Yesterday at this time, she was supposed to have been standing beside Emma discharging the happy duties of bridesmaid. Today unthinkable disaster had befallen both bride and groom. Screwing her courage to the sticking point, Daisy requested leave from the Ranger in the office to visit their prisoner.

"And who might you be?" The Ranger was very young—not much older than Daisy herself—and had not been among those who had marched Mr. Hansen away so callously yesterday. His uniform was khaki, with WILLETS stitched in blue thread over the chest pocket. On a coat tree near the door hung the short wool coat she presumed went over it. Prussian Blue—the color of Papa's old Army uniform. The color of the greatcoat Lady Hollys had said Papa had been wearing the last time she'd seen him.

*Oh, Papa ... wait for us. For how can we leave Georgetown now?*

She gave the young man her name and current place of residence. "I was the late Miss Makepeace's friend, and was to have been her bridesmaid. I wish to speak with Mr. Bjorn Hansen. To—to settle my mind."

He had her sign a ledger, then took a ring of keys from a hook. "This way, then. You won't get much more out of him than a lot of Norse gibberish, but he hasn't shown any signs of violence. Just the opposite."

Six cells made up the gaol beneath the building. Four were occupied by miners in various states of inebriation and remorse, one was empty, and in the last was Mr. Hansen. Gone now was the strong, capable carpenter who had looked at Emma with such awe in his eyes. Instead, a despairing man rocked back and forth on the cot, bent forward at the waist, holding his head and murmuring to the floor.

"Does he have no help?" she asked the Ranger in a low voice. "What is being done for him?"

"Doc Pascoe is rustling up a lawyer, but what few there are pretty much work exclusive-like for the mine owners. It's pretty clear what happened. Man finds out his fiancée is pregnant by someone else and kills her in a jealous rage." He shrugged. "Open and shut."

"Nonsense," Daisy snapped, irritated that this stranger should know such private details. "Mr. Hansen cared for his fiancée. He would never—"

"All the more reason," the Ranger interrupted. He turned away. "You have ten minutes. And don't get too close to the other cells. Some of these men haven't seen a woman in a while. They might not know the difference between a lady and a desert flower."

She'd already discovered *that*, thank you very much. Daisy swallowed her distaste and turned to Mr. Hansen. It took three attempts to get his attention before he realized he had a visitor, and even then he did not seem very happy to see her. "What are you doing here, Miss Linden?" he croaked in English more heavily accented than she had heard it before. "This is no place for a lady."

"It is no place for an innocent man, either," she said crisply. "You must tell them how much you cared for Emma."

"I have." His head dropped into his hands once more. "I told them I would have married her and raised the child as my own, and they did not believe me."

Between one blink and the next, one cry of the heart and the next, Daisy made up her mind to … to do something. Anything. This man was not going to stay down here under the ground one moment longer than necessary. "That is not what you told me yesterday morning. You had lost all faith in her. You could not even grieve her."

"Yesterday you heard a man crying out in his agony and loss. Today I have had time to think of all the if-onlys."

Those words again. Still connected with despair and death.

At her silence, he looked up. "Why do *you* not believe I have done this? You, who are nearly a stranger to me?"

"Because you were not a stranger to Emma. She cared for a man who revealed himself more in letters than in person. I trust her good judgment."

"Have you read my letters, then?"

"No, and I shall not." Were they in the valise? The traveling trunk? "What do you wish me to do with her things, Mr. Hansen—including any letters?"

"Burn the latter, for they have no meaning now. And I do not care what happens to her clothes, if she is not alive to wear them."

"There is one thing. Mr. Hansen, I painted her portrait as her wedding gift to you."

His gaze was bleak. "Did you? I should like to have seen it."

"She wanted you to have it. Shall I leave it in your house?"

With his fingers, he scrubbed his head all over so that his thick blond hair stood on end, and finally rose in an attempt to see out of the window set high in the wall. "What is the point, if I am to hang?"

"We cannot let that happen." The words were born of a bone-deep conviction.

He swung around. "We? I have no ... what is the word? I was asleep in my bed with no one to say any different. And they have plucked a motive from thin air. I can do nothing but repeat my innocence. How will you prevent it? You, a mere girl?"

"By finding out who really did it," she said, hoping he would not notice she had no idea how to accomplish such a thing. "It is clear the Rangers intend to do nothing further, and while the good doctor may flush a lawyer out of the bushes in time, he may need some prodding."

Now the silence held astonishment, along with the rude noises and groans of the other prisoners.

"You would do this for me?" he asked again. "I confess I am surprised. And humbled."

"Someone must do what is right, and I appear to be the only person at hand to make the attempt, other than the doctor. But he does not like me at all."

"He is a good man."

"Has he told you anything more about the—the circumstances of Emma's death?"

"No more than I told you yesterday. Except that she is to be buried this afternoon."

Daisy felt a tingle of shock. "So soon? A funeral cannot be arranged so quickly. And not without you!"

"It is the custom here. She will be buried in the pauper's field outside of town, where the whores and vagrants are buried when there is no one to pay for a plot."

Good heavens. This must not be. Not to a well-bred young lady. Not to a friend. "Can you not prevent it?"

"Not from here." His haggard face crumpled. "In any case, the town will not allow it to be otherwise. In the church cemetery, only good Christians and upstanding members of the community need apply. Not young ladies from foreign parts who anticipated the wedding." He turned away with a gasp, leaning on the bars as his shoulders shook.

Daisy struggled with her own dismay and sorrow. To be laid in the pauper's field—like something out of the Dark Ages. To go forever unremembered, with perhaps only a wooden marker for her final resting place that in time would crumble away to nothing. This was terrible.

He mastered himself after a few minutes. "If you are willing to help me, then please allow me to help you. You cannot stay at the Hotel de Paris indefinitely. You and your sister must stay at my house."

"Oh, but that is—" *Dreadfully improper.* "Very kind. But we cannot trespass upon your hospitality when you are in such dire straits."

A tiny glimmer of amusement lit his eyes. "Dupuy's place is expensive."

She had noticed. And they still might have months of living expenses yet before they found Papa. Propriety surrendered to practicality with only the briefest of struggles. "Very well, then. I accept with gratitude."

At the other end of the gaol, the gate was flung back with a clash. Her ten minutes were up.

"Good-bye for now, Mr. Hansen. Do not give up hope."

He shook her hand through the bars, his grip firm though his fingers were cold. But he made her no promises.

# CHAPTER 8

## FRIDAY, AUGUST 2, 1895

*1:20 p.m.*
*Georgetown*

*D*aisy and Frederica were forced to rent a pony and trap when they found out just how far out of town the paupers' field was, causing Daisy to feel slightly better about accepting Mr. Hansen's hospitality. The horse was cheap, and there were no steam vehicles to be had anyway. Perhaps it was just as well that Freddie's rudimentary skills at piloting a landau were not to be tried today.

"This is a disgrace," Freddie said, shifting on the thin leather padding of the seat. "Pauper's field, indeed. And you know what is worse? The Davises refusing to come. They are fair-weather friends, that's what."

"Be fair, dear. Mrs. Davis is distraught and cannot leave her room."

"She'd be quick enough to leave it if the funeral were in church."

Daisy sighed. "It is as useless to speculate about that as it is to try to guess who the father—" She stopped herself two syllables too late. She must be more upset than she realized if she could not control her tongue.

"Who the father of her child was, yes."

In sudden agitation, Daisy flapped the reins over the pony's back. Its hide was spotted and speckled in the most peculiar fashion. "Do not speak of it, Freddie. It is most unseemly."

"Unseemly? Goodness, Daisy, have you aged twenty years overnight? How like Aunt Jane you sound. I am not a child."

Stung, Daisy began, "I know, but—"

"I am perfectly aware that babies come to women who wear no wedding ring as well as to those who do."

"Neither of us should know that."

At the wobble in her voice, clearly audible over the rapid clop of the pony's hooves, Freddie slipped an arm around her waist. "I am sorry. I did not mean to upset you further. I just cannot help wondering, though. Who. And when. And why she would have permitted it when it seems she had already begun to write to Mr. Hansen."

"Perhaps she did not permit it." The words forced themselves from Daisy's lips even as in her mind's eye, Aunt Jane had the vapors and took to the sofa.

But that dreadful thought silenced Freddie for the rest of the way to their destination, where they observed a pair of undertakers on a slow march out into the field, a plain pine coffin borne upon their shoulders.

"I know it distresses you, but we must have them open the casket," she said to Freddie. "Moor the pony to that tree."

"I am already distressed. I have never been this close to a horse, either," Freddie objected. "What if it bites?"

"I have never opened a coffin," Daisy retorted. "We must call upon our resources under duress."

"That is what Maggie Polgarth always says," Freddie muttered as she did as she was bid. It apparently had not entered the horse's head that it might bite. "When you're in a tight spot, catalogue your resources, and apply your intellect."

Which was not quite the same thing, but if she did not intercept the undertakers, both resources and intellect would be of no use. When the men understood that two respectable-looking young ladies bearing flowers usually associated with a wedding wanted them to open the coffin, they looked at each other in confusion.

"Lid's nailed down, miss," one said at last, clearly concluding that Daisy was in charge of this outrage.

"I understand that. I trust you have the same hammer to hand with which you did the job? One pulls out nails with the same tool, does not one?"

"What fer?" asked the other. "Tain't right."

Daisy prepared to prevaricate. "We are her closest friends, and were not able to say good-bye. I have flowers and a keepsake from her mother that must go in the coffin, and then I beg you will allow us to pay our respects and say a prayer for her before you consign her to the earth. Since there is no one else to perform that office." Tears welled in her eyes.

Freddie's mouth trembled, and she fumbled a handkerchief out of her pocket with the hand not holding Emma's wedding roses.

The dreadful prospect of dealing with two weeping women galvanized the men into action. The hammer was produced, the lid pried up and set aside, and the pair withdrew a respectful distance and turned their backs to give them some privacy. One of them pulled out a pipe and lit it, as though he expected their prayers to take some time.

"Keep watch, Freddie. I do not want to be rushed."

Daisy knelt by her friend's side. Emma lay peacefully in the unadorned coffin, dressed in the clothes Daisy had seen at the doctor's office yesterday morning. Someone—his wife?—had laid two bright marigolds from the garden under her folded hands. Daisy took the roses and arranged them around her, tucking the wilted orange blossoms into her hair.

"Forgive me, dear friend," Daisy whispered.

What had caused the trickle of blood she had seen at the corner of her mouth? Did one spit up blood after having been beaten? All traces of it had been washed away, but whoever had done this had not taken the time to dress Emma in other clothes.

There were rips in the fine fabric of her blouse. Small tears, in a quantity of blood, which had stiffened as it dried. The stains had been concealed at the doctor's office by the purposeful folding of her underthings, leaving Daisy now feeling lightheaded from shock.

"Oh, dear," whispered Freddie.

"Please do not look, dearest."

"I am not. It is only that this is a most unsettling cemetery. A mist seems to be rising."

It took a moment of deep breathing to recover her wits. Daisy needed her wits now. Her courage. And not for something as insubstantial as a mist. If Emma had been set upon by persons unknown, perhaps the wounds might tell her something. What, she did not know—she had never been closer to what appeared to be a stab wound than cutting her finger while chopping potatoes for dinner. It would be distressing, but she must do this if it would help Mr. Hansen.

Gently, she unbuttoned Emma's blouse, noting that Mrs. Pascoe had not seen fit to put the corset or corset cover back on. The chemise was the layer closest to the skin, delicate lawn finely tucked and trimmed. And torn. All four layers— blouse, corset cover, corset, and chemise—had been violated by the knife in the same manner, one below the other.

"How did the doctor's wife not think to ask us for fresh garments for her to be buried in?" Somehow this seemed horribly disrespectful.

The least of several distressing facts. Daisy had never seen such wounds in her life, and she swallowed the bile that rose in her throat.

"Daisy, are you all right?"

She looked up at her sister, tears leaking from her eyes. "You were saying about the mist?" she croaked.

Looking as pale as Daisy felt, Freddie understood at once. "It seems to be agitated. Mist rises in the morning, not at two in the afternoon. I do not know how to reassure the, er, inhabitants that we are not ghouls. That our intentions are good. That we mean Emma no harm."

"I will try to be quicker."

Taking a deep breath, she focused upon her task. Emma's chest had been pierced once—twice—thrice—by a blade seeking her heart. The cuts were not very wide, an inch at most, perhaps less. She had no way to know how long the blade was unless she summoned the nerve to turn Emma over to see if it had pierced her through. Which she could not.

Despite her need to discover who had done this, the fact

remained that she was being a ghoul. A loving, kindly intentioned ghoul with tears dripping off her nose.

Never mind. She wiped her face on her jacket sleeve. However long it was, the blade's force seemed clear. Bruises had formed around the cuts from the violence of it. Bruises formed when blood vessels broke under a blow, did they not? Mr. Hansen had said something about her protecting herself—if so, would her hands not have been cut as well?

Tenderly, Daisy lifted them both. They were unmarred, except for a scrape on the right palm. Perhaps she had flung out a hand to break her fall.

Emma had not even had a chance to defend herself. Had the attack been so quick—from the front, not from behind, at that—and yet he had taken the time to kick a fallen, dying woman?

*Do not dishonor your friend by being sick.*

What could have done this? Did the miners' tools include a blade? Had it been a saber like those the Rangers wore, a kitchen knife, a hunting knife—some kind of blade in common use in the Wild West that she had not yet seen? With so many possibilities, their errand here seemed even more foolish and frustrating and horrible. Too many answers were as bad as none.

She smoothed the hair from her friend's face and, still kneeling, pulled her sketchbook and a pencil from her reticule.

"Daisy!" Freddie hissed. "The undertaker has finished his pipe. And now—the mist—I cannot see the farthest row of crosses."

A few strokes had the location and contours of the wounds approximated, careful smudges of the pencil indicating the tight, circular bruises. A few more formed the peaceful outlines of her friend's throat and chin. Then she buttoned and tucked in her clothes the way she had found them. Lastly, she crossed her poor hands once more upon the marigolds.

Under the guise of pulling out a handkerchief, she stashed the sketchbook in her reticule once again, and remained for a few moments in the pose of prayer. An appeal to the Almighty for mercy was all she could manage. Her resources were expended.

To her surprise, Freddie's voice came steady and clear.

"The Lord is my shepherd, I shall not want ..."

The Psalmist's beautiful words flowed over the casket and Daisy's shattered feelings, and even the mist ceased its terrible advance to hover amid the trunks of the pines.

"...and I will dwell in the house of the Lord forever."

Daisy rose and dusted off her skirts. She and Freddie bowed to the undertakers, who were shifting from one booted foot to the other, and made their way slowly back to the patient pony. She felt exhausted.

Freddie patted its nose. "We no longer seem to be in any danger." No one living was present save themselves, the undertakers now bending to their work, and a pair of jays frisking in the pines.

"I am glad to hear it. Thank you for the psalm. I think she would have liked it."

"Come. I will drive us back to the blacksmith's. Imagine a town that is so up-to-date with Mr. Tesla's electricks still keeping a blacksmith in business."

Leaning on each other, they had two miles to recover. Daisy was forced to consider the magnitude of the task she had before her. She was no Texican Ranger. She had no skills other than her powers of observation, and what good were they when outnumbered by dozens of possibilities?

But as they passed the doctor's house, she wondered if perhaps he might be of some further help. "Freddie, pull up. I wish to call upon the doctor."

"Are you not well? Outside of what we are both feeling at the moment, I mean. You were looking dreadfully pale earlier."

"I am perfectly well." She moored the animal to the fence and Freddie followed her around to the surgery, where they found the doctor seeing a patient out the door.

No throwing people off the steps today, then. He bowed politely to the departing matron and watched the girls approach. "Miss Linden."

"Dr. Pascoe. This is my sister, Frederica."

He inclined his head as Freddie dropped a curtsey. "What may I do for you? I am between patients for the next five minutes."

"I need no longer than that," Daisy said. She did not even require an invitation to step within. Which was a good thing, since one did not seem to be forthcoming. "Doctor, we have just had quite a long drive to pay our last respects to Miss Makepeace. She was not buried in the church cemetery, you see."

His face flushed in that mottled, heavy way she had seen yesterday. "I am aware of that."

"I understand that the paupers' field is for—for fallen women and criminals. But surely—given the place she was to hold in society here—and Mr. Hansen's wish that she be given this respect—there is still time to move her coffin to the church cemetery and give her a proper funeral. They were only beginning to dig when we left."

He eyed her, his civility diminishing in direct proportion to the height of his color. "Allow me to educate you, a stranger in these parts. Mr. Hansen is a respectable man despite these accusations against him. Immediately after I administered salts to Eveline yesterday at the Davis home, I returned to visit the good reverend at First Presbyterian on Bjorn's behalf. He is adamant that a fallen woman may not be buried in sacred ground alongside our finest citizens."

"But sir—for all we know, the child may have been the result of some earlier attack. She may have been innocent."

"That is a subject a *well brought up* young lady should have no knowledge of and may certainly not discuss. I am ashamed for you." *Since you have no shame yourself.*

Daisy clenched her molars upon the words that wanted to fly out of her mouth and beat him about the head. How dare he imply that Mama and Papa had done a poor job of her upbringing!

"You may be on your way now," he said stiffly. "I have done my best and can do no more."

"Just one thing—have you had any success in finding someone to represent Mr. Hansen?"

"And how is that your business?"

"I was to be bridesmaid at his wedding. I believe I may be forgiven an interest in his welfare."

"An interest, indeed," he replied. "Be careful it is not enough to give the impression you wish to step into a dead woman's shoes."

Frederica took her hand with cold fingers, for Daisy had been shocked into silence.

Into her struggle to form words, he went on, "I cannot think that your friendship with that young woman is anything to recommend you. I regret being the cause of further distress to you, but she has disgraced and endangered my friend, and to my view, has come to an end no better than she deserved.

"But to answer your impertinent question, no, I have not yet found someone to defend Mr. Hansen. There are three lawyers in Georgetown, all attached to the mining companies. They take care of land interests and any trouble the miners get into, which keeps them occupied on a daily basis. If someone unconnected with the mines needs representation of a legal or civil sort, they call upon Jake Stuyvesant in Silver Plume—if they can catch his attention between drunks. I will not speak to him even in these desperate straits."

"Then how is Mr. Hansen to be defended?" Freddie burst out, since Daisy could not.

"These are the Texican Territories, young lady. We do not have Philadelphia lawyers parading through the streets handing out cards. The only man I could find with anything close to legal experience is a greenhorn by name of Meriwether-Astor. He has not taken the bar exams, nor is he even a resident here. But he may be my only prospect."

"Hugh Meriwether-Astor?" Frederica said in surprise.

"You seem to know all the transients hereabouts."

Now it was Frederica's turn to be silenced.

"Have you hired him?" Daisy's powers of speech returned in the face of this fresh insult.

"I have asked him to look into the case, but I hold out no hope that he will take it—or succeed if he does."

Daisy lost her tenuous grip upon her temper, feeling it slide away like a piece of wet rope off the end of a quay. "You do not seem overly concerned about the impending hanging of a man you call your friend. I should be moving heaven and earth to secure him a good lawyer, even if it meant sending to Denver for one."

Now she had flicked his self-respect on the raw. Standing on the top step, fists clenched, he seemed to loom over them. "Your opinion is both unwelcome and irrelevant. If necessary I will defend him myself. We look after our own here. Now, I beg you, remove yourselves from these premises. I hear my next patient's buggy."

With that, he turned and strode into the surgery, the door closing behind him in a manner much too firm for civility.

After a moment, Frederica took a breath. "If that is how he acts as a friend, I should hate to experience his bedside manner as a patient."

Daisy turned and walked back to the pony and trap, her skirts snapping. She took some satisfaction in the sight of the animal placidly consuming Mrs. Pascoe's perennial border. "At least we have learned something," Daisy said as they climbed in and she picked up the reins. "Mr. Meriwether-Astor seems like a kind and capable person. At least we can tell him what we have discovered. And there is someone else."

"Someone else to defend Mr. Hansen?"

"No. Someone we should talk to. The young man who gave me that potion for Emma yesterday. The doctor threw him out of his surgery where we were standing just now."

Rapidly, she told Freddie the circumstances. "What if it was not the cure he promised? What if he is the villain the doctor suspects him of being, and it was some kind of slow-acting poison?"

Had William Barney—Barnum—oh, what was his name?—

been the man Emma had encountered on that dark street? Had she known something was horribly amiss, and accused him of it? Would that not incite a man to rage if he thought she would tell the doctor and the authorities, thereby exposing him and his crime?

When they returned the pony and trap to the livery stable, she and Freddie walked in the direction of Argentine Street.

"Are you sure you want to do this, dear?" Freddie sounded worried now. "It seems far too dangerous. Should we not simply tell Mr. Meriwether-Astor and board the late train?"

Which seemed a good opportunity to tell her of Mr. Hansen's invitation to use his house.

"Stay here? For how long? What about Papa —Emma said—"

"Freddie, we are unable to do anything more for Emma than we have already done, little as it was. But we must do something to help Mr. Hansen. He is innocent, and it seems the Texican Rangers have condemned him already. They are not even looking for the real murderer. It seems to me that our finding that person is his only hope of avoiding the rope."

"*Our* finding? What do *we* know of such things?"

"Little enough, I grant you. The doctor may be Mr. Hansen's friend, but I am not sure he can be depended on. He did not even tell Mr. Hansen the extent of Emma's injuries." She did not say so to Freddie, but perhaps this was deliberate —so that Mr. Hansen might trip himself up with knowledge only the murderer possessed.

Perhaps the doctor was the kind of friend who made a good enemy.

## CHAPTER 9

SATURDAY, AUGUST 3, 1895

*5:05 p.m.*

*I*t took a fair amount of time for Freddie to resign herself to staying in Georgetown instead of pursuing their search for their father. But she was not resigned to the pursuit of murderers. Neither was she about to allow Daisy to talk to any gentleman alone, so they reached a truce at the tavern door. The snake-oil salesman, however, was not at home. Daisy's disappointment battled with relief.

Frederica tapped her sleeve and indicated the field behind the building. "That is where I picked the flowers for Mr. Hansen's house."

A figure holding something rose from where it had bent in the waving grass, which had not been cut and which swayed about his waist. Daisy recognized him at once, and her resolution returned. "There is the man we seek, occupied in much the same way. Come."

The long light of a late summer afternoon gilded the grass,

illuminating the brown-eyed Susans and Queen Anne's Lace from behind so that they seemed to glow. Daisy felt a pang of regret that she did not have her paints with her, only the sketchbook, for the effects of light and shadow were an ongoing and delightful study. But they had more urgent business now.

The snake-oil salesman saw their approach and waggled a plant with white flowers and feathery leaves in greeting, in the process showering himself in dirt from its roots. Apparently unconcerned, he called, "Why, hello. Are the wedding festivities concluded satisfactorily?"

"He does not know," Freddie murmured in some wonderment.

"How can that be possible?" Daisy muttered back. "The entire town knows." More loudly, she said, "I hope we are not disturbing you, sir."

"Do I look disturbed?" Again he waved the plant, but thankfully, all the earth that could be dislodged from its roots already had been. "I am digging yarrow. It is extremely beneficial for cough and fever, and difficult to find during the season in which one catches cold. Therefore I am like the ant in the fable, prudently putting it by for the winter." He bowed to Frederica. "William Barnicott, at your service, miss."

*Barnicott.* She must remember it in case she was obliged to pass it on to the authorities. "This is my sister, Frederica," Daisy said. "I am afraid we bring sad news."

"Oh?" The appealing triangles of his face fell into an arrangement of distress. "Are you both well?"

"We are, but one of your patients is not. I regret to inform you that there has been no wedding. Miss Emma Makepeace died sometime in the early hours of yesterday morning."

He stared at her, and Daisy realized that his very nice russet-brown eyes were shaded by enviably long lashes.

Which were utterly irrelevant to the task at hand.

"The young lady about whom we spoke on Thursday?" he asked in tones of disbelief. "The one with the stomach complaint? It was that serious?"

"It turns out that the doctor's wife was right after all," Daisy said stiffly. She did not want to betray her friend's secret, but she could see no way out of it. "It seems Miss Makepeace was expecting a child."

Mr. Barnicott's eyes darkened in sympathy, not censure. "Miss Linden, I am dreadfully sorry for your loss. But I hope you will take comfort in the fact that you did your best to help her."

"That is why I am here. Do you remember what was in that potion you sent with me?"

"Just what I told you. Lady's mantle, lemon balm, chickweed, and a little ground ginger root, concocted into a tincture."

"Could it have killed her?" Freddie blurted.

"Certainly not," he said with the firmness of a man who knew his business. "In fact, lady's mantle is particularly beneficial to ladies in a delicate condition, though of course it would do no harm in the case of a simple stomach upset."

"Did you ever see Miss Makepeace?" Daisy asked. "Or did she visit at any time Thursday?" Of course she knew the answer; Emma, Freddie, and Daisy had been together for most of the day and evening.

"Sadly, no," the young man said. "But I can tell she was a young lady who inspired devotion in others. She seems to have been very fortunate in her friends."

This was just too civil and kind. Perhaps Daisy was taking the wrong approach.

"And Thursday night? Did you happen to see her? She was known to have been walking back to the Hotel de Paris around midnight."

"Alone? Unescorted?" The pitch of his musical voice rose in dismay.

"There were ... mitigating circumstances. Perhaps you might have offered your assistance?"

"I certainly would have, had I seen her. This is a fairly safe town, but still, a young lady of good family should not be walking alone at night, and certainly not once the taverns close and the streets are flooded with unruly miners."

"So you were not in town at that hour? Perhaps enjoying supper or companionship yourself in a tavern?"

He shook his head. "As it happens, I was attending a young laundress at the house of, er, Madame Ophelia. She took a beating from one of the customers that evening, poor thing. The, ah, owner of the establishment called for my services since Dr. Pascoe was, um—"

"Unwilling to attend her?" Frederica asked with the smallest edge to her voice.

"I would hate to cast aspersions on a fellow medical professional in the upholding of his oath. I am sure he was called away on another case."

"Ophelia's, you said?" Daisy asked. "Which house is hers?"

He nodded over one shoulder. "The oxblood—" He stopped himself, clearly remembering too late how unsuitable such a subject was for the ears of unmarried young ladies. "Why would you want to know that? Most here pretend the houses across the river don't exist."

"I am not most people."

That penetrating russet gaze rested upon her for a moment, as though trying to read her expression. "Why all these questions, Miss Linden?"

She raised her chin and plowed on. Emma deserved nothing if not persistence. "Please forgive me, but ... do you own a blade of any kind—perhaps for cutting plants?"

"A blade." Now the eyebrows lowered and his gaze became so intent that she took a step back and crushed an entire clump of buttercups. "This is more than a walk home at night. Was your friend attacked by someone wielding a blade? Is that the purpose of all these questions? You suspect me to be that someone?"

Clearly she was not cut out for a career as a Texican Ranger or one of Sir Robert Peel's constables or any other kind of investigator. The bitterness in his tone was perfectly audible, and in the best case, he would turn on his heel and leave. In the worst case, he would attack them and leave their bodies in the long grass for the carrion birds to find.

He turned away for a moment to take several deep breaths. Then he bent to pick an odd-looking flower bearing a slight resemblance to a daisy, as though its cheerful aspect would lighten his mood.

"Yes, I own a blade. It is eight inches in length, made by Mr. Bowie in Houston, and I do not cut plants with it. They give up their secrets under much gentler persuasion. This coneflower, for instance, is also useful for cough and congestion.

"The Bowie knife and an Enfield rifle are my only means of protection during the long stretches of wilderness between settlements. When forced to, I use them on coyotes and pumas. Not young ladies of good family. Or anyone else, for that matter."

"How … how wide is the blade, sir?" Daisy managed through lips that seemed to have forgotten how to move. But she must ask this last question. She must end this, so that she would not have to return and go through it again. Would not feel this shame at being so duplicitous when he had been nothing but considerate and kind.

"Nearly two inches at the crossbar, narrowing to a tip suitable for skinning rabbits and gutting fish, if necessary. I can show it to you, if you like. It is in my conveyance, there." He nodded toward the back of the tavern.

Daisy realized she had earlier misunderstood the nature of his lodgings. When he had said "behind the tavern," he had not meant a room, he had meant this very field, wherein rested the most extraordinary vehicle she had ever seen. It combined a landau-like front with a rear that was solid on one side and on the other resembled nothing so much as an apothecary's shop, with rows of windows that allowed the proprietor to show the wares within without risk of their being pocketed. A steam pipe issued from a chamber between front and back, where it appeared a fuselage would be attached by a series of rings and ropes, to make the entire contraption float. The fuselage was currently in a heap on the ground, leaving the gasbags hovering naked in the air.

It seemed that Mr. Barnicott had been grounded for repairs.

Curious though she was about how one operated such a thing, and its efficacy in this steep and mountainous country, she must recall herself to her errand.

A blade such as he described could not have left the

wounds she had witnessed. He must be telling her the truth. He could not be the guilty one.

She let out a long breath and was finally able to reply. "That is a most extraordinary vehicle, but I will not inconvenience you. Thank you for your honesty and forbearance, sir. We will trouble you no longer."

She inclined her head, her straw hat brim briefly blocking her view of his gaze upon her, and turned away.

They had not taken half a dozen steps when he called, "Miss Linden, wait. Do you intend to pursue this line of inquiry? While it would be sensible of you to give my name to the Texican Rangers as a suspect, I pray that you will not. I have had a number of run-ins with them already since leaving the Fifteen Colonies, and do not wish to repeat the experience."

"I am satisfied concerning your innocence in this matter, sir," she managed. "Besides, the Rangers are not making any inquiries at all. That is why we are doing so."

"That does not sound like them," he said rather flatly.

"They have already put Miss Makepeace's fiancé in gaol," Freddie told him, in a forthcoming way most unlike her. "They believe they have their man and are looking no further."

"Did he do it?" the young man asked in some surprise. "I've met him. He doesn't seem like the sort. But then, murderers hardly ever do."

"Of course he didn't," Daisy said briskly. "That is why, in the absence of any kind of legal representation for him at the moment, we are doing what we can to help."

"He is fortunate in his friends, too, then."

"He is lucky he has us," Freddie agreed. "That grumpy

doctor says he is his friend, but I'm not convinced. He will not even send to Denver for a lawyer."

"In the Territories, you will not find people sending to the city for others to solve their problems," he told her, nodding. "They will hold him in gaol until the circuit magistrate makes his way here. Will the poor man defend himself, then?"

"No, but someone else may." Freddie turned to Daisy. "We ought to speak with Mr. Meriwether-Astor, sister. He will want to know what we have discovered."

"Meriwether-Astor?" Mr. Barnicott said in some surprise. "Any relation to Mrs. Stanford Fremont, née Gloria Meriwether-Astor?"

"They are cousins, I believe," Daisy told him, half of her wondering why they were telling this man all their nearest concerns, the other half finding a certain relief in sharing the burden. She must impress upon Freddie the need for confidentiality. It would not do to be blabbing their business to all and sundry and putting a murderer on alert that people were taking an interest in his activities.

"So you are acquainted with Meriwether-Astor?" he persisted.

"We met him on the airship coming over from London. The same ship on which we met Miss Makepeace. He has been very kind." Words came out of Daisy's mouth, telling him more and more, while her mind shouted that she ought to listen to herself and be more circumspect. What was wrong with her?

This must end at once.

"Come, Frederica. We must not detain Mr. Barnicott any longer."

"But Daisy—"

"At once, dear. Good day, sir."

As they crossed the field, wading through drifts of yellow and gold and blue, it became clear that her sister was not appreciating Daisy's whispered lecture about correct behavior in the least.

"He is a kind man," she said obstinately, as if one could make such a determination on five minutes' acquaintance. "Especially after we as much as accused him of being a murderer. Most men would have become angry—at least, I imagine so. One is not in the habit of making such accusations as a general rule, so one does not have experience to go by."

"I am just saying that *one* had better be more discreet. If we share confidences with the wrong party, it is not inconceivable that we could find ourselves on the wrong end of a knife, too."

Which horrifying prospect was enough to silence her sister for the entire length of the walk to the hotel.

# CHAPTER 10

SATURDAY, AUGUST 3, 1895

*6:30 p.m.*

Since their luggage was already in the storage room behind the reception desk, it was only a matter of minutes to bring down that of Miss Makepeace and check out of the Hotel de Paris. Daisy paid the ever-present boy lurking around the unused coal chute to trundle along behind them with Miss Makepeace's lovely travel trunk, her wedding suit once more in its bag and all her effects safely enclosed therein. They could not bring themselves to dispose of it as Mr. Hansen had suggested. Instead, once he was free and enough time had passed that the sight of her things did not grieve him, he might reconsider.

The door of the little house at Eighth and Rose was unlocked, and after the boy had deposited his burden in the entry and collected his coin, he frowned down at the trunk.

"This belongs to that lady what were murdered Thursday

midnight? Her what was to be Mrs. Hansen, who was in your party?"

Daisy briefly considered telling him what happened to little boys who poked their noses into other people's business, then abandoned the idea. She had been told often enough that children ought to be seen and not heard, and look how well that had turned out. "Yes, I am afraid so. Thank you for helping us. You may be on your way."

"How did you know?" Freddie asked.

The boy shrugged his thin shoulders under his dirty coat. "Usin' me noggin. I saw you three together at the 'otel, then I heard wot 'appened to her, then I'm paid to bring a trunk bearing 'er name to Mr. Hansen's address. Pretty simple. Is it true he done it?"

"It is not," Daisy said crisply. "And if you are any friend to him, you will keep your ears open for any hint of who did."

"I ain't friend to anyone, but for another penny I could be talked into keepin' an ear out." His eyes, gray as a stormy sky, held hers as bold as could be, though the top of his cap barely came to her shoulder.

Possibilities were not exactly raining down upon their heads, so Daisy nodded. "We have an agreement, then. What is your name, young man?"

"*Hey you*, mostly, miss. Or *boy*."

"What did your mother call you?" she said more gently. "For I certainly do not address people who are kind enough to help me as *hey you*."

His brows furrowed and his lips formed a narrow line. "Don't you talk about my mother. It ain't her fault we fell on hard times."

"I should think not. Clearly, she was a woman of character to have raised such a brave and enterprising son."

He looked a little mollified, and his tanned fists relaxed. "She called me Davey."

"Thank you, then, Davey. I am Miss Daisy Linden, and this is my sister Frederica. We will be staying here for ... a few days. If you hear of anything that might help us discover who killed our poor friend, we would be very grateful."

With a nod, he ran down the path and the gate banged shut behind him.

Daisy and Freddie looked about them.

"Can it really be only only yesterday that disaster befell our friends?" Daisy wondered aloud. "The house feels abandoned already."

"Then I am glad we are permitted to bring it back to life," Freddie said. "Where are we to sleep?" She prowled through parlor, kitchen, dining room, and office, and finally called, "Daisy, come and see."

Her voice had come from the only bedroom. "We will need to change the sheets, if there is such a thing as a second set," Daisy said, joining her. Then— "Oh."

Her heart gave a strange thump as she gazed at the bridal bed, its beautifully appliquéd quilt strewn with rose petals that had curled up at the edges. The pillowcases were white as a drift of snow and trimmed in handmade lace—perhaps the gift of a faraway mother or sister. It was clear that it had been freshly prepared early on the wedding morning, with every effort made to please.

"A man who would do this would never raise his hand to a woman, much less ... anything else," Freddie said, her voice trembling a little. "How can we possibly disturb what was meant for her?"

"He offered it to us," Daisy said. "It is all he could do in exchange for our help. Let us accept his gift as gracefully as we can. Help me clear away these petals, dear."

It did not take long, nor did the unpacking and hanging of their few skirts and blouses and Daisy's one dinner dress. "I believe Mr. Hansen made this wardrobe," Daisy said, running a hand down the satiny finish. "Look at the carving of the doves—for peace. *Make peace*, don't you see?" Her throat tightened, but she pressed on. "And the usefulness of the shelving on the inside, here, all the way down."

Freddie inhaled the scent of the wood. "It is lined in cedar, to keep the moths out. He thought of everything."

And Emma would never now enjoy such consideration, such attention to her smallest happiness. Daisy turned away to hide her wet eyes, opening a drawer built into the base of the wardrobe.

It contained shirts, collars, and a bundle of letters, all addressed to Mr. Hansen in a feminine hand. "He said he wished me to burn his letters to her, should I find them among her things," Daisy said, "but gave me no instructions as to hers to him."

"We cannot burn them, sister." Freddie's gaze was solemn. "Outside of the contents of that trunk and your portrait, they are all he has of her."

"I do not know whether they will comfort or distress him," she said. "He told me he did not care what we did with everything, but I cannot help but think he may care later." Once he was vindicated and set free.

She gazed at the packet of letters. "I wonder..." Heat

burned into her cheeks and she could not quite meet Frederica's gaze. "Do not think me horrid, but what if there is some clue as to her assailant's identity in those letters?"

Freddie's whole body stiffened in offense. "Daisy, you cannot be suggesting that we read them. That is disgraceful. First her coffin—now her confidence—where will it end?"

Daisy had had enough of a struggle with her behavior today. She did not want to augment it by snooping and being exposed to expressions of feeling that were private. But at the same time, what if a clue lay there, unseen and overlooked? "I only thought—"

"Mama would be ashamed of you. Besides, Emma said she and her papa had been living in London for six months. Her assailant is almost certainly from here. A stranger—a miner— someone we have no way to know. You cannot tell me that someone from England would travel across the world to carry out such an act. Aunt Jane hid the newspapers from us, but we both know that London is a much better location for terrible deeds."

"I know this will distress you, but there is one person of our acquaintance who did, as you say, travel across the world. Who has been in London at least part of that time."

"Who?" Freddie demanded.

"Mr. Meriwether-Astor."

Silence fell in the simple but comfortable bedroom, their agitated breathing and the rustle of their skirts the only sound.

When Freddie finally spoke, it was in the measured tones of one attempting to be logical in the face of madness. "Nothing will induce me to believe that the man who has been so kind to us, who has gone out of his way to see to our comfort, who is the friend of my friend, can possibly have anything to do with what happened to Emma."

"What if they were acquainted in London? What if he is the father of the child?"

"How can you say such a thing? He is the last man who would ruin a woman's reputation, to say nothing of harming her."

"Justice may not be the only one who is blind. I saw your partiality for him, despite his for your friend Maggie."

"Which makes him even less likely to be the father," Freddie said triumphantly, though the flags of high temper flew in her cheeks.

"But you must admit it could be possible."

"I admit no such thing. What possible reason would he have for committing such a crime?"

"Why, jealousy, I suppose," she replied, miring herself even further now that she had to consider it. "To prevent her marrying Mr. Hansen. Though I admit that would make two men with a motive of jealousy. Mr. Hansen of the father, and Mr. Meriwether-Astor of the husband. Only one can have done it."

"Nonsense," Freddie snapped. "Neither did it. It was someone from here—some terrible impulse in a madman's heart. Besides, Emma and Hugh did not even know one another. You saw them on *Persephone*. There was no recognition at their first meeting, that day at breakfast."

"Hugh, is it?" Daisy observed in passing. "He could be a good actor."

"No one could keep up the act without betraying the truth by a glance, a touch."

"Oh, and are you so wise in the ways of men that you know this, a girl of eighteen?"

Freddie's color faded and she turned away.

"I am sorry." Contrite, Daisy laid a hand on her shoulder. She was grateful her sister did not shrug it off. "That was unkind. You are a good judge of character and an observer of human nature on both the natural and spiritual planes. But getting back to the matter at hand, I think we must do our best for Mr. Hansen, and read the letters."

"Let it be on your conscience." Freddie walked to the door. "I am going to make tea."

It did not take long—there were only a dozen or so in the little bundle, none taking more than four sides of the thin paper designed for airmail via pigeon. Daisy scanned them, noting the details of Emma's daily life, her discreet shopping for her trousseau, her meetings with the mail-order brides in the guise of the literary club. There were brief accounts of dinners at which she acted as her father's hostess, the occasional flicker when she could escape the house, and several balls.

Daisy held a letter dated late April, one name among several that littered the page standing out in its familiarity.

"The tea is ready," Freddie called from the dining room. "Come have a cup. To drink, not to paint."

Daisy had a feeling that painting teacups, which usually soothed and comforted her, would not be so effective today. She went in, the fragile sheet in her hand. "Freddie, look."

Freddie's expression became fixed as she read.

*Papa insists on my going to these affairs, though I cannot imagine why when the likelihood of my marrying anyone there is nil. But he does not know that, of course, so I make an appearance, and dance with a Mount-Batting here and a Meriwether-Astor there, always in the particular set with whom he wishes me to be seen. The Dunsmuir set, you know. But they are boys, and I wish to love a man.*

*One man, my dearest. You.*

# CHAPTER 11

## SUNDAY, AUGUST 4, 1895

*3:40 p.m.*
*Georgetown*

illiam Barnicott had been booted out of Harvard some three years ago, four months short of the conferring of his degree in chemistry. The school had no tolerance for people who blew up entire buildings by mistake, even if they apologized. Since he had been in the building at the time, though thankfully in the stairwell (he had been on his way to the dining room for a midnight snack), he thought they might have shown a little clemency to an injured man.

They had not.

His departure was swift and merciless, though not half so merciless as his father's subsequent cutting off of his stipend and the removal of his name from the family Bible.

He had the foresight to empty his slender bank account before his father got to it, however, and took the first train out of Boston without caring very much where it went. When he alighted in New Orleans, capital of the Louisiana Territory, he had his eyes opened to a society that operated in ways very different from that of the Fifteen Colonies. He'd lasted there for a year before being swindled out of the remainder of his money by a pair of long-lashed black eyes and promises of forever. He'd learned later that he was not the first to have lost his head in this way. He was the first, however, to turn the tables on the lady and her protector, using the skills that had had such dire results at university to much better effect.

He had blown up the carriage house under which they kept their valuables. He'd only intended to bring down one wall, but once again he'd underestimated the power of chemicals (which only made him more eager to study them further).

In the ensuing free-for-all that enriched the poor of the Vieux Carré with as much as they could carry away, he took back what was his and escaped to the railyard, where he caught the midnight train. He'd fallen in with a snake-oil salesman far to the north of New Orleans, who rather enjoyed aping the mannerisms of the characters in the flickers. He taught William about the power of perception. He also taught him what little he actually knew about cures.

Sadly, he'd been shot by a jealous husband, leaving William with his peculiar vehicle and a shady reputation. William regretted the loss of his friend and mentor, but he would always be grateful to him. For the first time, he was in control of his fate and now possessed a means of making his living.

He applied himself to chemistry, to cures, and to the botany all around him, with the help of the occasional book from the lending libraries of those rare towns that supported one. By the time he reached the Texican Territories, there were no more libraries, and he had been arrested twice for vagrancy and the illegal sale of liquor. The fact that a tincture required potato liquor in tiny amounts meant nothing to the magistrates, who were often as not offended hotel and tavern owners anxious to preserve their own living.

The last time, he had been quick-thinking enough to hand over a glass jar to the Texican Ranger as he thrust him into the gaol cell, suggesting that he apply it to his rather awful skin condition. The man was cured in three days, and William set free with only a warning.

A chance meeting with a Navapai engineer in Santa Fe had taken him to a cliff-top village, where he had spent nearly nine months learning all he could about plants and cures from a female shaman called Alaia. The engineer—who turned out to be her son—retrofitted his vehicle with a balloon to make it easier to traverse the canyons and arroyos of the Wild West, and he had proceeded on his way with a better education than Harvard had ever given him, and enough of the Navapai tongue to keep him from getting killed every time he approached the sandstone canyons of the Rio Sangre Colorado de Christo.

Though the Rose Rebellion had put the Viceroy firmly back on his throne in the Royal Kingdom of Spain and the Californias, and with changes in the laws that now allowed foreigners to travel there free of let or hindrance, he preferred to give the place a wide berth. He was content to make his living on this side of the mountains helping those he could, supplementing it by writing mostly true articles for the newspapers back in the Fifteen Colonies. It amused him to think of his parents and sisters reading the latest in An Educated Gentleman's *Tales of a Medicine Man*, with their lurid engravings, innocent of the fact that they were steadily fattening the discreet bank account in Santa Fe belonging to their cast-off son.

"Barney?"

He straightened, a bouquet of precious coneflower in one hand. The girl approaching him from the far side of the meadow was half dressed in a red corset and multicolored can-can skirts, a purple shawl around her bare shoulders. Madame Ophelia's was the only house of desert flowers to feature "can-can dancers straight from the Paris stage!" and his heart sank.

"Good afternoon, Kathleen. Is everything all right?"

She shook her head. "It's the little Canton girl. Madame don't want our place getting a bad reputation, and she's wailing so loud the gentlemen are getting spooked."

"Her pain has increased?" He was already heading for his vehicle and his medicine box, speaking over his shoulder.

"Seems so."

"Thank you. Tell Madame I'll be along shortly."

He set the coneflower to drying, washed his hands in the horse trough next to the tavern, and collected his box. Then he made his way among the trees to one of the discreet bridges that crossed Clear Creek, the dividing line between the acceptable side of society and the unacceptable.

They were sturdy bridges, well able to take the considerable foot traffic.

He found the little Canton laundress on a pallet in the kitchen next to the stove, her eyes glassy and one hand pressed to her side. "Hurts—" she gasped.

"Let me see." Gently, he unbuttoned her unbleached cotton shirt, which had probably once belonged to a boy and he hoped formed its own kind of deterrent on this side of town. Her hair had been sheared off below the ears some time ago, and whatever gloss it might once have possessed had dulled with pain and trauma. Kathleen, who had fetched him Thursday night, had said a gentleman had mistaken the laundress for a desert flower, and when she had refused him, had done a thorough job of exorcising his disappointment. Today the bruises had blossomed on her abdomen in shades of purple, yellow, and green, partly covered by the bandage he had wound about her chest and middle.

"Have you been applying the salve I gave you?" He could smell it, so he knew she had. That was progress.

"Aye, sir." She groaned as he touched her, though he was using all the care he could. "Hurts, sir."

"I'm sure it does—an ebony cane would feel like a crowbar to a delicate frame such as yours."

She screamed as his fingers touched the bruise over her lowest rib, and Ophelia popped through the doorway as though she'd been listening in the corridor.

"Stop that caterwauling at once! One of our best customers just left because of your racket." Ophelia had once been on the stage, he had learned at great length as he tended to the laundress Thursday night, and she had no difficulty in projecting to the third balcony now. "I've given you my hospitality and this is how you repay me? Be off with you. I won't have it."

"Madame—please—" The girl's dark eyes begged indulgence as she lay on the dirty pallet.

"If you can't work, you can't stay, and that's that." She turned and marched back to the parlor in the front.

The girl's eyes filled with tears. "What I do?"

William made up his mind. "You're coming with me until you are well, and then you may make your own choice in the matter."

He picked her up and carried her back to the conveyance, doing his level best not to jostle her, and she doing her best not to groan when he did. She weighed next to nothing. The first thing he must see to was a restorative draught and some beef soup. Despite his care, she was weeping silently by the time he laid her in the sleeping cupboard in the rear of his vehicle.

"If—if you will wait until I can sit up, sir, I will pay you in kind."

It took him a moment to recover from her perfect diction, when since their meeting last night she had been speaking in the pidgin many of the Canton people employed. It took another moment to comprehend her meaning.

"Good heavens. I am not that sort of man. There will be no payments of that or any other kind while you are my guest— or at any time thereafter."

"But I have no money, sir. And now, no job or place to live."

"You do not need to think of all that now. Rest, and I will see about food for both of us. What is your name?"

"They call me Washie."

William frowned. "That is no name for a young lady who has clearly had an education. Where is your family?"

She nibbled her upper lip. "Papa was a teacher in the old country, but he came to Gold Mountain to find my auntie— his sister—who had come here to marry. But he could not find her, and had to take work on the railroad. I was born in Gold Mountain, and went to a school that taught English."

She took a steadying breath. "He and Mahmee both caught the typhoid last winter. I did not want to work on the railroad or in the whorehouses, so I ... departed."

If those were her choices, William could hardly imagine what life must have been like for her. "What is Gold Mountain?"

"The Californio capital."

"You mean San Francisco?" While the young Viceroy's official residence was upon one of the hills crowning the city, and gold had created a rich and elegant society, the water-front was known to many as the Barbary Coast, home to merchant vessels, criminal gangs, and corruption. "Before they passed, what name did your parents give you?"

"You will not be able to say it."

"I should still like to know, if we are to be friends."

Somehow she managed to lift her chin, and William briefly glimpsed the strength that must have brought her all the dangerous miles across the Royal Kingdom to the mountains of the Texican Territory.

"I am Yang Lin-Bai."

He knew enough of Canton custom to remember that when introducing oneself, one used the surname first. "I am honored, Miss Yang."

But she shook her head. "You should call me Washie."

"I shall not. You will not be a laundress forever, and it would be most inappropriate. In the Canton tongue, what does Lin-Bai mean?" As she had predicted, he could not reproduce her inflection of the syllables, but she understood.

"White jade," she whispered, as though the words themselves were a treasure.

"If *Miss Yang* and *Washie* are off the table, would you object to my addressing you as Lin? It has the advantage of being both musical and brief."

A smile touched her lips. "You may. What is your name, then, sir? I heard Kathleen call you Barney."

"William Barnicott. But feel free to call me Barney if you like. Everyone does."

"Is that not like Washie? Everyone calls me that. They call all the laundresses that."

"Not in the least. My friends used it at school in Boston. A sobriquet was a mark of—well, camaraderie, I suppose."

"And it is brief." She attempted a smile, and her face spasmed instead. "What is Boston?"

"A place I hope you never go, many thousands of miles from here. How old are you?"

"I was thirteen on my last name day, when the wild roses were blooming along the creek."

Thirteen in June, then. She looked no more than ten. His heart contracted in compassion as he wondered how in God's name a man could take a cane to someone so small and defenseless. Such a man deserved to be swiftly hanged.

He took a packet of herbs out of one of the narrow drawers behind him and said, "I will return in a few minutes. Apply more salve while I am gone."

"Barney?"

He turned at the foot of the steps and leaned in the door. "Yes?"

"Thank you. In my father's tongue we say *xie-xie*."

"Shay-shay?"

"Well enough." He rejoiced to hear a smile in her voice.

"You are most welcome. Do not forget the salve."

The tavern's steam cooker supplied hot water for Alaia's

magical meadow tea, the bar a couple of bowls for the beef barley soup much favored by the miners for its substance, and a bottle of red wine. He carried it all back to his vehicle and spent a most congenial supper hour with his patient. When her strength flagged and her eyelids drooped, he took the bowl from her, encouraged her to finish the tea, and gently slid the cupboard door closed. "Good night, Lin. Rest now."

"Good night, Barney," came the nearly inaudible reply as she lapsed into an exhausted sleep.

Barney returned the bowls and mug to the tavern and made up a bed for himself on the leather-covered bench in the front of the vehicle. He would need to be careful not to brain himself on the acceleration bar when he turned over, but in his travels he had slept in many a less comfortable place.

Returning to the rear, he slid a stool from its aperture and seated himself once again at the tiny, hinged table opposite the sleeping cupboard. This day had been the strangest he had experienced in a long time—and he had experienced some strange ones. First that graceless young Englishwoman and her sister had practically accused him of the murder of a woman he had never met. Then he had rescued an abused child without thinking farther into the future than getting her on her feet.

It had been a day full of singular young ladies, to be sure. There must be a story for the Medicine Man's readers in all this.

He reached for his travel case and took out paper and ink. By the light of the lamp hanging from its hook behind his shoulder, he began to write.

## CHAPTER 12

### MONDAY, AUGUST 5, 1895

*10:25 a.m.*
*Georgetown*

*S*unday morning, Daisy and Frederica had eschewed the company of the congregation at First Presbyterian Church ("I am quite sure we are the wrong sort of people for them, Freddie,") and attended the service instead at a humble clapboard chapel where the singing was fine and the congregation made up of miners, laundresses, and those who might have been of Creole, Moorish, and Texican descent. Later, declining the delights of oysters and buffalo steak at the Hotel de Paris, the young ladies instead had taken their evening meal at a much more modest establishment.

Their first night in Mr. Hansen's house had been quiet, though Daisy could not say she slept well in a bed that did not belong to her.

This morning, they had ventured to the general store to lay in a few supplies. Then, after breakfast, it was time to gird up their loins and continue with their inquiries, pitting hope against futility every step of the way. Mr. Hansen had been in gaol three days already. Emma's murderer had been at large for longer. They must be brave.

Following directions from the clerk at the offices of the Pelican Mine, Daisy and Frederica found Mr. Meriwether-Astor at home in a tiny house he had rented on Ninth Street, just around the corner from that of Mr. and Mrs. Davis.

"We are very close to the Davises', Freddie," Daisy said at the gate. "We ought to call upon Mrs. Davis and condole with her."

"Can we do it some other time? By the time we finish here, it will be noon, and it would be the height of bad manners to arrive uninvited as Mrs. Davis and her husband sit down to luncheon."

Daisy had to admit she was probably right. Mr. Davis had not struck her as the kind of man who tolerated interruptions to his meals.

"To what do I owe the pleasure of this call?" On the other hand, Mr. Meriwether-Astor looked delighted, despite his collar being removed and ink stains upon his fingers. "How did you find me?"

He waved them into a pair of chairs upholstered in dreadful turquoise brocade that had clearly been mass-produced in a manufactory. He must have rented the house furnished, for no one could live with such a color by choice.

"We asked at the mine offices," Frederica said, then added a little anxiously, "I hope we are not intruding."

"No indeed. In fact, I am flattered that you took the trouble, and did not leave our next meeting to the whims of fate."

Frederica blushed, and Daisy judged it time to forestall a flirtation by telling him the reason for their call.

"To own the truth," she said, "we are here to tell you—I mean, I suppose you must have heard that Emma Makepeace was taken from us Thursday night?"

His bright pleasure in their company seemed to dim, making him seem older. "I am sad to say that I have. Please allow me to extend my condolences upon the loss of your friend. It is shocking. Terrible for such a beautiful person to be taken so soon."

"Thank you." Daisy gazed at him, attempting to discover any hint of dissembling in his eyes or expression.

"We cannot quite believe it is true," Freddie said, "except that we went to the cemetery Saturday to pay our final respects at the graveside. That was very real."

"I am glad," he said unexpectedly. "She deserved to have her friends with her, if her intended could not be."

Was there a faint note of judgment in his tone? No. She must be mistaken.

"It all happened so fast I apologize that we did not think to visit before this," Daisy told him. If he did not know Emma had been interred in the paupers' field, she would not be the one to tell him. "You were her friend, too."

"Not to the extent that you were."

"But you knew her longer," Frederica suggested.

His gaze came up, puzzled, to move between them seeking clarity. "I beg your pardon?"

"She simply means that—from something Emma said on the journey—it seems you met earlier, in London, perhaps at a ball or some other crowded occasion? I thought it was curious, you know, on *Persephone*, that you did not acknowledge the acquaintance."

He gazed at them, utterly at a loss. "You believe me to have been acquainted with Miss Makepeace before we met on *Persephone*?"

"Yes, I am quite sure she mentioned a ball, did not she, Freddie?" Daisy turned to her sister.

"It was in the spring." Oh, how innocent she looked! "It was definitely at a ball, because she said she had danced with a Mr. Meriwether-Astor."

The young man took a breath that seemed to indicate a sudden understanding, and relaxed against the wooden slats of his chair. "She must have meant my brother, Sydney. He was in London at about that time, on his way to Egypt, where he is now."

"Your brother?" Daisy said a little flatly as their theory evaporated. "I did not realize you had a brother. Goodness, what assumptions we have made. You will think us dreadfully silly."

His face warmed once again into a smile. "Never. It must have seemed very peculiar to you, to think of my introducing myself as though I had never laid eyes on her in my life. Which, as it turns out, I had not." He laughed. "I have been at university in Philadelphia, studying law. I have been in London very lately, though, to visit friends—including your friend Miss Polgarth, Miss Frederica—and to celebrate my surviving my first year. I was on my way home when I met you all."

Which is exactly what he had told them on the ship. How foolish they had been! If he had not been in London in April, then he was not the father of Emma's child, and had no reason to be jealous or to harm her. And if his brother was in Egypt now, then while a miniscule but doubtful chance existed that he might be the father, it was certain he could not be the murderer.

"I am so sorry you were not able to come to the groom's dinner on Thursday night," Daisy said. "If you had, this might have turned out quite differently. We know now why she was alone on her walk home. Mr. Davis was called to some crisis at the mine."

Hugh nodded. "I was there, too. And much as I would have enjoyed the dinner, I was one of the men down that tunnel when the beam collapsed. I came here to be educated about mining, but believe me, that was more than I bargained for."

Daisy exchanged glances with Freddie. He might have thought it a mere expression of relief, but Daisy clearly saw acknowledgement in Freddie's eyes. *Hugh could not have killed Emma, then, no matter what his brother might have been up to in the spring.*

Anxious to change the subject, Daisy said, "So you have a year of law school to your credit. Dr. Pascoe says that is more than many possess if they wish to come to the defense of their friends here in Georgetown."

"So you know he has been to see me."

"He told us. I will be honest—I am very worried for Mr. Hansen," Daisy confided. "The Texican Rangers have as much as tried him and found him guilty of Emma's death already."

"And you do not share their belief?"

"Certainly not," Daisy said.

"He was in love with her," Freddie added, as though this were the conclusion of the matter.

"Love can trigger passion of both the positive and the

negative kind," Mr. Meriwether-Astor replied thoughtfully. "Considering that in Georgetown we and the Davises are the only ones who knew the young lady, he is the most logical suspect. I know with certainty none of us harmed her, so that leaves only the man she was to marry."

This observation, in all its cool logic, did not seem to be leavened by the friendship or concern that would cause a man to take up the defense of another.

"But sir, Emma met many a person outside this room—the gentleman at the reception desk at the Hotel de Paris, Mr. Dupuy himself, some of the other guests. Why should not the pool of possibilities include them?"

"You believe it to have been the work of a random stranger?"

"It could have been," Daisy said. "With the mines and constant arrivals on the train, it seems worth considering, at least."

"But does it not seem much more likely that such a passionate crime—ladies, forgive me, but I only repeat what the doctor said—a beating on top of a knife attack, would have to be committed by someone in a highly emotional state?"

Silence fell in the room on the heels of an insight Daisy had never before considered. A chill settled on her shoulders and crept down her back, and she wished she had brought her shawl. "Do you plan to defend him?"

"I have not decided." He indicated the desk against the wall behind him, covered in papers and drawings. "My purpose here is to learn about mining. In any case, a year of law school does not prepare one for criminal defense, especially when that year has been in the field of claims and conveyances. If he had built a barn or staked a claim on someone else's land, I might be able to help. But not this."

"But surely you will try," Freddie pleaded. "If you do not, it will be up to Daisy and me, and so far, no one is listening to us."

His brows rose. "Daisy and you? What on earth do you mean?" In his astonishment, he did not seem to realize he had used Daisy's given name.

"Someone must discover the real culprit." Daisy held up a gloved hand and counted off on her fingers. "The Rangers are not investigating, believing they have their man. Dr. Pascoe believes he is innocent, but unlike you, thinks it was one of the miners or a stranger whose identity is impossible to determine. He will take up Mr. Hansen's defense as a last resort, but holds out no hope that he will succeed."

"I have my doubts about the depth of his friendship," Freddie said darkly. "That is no attitude to take before a magistrate."

"And you?" Mr. Meriwether-Astor said again. "What hope do you have of mounting a defense?"

"If we can find the culprit, that will be defense enough, don't you agree?" Goodness, he *could* be a little more supportive. After all, he had admired Emma. Should he not want to seek justice for her?

Mr. Meriwether-Astor seemed to be deciding upon the proper approach to his next words. "My dear girls, you must put this utterly out of your minds. It is not to be thought of."

"We are the only ones who *are* thinking of it," Daisy pointed out. "Neither of us wishes to see Mr. Hansen hang for a crime he did not commit."

"He has offered us his house to stay in while we are here,"

Freddie put in. "A man so thoughtful and kind could not be guilty."

"He has nothing to lose in making such an offer if he thinks you can get him off the hook," Mr. Meriwether-Astor said with truly demoralizing effect.

Daisy shot to her feet, and Freddie with her. "We may gather, then, that in fact you will *not* be taking his case?"

He rose, too, making patting motions in the air as though attempting to settle them down. "Let us not be hasty. We are friends, are we not? I simply need a little more time to find the best route to success. I am to dine with Dr. Pascoe this evening to discuss it. Ought I to ask if I might bring two guests?"

"Oh, no," Freddie blurted.

"Thank you for such a kind offer, but I think not," Daisy said a little more gracefully. "We will be about our business. Would you like to know the facts as we unearth them?"

The alarm returned to his eyes. "I would like no such thing. Girls, I beg of you, put this scheme out of your minds. This belongs in the hands of men, not gently bred females who are innocent of the world, and who do not know the town or its people."

"You don't either," Daisy pointed out with admirable logic and self-control. *Girls, indeed. Hmph.*

"But the doctor does—intimately—and he and I will confer. Promise me that you will not go around getting your-selves into trouble."

Daisy hesitated, then gave a sigh. "I promise."

Relief spread across his features, dismay across Freddie's.

"I am glad to hear it. I will let you know the results of our meeting. For now, may I offer you some luncheon? This house, small though it may be, comes with a respectable housekeeper and cook."

Daisy was still standing. "No, thank you. We must be on our way. Please give Dr. Pascoe our compliments."

He bowed them out and stood on the porch watching as they strolled away arm in arm. When they had turned the corner and could be reasonably certain the soft summer air would not carry the sound of their voices, Freddie said, "You do not really intend to keep your promise, do you, Daisy?"

"I do."

"But ... but what if both the doctor and Mr. Meriwether-Astor decide that the Rangers are right and the case is closed?"

"You mistake me, Freddie. I promised not to get myself into trouble. I did not promise to cease our inquiries, or to give up on Mr. Hansen as I fear both Mr. Meriwether-Astor and the doctor may do."

Freddie squeezed her arm. "Oh, I am glad. You quite frightened me back there."

"I am surprised at Mr. Meriwether-Astor. Clearly he did not have the regard for Emma that I thought, or he would not be so cavalier about determining the identity of the person who killed her."

Freddie walked on a few paces. "I do not understand it either. How can a man simply allow another to be condemned?"

Nothing in Daisy's experience equipped her to answer such a question. "We simply must find the real culprit," she said at last.

"And keep ourselves out of trouble," Freddie said. "It would never do to break a promise."

# CHAPTER 13

## MONDAY, AUGUST 5, 1895

*1:50 p.m.*

After a heartening lunch of tea and bread and cheese, Daisy pulled on her gloves. "I shall visit Mrs. Davis to condole with her. It is the proper thing to do."

"Would you like me to go with you?" Freddie picked up the empty plates. "For if not, I thought I might visit Mr. Hansen and take him one or two of these apples, and perhaps some bread and cheese."

The thought of her younger sister exposed to the prisoners in the gaol sent a dart of apprehension through Daisy's stomach. "Your compassion is commendable, but believe me, the gaol is no place for a young lady of tender years."

"I am only three years more tender than you, and you have gone," Freddie retorted with more truth than sense.

"I do not wish to repeat the experience. It was dreadful."

"Imagine how Mr. Hansen feels."

Daisy thought quickly, lest Freddie get her back up

and do as she planned regardless. "But mightn't you leave the food in the care of one of the Rangers in the front office to be delivered to him? And keep your ears open. Perhaps engage one of them in discreet conversation. Drop a hint or two that they might look elsewhere for their suspect."

"An excellent idea." Beaming, Freddie took the plates into the kitchen and went in search of some paper with which to wrap the food. "I will meet you back here."

Pleased at the success of her stratagem, Daisy set off. A short walk took her to the Davis home, where she found no response to her knock. As she came down the steps, a voice hailed her from the overgrown garden next door.

"Are you looking for Eveline?" A woman in her seventies waved a trowel from behind a newly planted ornamental maple and pushed herself to her feet.

"Yes, I am," Daisy said. "My sister and I were here to dinner on Thursday night and I wished to call upon her. But I see I shall have to leave my card."

"Oh, goodness, we don't stand upon such ceremony here." The woman thrust out a hand, remembering at the last moment to pull off its gardening glove. "Mrs. Tillie Tregoth. And you must be Margaret Linden. Eveline told me about the dinner."

"Margrethe, actually. But everyone calls me Daisy. I have come to condole with her on the death of a mutual friend."

"Well, Miss Daisy, you'll find Eveline recovered somewhat from the shock. She's at the quilting bee, three doors down." She pointed west. "Just knock and go in. If you can use a needle and thread, so much the better."

"Oh, I couldn't intrude—"

"Of course you can. It's been an hour, so they'll need something fresh to talk about. Your timing will be perfect."

A group of ladies, all talking about the doings of the town? How lucky—and how terrifying. "Perhaps I will—how kind of you to suggest it. Mrs. Tregoth, I take it you know of the death of our friend Emma Makepeace?"

"Bjorn Hansen's fiancée? Oh yes. I had it from Mary Pascoe after the wedding that wasn't. Such a loss for the poor man! You can bet it's been well chewed over around the quilt frame by now, and Eveline the center of attention again, just the way she likes it."

"Oh?" Mrs. Davis hadn't seemed to be that sort of person. Then again, perhaps her husband made sure she wasn't, in his company at least.

"You see, *Eveline* was supposed to be Mr. Hansen's mail-order bride. She came out from London last year, but she was in too big a hurry. Bjorn had asked her to wait, but she came anyway. Poor man, living in a boarding-house and the Rose Street cottage not even built yet. And there was Patrick Davis with not only a house, but two children in dire need of a mother. Mr. Davis swept her off her feet, leaving Bjorn to start over with someone else."

"My goodness," was all Daisy could think to say. It was not surprising that none of *this* had come out at dinner. Perhaps Emma had never known.

And poor Mr. Hansen, to have two brides in succession snatched away from him!

"Look at me, ratchet-jawing away when you're wanting to get on." The old lady pointed down the street again. "Third house, the one with the yellow roses. You can't miss it—it will also be the one with all the racket."

Mrs. Tregoth's description was correct in every particular, even to the welcome Daisy received. Mrs. Davis introduced her as "my poor dear friend's erstwhile bridesmaid" and after that, she was ushered into a chair around the massive quilting frame and handed a needle as though she had been a member of the circle since its inception.

She had never quilted before, but anyone living in the house of Aunt Jane learned how to sew a fine seam, knit blankets for charity, and crochet lace ... or else. Her even stitches were much admired, and before six inches had passed under her needle, the ladies of Georgetown had returned to the topic at hand.

"I think you had a very narrow escape, Eveline," said a woman at the opposite corner. "Imagine—it could have been *you* laid to rest yesterday. Though not, of course, in *that* cemetery."

"Surely not," Eveline demurred. "We all know Mr. Hansen to be a kind and obliging man, talented in his trade, and incapable of harming anyone. I refuse to believe he is guilty."

"The Texican Rangers disagree." With a start, Daisy recognized the voice of the doctor's wife. Mary Pascoe was sitting square on the end of the quilt frame like the chairman of the board. "Dr. Pascoe says it is the quickest arrest they've made in the last year."

"It is a pity they have the wrong man," Daisy blurted before she could stop herself. "It is taking convenience too far, in my opinion."

"Convenience!" a lady to her left repeated in rising tones. "The Rangers do not take convenience into their estimations of a man's guilt. Only facts."

In for a penny, in for a pound. "They are clearly unaware

of some facts, then, despite my attempts to bring them to their attention," Daisy's stitches were still even, though the needle was becoming slippery under her fingers. "The most important one being that Mr. Hansen was in love with his fiancée, and the last man on earth who would harm her."

"I am sorry to be the bearer of bad news," Mary Pascoe said in a voice that wasn't the least bit sorry, "but even a man in love could not overlook his bride's delicate condition."

It became obvious to Daisy that doctor/patient confidentiality did not extend to the doctor's wife. And from the faces around her, she had already vouchsafed this stunner earlier. The fact that Mrs. Pascoe would divulge such details to an unmarried woman said much more about her character than Daisy suspected she realized.

Daisy appealed to Mrs. Davis on the opposite side of the quilting frame. "I understand that you knew him better than most, Mrs. Davis. It sounds as though you agree with me."

Eveline Davis blushed. "A few letters hardly count toward knowing a man, Miss Linden. But I must say that like you, I have a difficult time believing it." Her face crumpled. "Oh, my poor dear Emma."

The woman next to her put an arm around her and offered her a handkerchief, with which she dabbed her eyes. At least the tears were real.

"I've always admired your husband, Eveline, and now more than ever," said the woman, giving her a squeeze. "Always willing to let bygones be bygones. Despite Mr. Davis's stealing you away, he and Mr. Hansen have become good friends."

"Such good friends that we hosted the groom's supper," Mrs. Davis wailed into the handkerchief. "And now Patrick is to be deprived of another friend, if the Rangers have their way."

Daisy frowned at the feather pattern taking shape beneath her needle. If Mr. Davis was such a good friend, why was he not seeking the murderer, too, and working with Dr. Pascoe to free him?

"Perhaps someone resents Mr. Hansen's affable character and business success," the lady on the corner suggested, "and does not want to see him happy."

"Or alive," someone else muttered, but Daisy could not see who it was.

"His past is not entirely blameless, after all," Mrs. Pascoe pointed out in the mysterious tone that only serves to aggravate those not privy to the details.

"One's past hardly exempts one from being a good friend," Daisy said, unable to keep quiet.

"You are much too young to know anything about it," was the crushing response.

"Oh, goodness, Mary, go easy on the poor child," said their hostess. "You've already told her the worst. And everybody knows about that poor desert flower—and the lieutenant's wife—though both are in the past and ought to be forgotten."

"I don't," someone else said. "You cannot leave me in suspense, Louise."

Daisy did her best to keep her gaze on her stitches and disappear from view between her two neighbors, while listening with all her might.

"We do not speak of desert flowers in this house," their hostess said stiffly.

Mr. Hansen had fallen in love with a desert flower?

"She wasn't always one of … those," someone else said.

"Though Kathleen Shanahan was probably no better than she should be. I knew her mother. She took in sewing and did what she could to keep body and soul together, rest her soul. As for Kathleen, she waited upon us once or twice in the dining room at the Hotel de Paris, before the scan—"

"I *said*, we do not speak of desert flowers in this house," Louise repeated, glaring. "As to the other, it happened a good decade ago, though I imagine Lieutenant Ross cannot help but think of it every time he looks at that frivolous creature he's married to."

Daisy tucked the hints about Kathleen Shanahan away for later scrutiny. Would a jealous, desperate woman be capable of injuring the one who had supplanted her in Mr. Hansen's affections?

"Frances, she means," someone supplied helpfully. "She is twenty years his junior at least."

"Oh, she runs the foreign missions effort at church," the woman new to the group said on a note of recognition. "She's lovely. A bit standoffish, though."

"Quite so," Louise said. "Butter wouldn't melt in her mouth now, but ten years ago she was a very young twenty—spoiled and cosseted by her parents, who own the Pelican Mine. Her marriage to Gavin Ross was the event of the year, believe me, with a dress ordered all the way from New York. Mr. Hansen was newly arrived in town, and a fine figure of a man he was, unlike the lieutenant, who had allowed himself too many good meals. She trapped him into an affair—"

"Louise, I'm quite certain the trapping was mutual," Mary Pascoe said, correcting their hostess. "Men will be men, and Frances Ross drank flattery and compliments the way some people drink wine. In excess, and to the point of senselessness."

Daisy wondered if she meant *insensibility*, but not for worlds would she interrupt the babbling brook of gossip by asking.

"In any case," their hostess went on, "it all came to a head when Mr. Hansen took her up in that touring balloon with no chaperone or witnesses and ... nine months later she presented her husband with a healthy baby boy."

"But that doesn't mean—"

"With *blond curls*," Mary Pascoe interrupted. "Frances has brown hair, and the lieutenant comes from a long line of black Irish. His two younger sisters have the widow's peak anyone can see in all the family daguerreotypes. It was quite clear who the father was, and remains clear to this day."

"Goodness," breathed the woman to whom these interesting details were as new as they were to Daisy. "You don't suppose that the lieutenant has been waiting for his chance to get his revenge, do you?"

"If you mean could Lieutenant Ross be guilty of murdering that girl and her unborn child, of course not," snapped Louise.

"But we don't know," the woman pointed out, very reasonably, Daisy thought.

"What, risk his career and position, and a possible future as a magistrate when his brother-in-law leaves the bench?" Mary Pascoe snorted. "If he didn't cast off his guilty wife and clap Bjorn Hansen in gaol on a trumped-up charge ten years ago, it's not likely he'd go to the extreme of killing the man's fiancée in some kind of mad revenge now."

"You have to admit, though," said the lady on the corner,

"he must feel some satisfaction in seeing his men conclude the investigation so swiftly with his rival in gaol."

"I would not know," the doctor's wife said, her lips primming up. "Lieutenant Ross is a good Christian man to have forgiven his wife and given her child a home. I am quite sure he remembers that Scripture says vengeance belongs to the Lord."

Perhaps, Daisy thought. But it might not stop him from using his position to delay and prevent any investigation into Emma's death. Or to convince a magistrate that any proof to the contrary brought before him was irrelevant or false. A good Christian man could allow the law to take its course and feel nothing but sober satisfaction in justice being done, having finally come full circle.

# CHAPTER 14

## MONDAY, AUGUST 5, 1895

*3:45 p.m.*

*W*hen Daisy took her leave amid a flurry of invitations to come again, to take tea, to join the Ladies' Aid, she gained the safety of Mr. Hansen's front garden with a gasp of relief. She hadn't told anyone that she and Frederica were merely in transit; nor had she mentioned that they were staying in the home of the deceased and the accused.

That would probably have dried up the invitations on the spot.

But she did want to remain friendly with the women of the town while she was here. One never knew when the observations and conclusions of a woman might hold just the bit of information that would help save a man's life.

That odd little snippet about the desert flower, for instance. They'd been perfectly frank about speaking of the lieutenant's scandal. Why not speak of one involving her?

She found Frederica's coat hanging on a peg by the door, but she was not in the house. A look outside revealed her in the back garden, bent over a small enclosure. She pulled her sketchbook and a pencil out of her reticule and went to join her.

"What do you have there, Freddie?" she asked as she crossed what was meant to be a flagged walk bisecting a lawn, but the latter had no grass yet, despite the fact that it was summer. Only a wilderness of weeds, waiting for someone to care for it.

"I thought this was a tool shed back here, but it isn't. He keeps chickens." Freddie indicated several hens whose avid gazes soon returned to her when they realized Daisy had nothing edible in her hands. "I had no idea. Why didn't he mention them, I wonder? Look, they have nothing to eat."

"I expect he has had weightier matters on his mind. Let them out for a while ... though it is clouding over. I believe it may rain."

As though they perceived their time might be short, the birds began to dig and weed energetically, and the heels of the loaf Freddie brought out were most welcome. She filled a pan with water and eventually located a burlap bag of dried cobs of corn that seemed to be intended for their consumption.

"I did not know you knew the first thing about chickens," she observed as Freddie joined her upon the back step to watch the birds' industrious tilling and weeding of the ground. She began to sketch their pleasing shapes in their various poses.

"I learned during my visits to Carrick House. Lady Claire keeps chickens in the garden, and at night they roost in a coop that walks about. I did not see that, however. But Lewis—I mean, Mr. Protheroe, her secretary—showed me how one cares for them. And you saw that there were a small number aboard *Swan*, did you not?"

The less said about poultry roaming the decks of otherwise respectable airships, the better. At length, shading in feathers and tails, Daisy said, "Was your visit to the Rangers useful?"

Freddie clasped her hands over one knee. "It was certainly illuminating. That young officer took my packet of food and promised he would deliver it. Then, as you suggested, I engaged him in conversation."

The smile in her tone prompted Daisy to say, "And was it enjoyable?"

"It was. Apparently his younger brother is ... was ... employed by Mr. Hansen as an apprentice carpenter to learn the trade. The family is most distressed, and seem to be holding poor Ranger Willets personally responsible for his brother's inability to work. He is terribly conflicted, because by all accounts Mr. Hansen is a good, fair man."

"Not *all* accounts." While she drew in a large cluster of lupine as a background, Daisy told her what she had learned about his indiscretions with the lieutenant's wife and the desert flower.

"Dear me." Freddie seemed quite taken aback. "Is this common knowledge among the Rangers?" Then she answered herself. "It cannot be, or Ranger Willets would have hinted at it."

"To a young lady, unmarried and unknown to him? I think not. I am surprised at the ladies talking about such things in front of me. But the point is that while the lieutenant might not have accosted poor Emma himself to hurt Mr. Hansen, he certainly has all the reason in the world not to pursue an investigation further, but simply to let the wheels of justice grind him to powder."

Freddie was silent for some minutes, watching the hens. "Are people so ill behaved everywhere, or only in this town?"

Daisy's heart softened at the wistful tone in her sister's voice, almost as though she were bidding her childhood farewell once and for all. "I think we will find people behaving well and ill wherever we go. But I hold out hope that the majority of people are good, and kind, and wish the best for one another."

"Then I wish we could leave soon. I want to be about the business of finding Papa. That was Emma's dying wish, you know. We cannot disregard it forever."

"Nor shall we." She held up her book for Freddie's inspection, and the freshening breeze riffled the pages.

"You have captured the hens perfectly." Her sister rose. "I had better put them in their house—was that thunder?"

Indeed it was. When Freddie finally chivvied the birds into their dry little home with a good supply of corn, she barely made it across the garden before the skies opened up on a deluge so fierce they could hardly see the coop.

"Goodness," Daisy said. "Have you ever seen rain like this in your life?"

"I thought London was bad, but even it is not like this." Freddie pushed the back door open and they stepped into the kitchen. "The skies are much wider here than in Bath, and hold ever so much more water. Come. We have been putting off going through Emma's things. We cannot go out, so we may as well do it now."

"I do not much relish the prospect of tracking down this

Kathleen person," Daisy confessed as they returned to the foyer, where Emma's travel trunk and valise still sat. "My resources are at an end—or rather, they are not up to making a beginning. I wonder if Sir Robert Peel's men feel this way during an investigation? As though anyone in an entire city could have committed the crime, and they have no way to winnow through the population to find the culprit."

"That way lies despair," Freddie said, pulling the trunk into the bedroom on its tiny wheels. "Let us set ourselves to a concrete task. Emma's family must be notified. Let us see if we can find an address."

Daisy's sense of loss returned again as they gently removed Emma's clothes from the travel trunk, searching pockets and hanging each item in the wardrobe as they finished with it. Each drawer, each cubbyhole was turned out, yielding at last nothing more than a scrapbook album and an engagement diary.

The diary was filled with notes of balls and exhibitions, reminders, and appointments that seemed to Daisy to roughly correspond with the events in Emma's letters to Mr. Hansen. As the date of her departure approached, the notations became more cryptic, with initials and numbers jumbled among the names and events.

"It seems she might have worried about being discovered," Daisy finally said. "Look. July tenth. *P7201410*. Is that a magnetic code for a pigeon?"

Freddie studied the page, the rain pounding upon the roof as though it were determined to find a way past its snug shingles and sturdy construction. "What time did *Persephone* lift from Paris?" she asked suddenly.

"After lunch," Daisy replied. "Don't you remember? We were served while still moored to the Eiffel Tower."

"That's what this is, then. *Persephone*, July twentieth, at two-ten. I'll wager that all these notations have something to do with her travel plans, and she did not want her father or the servants knowing about it."

"I suppose not, if she was planning to be a mail-order bride and her papa was busy drumming up a wealthy man for her there in town."

"One must admire her courage, to embark on her own course instead of accepting the one set for her," Freddie said. "Is there anything in that scrapbook album?"

Daisy turned the pages, which illustrated the other woman's life in riotous, cheerful disarray. Picture postcards, dance cards bearing one or two quite illustrious names, theatre programs. Stamps from foreign letters, a few daguerreotypes scattered between pressed flowers and engravings cut from magazines. Recipes, poetry, an article about an art exhibition in Venice.

They looked at the daguerreotypes, but could find no indication of who the people were. A child with golden hair. Two ladies flanking a plinth and holding books, who might have been fellow mail-order brides poking sly fun at their literary club. And a gentleman with—

"Freddie! Look at this." Daisy slipped the stiff image out of the corners that held it. "I've seen this man."

"What? Where?"

"In the Hotel de Paris, Friday morning. There was a group of businessmen at breakfast, and he was among them."

"How could someone in Emma's album of her London life

be here?" Freddie objected. "She knew no one but us and the Davises."

And she had made no mention at all of family coming for the wedding, choosing instead to ask acquaintances of only a week to stand up with her.

Freddie, observing her frown, said, "You must be mistaken, dear. A room full of strangers—we so excited on the wedding morning—Emma missing. How could anyone fix a single individual in memory—especially with what came after?"

Because he had looked her over as though she were a desert flower, and found her wanting, that was why. But she was not about to tell Freddie she had endured such an insult.

They could not be the same man. Emma simply would not know such a horrid person.

The rain was draining Daisy's optimism as surely as it had drained the sunlight. "You are probably right. I need a cup of tea."

The tea proved comforting, as did finishing the sketch of the hens and opening her palette to add the greens and blues of the garden and the sunny gold and red of their feathers. While Freddie turned the pages of the album more slowly, taking them in, Daisy considered the short list of options open to her.

One—pay another call upon Mr. Meriwether-Astor to discover whether he and Dr. Pascoe had come up with a means to help Mr. Hansen.

Two—locate a desert flower named Kathleen to discover whether she was of a jealous disposition and had been out and about at midnight Thursday.

Three—inquire of every miner she met whether he had

been out at the same time and seen or heard anything. Or done anything reprehensible himself.

Four—take the steam conveyance up to the train station and book two tickets to Santa Fe.

Daisy considered the tea leaves in the bottom of her cup, struggling with the depressing conviction that really, option four was the only one that looked as though anything positive might come of it.

# CHAPTER 15

MONDAY, AUGUST 5, 1895

*5:50 p.m.*

The rain finally stopped close to six o'clock, allowing Daisy and Freddie to venture forth in search of dinner. Though it was August, and one might assume the streets would be dry, packed earth, it was abundantly clear that the raised wooden sidewalks were an absolute necessity when the weather could be as savage as it had been this afternoon. Clear Creek roared as they crossed one of its many bridges, and even Sixth Street had a rill running down the middle that was cut deeper with every carriage and steam dray that splashed through it.

As they approached the restaurant where they had eaten the previous evening, Freddie gasped and clutched Daisy's arm, dragging her back. "Look out!"

"What is it?" Had she seen a vicious dog, or someone lurking in the twilight depths between the buildings?

"That man—he was tossed out of the place right in front of you! Dear heaven—he is covered in blood!"

Cold fingers prickled down the back of Daisy's neck. The street was empty save for a horse tied up to a rail opposite. "Freddie—dear—"

Something in the tone of her voice made Freddie blink, and the alarm drained out of her face. So did the color.

"Oh." Her tone flattened as she stared at the empty street and grazing horse. "There is no man. It is quite obvious there is no one here but us."

"No, dear." Daisy slipped an arm around her shoulders. "Never mind. Come inside and we'll get some food into you."

The proprietor cleared his throat as he seated them. "Had a bit of a turn, did you, miss?"

"I did, but I am quite well now, thank you," Freddie answered a little stiffly.

"Thought you might've seen old Ed Bainbridge. He's given plenty of people a turn in the last twenty years, though he's dead as a doornail. Killed a man over a tin of oysters in the saloon next door. They hung him, but his ghost is still about, frightening folks with its violence."

Goodness, could he not see how pale Freddie was? Did the people here not realize that one did not speak of such things to young ladies?

"I was not frightened, nor did I see anything," Freddie said in an empty echo of her usual musical tones. "Thank you for inquiring."

"Glad to hear it. We're serving Texican chili and cornbread this evening, if you'd like some."

They ordered it, ate as quickly as its heat would allow, and found themselves back outside in forty-five minutes.

"I wish to go home," Freddie said. "I don't like that place as much as I did last evening."

"Home?" Daisy repeated in some alarm. "Do you mean home to Bath?"

Her sister glanced at her as though she were mad. "Of course not. I meant home to Rose Street. I suppose it is as much a home as any we are likely to see until we find Papa."

"Oh. Of course." Her fingers tightened on the herringbone sleeve of Freddie's walking suit as she recognized two figures coming out of the Hotel de Paris. "Is that Dr. Pascoe and Mr. Meriwether-Astor?"

"Yes, it is."

The two men shook hands, and then crossed Sixth Street. Dr. Pascoe went into a saloon, where the occupants greeted him with a roar of welcome, while Hugh Meriwether-Astor walked down another block to Rose Street and turned right into it.

"He is going to call upon us, as he promised," Freddie said. "Come."

Daisy was just about to step off the sidewalk in order to navigate the morass in the middle of the street, when she heard a low whistle.

"Psst! Miss Daisy!" Davey the errand boy slipped out of the shadows between the hotel and the opera house, whose play-bills advertised the impending arrival of Madame Nilsson to sing selections from *Lucrezia Borgia*. "Don't cross there— you're like to drown. Come higher up."

"Thank you, Davey. Your timing is fortuitous."

"I was not looking forward to having hems six inches deep in mud, either," Freddie added, her spirits clearly rising at the sight of the boy's cheerful face.

As they crossed the street on higher ground, lit from moment to moment by the dazzling bolts issuing from Mr. Tesla's power plant above, Daisy said, "Davey, how long have you been, er, working at the Hotel de Paris?"

"A year, mebbe."

She was tempted to ask where he and his mother lived, but a more important question pre-empted it. "Did you know a young lady who used to wait upon the tables there—a Kathleen Shanahan?"

"Oh aye, I know Kathleen. She works for Madame Ophelia now, on Brownell Street. Sometimes I run errands for the girls. Saves 'em from having to come into town on wet days. They're obliged to step off the sidewalks into the street when the gentlefolk pass by, see."

Freddie drew in a breath, clearly imagining the same awkard sight, and feeling the same compassion for the unfortunate girls who had to scramble up and down from road to boardwalk regardless of the mud.

Asking these questions was most improper. But at the same time— "She was once a friend of Mr. Hansen's, I understand."

"She was, miss. Set on being his wife, more like."

"What happened to change her mind?"

Davey shook his head, clearly marveling at her lack of experience of the world. "Kathleen, she's a man's kind of woman. She was waiting on tables at the hotel and got friendly with a commercial traveler. Mr. Dupuy has a lot of 'em come through—even fitted up sample rooms for 'em to show their wares. Anyhow, Kathleen, she got caught in one of those cabinet beds and there was a big to-do."

Daisy didn't even want to speculate what a cabinet bed

was or how one got caught in it—whether literally or metaphorically. "Was she sacked?"

"Oh yes, miss, though it wasn't hardly her fault. Salesmen'll go after anything in skirts. But after that, all them fussbudgets in town made sure she couldn't get work—not even washing —except over on Brownell Street. She's still a decent sort. To me, anyhow."

"I'm sorry to hear of her ill fortune," she said.

Davey grinned. "Not so ill, miss. There's only five flower houses on Brownell Street, but they're on the richest square mile on earth. Lot of silver in these parts, miss. She ent doing so badly. She gave me a fifty-cent piece just for fetching a letter at the post office."

"Daisy." Freddie tugged on her sleeve. "Mr. Meriwether-Astor will not find us at home."

"You are right. Thank you, Davey. For ... everything. You've been very ... informative."

"What'd you want to know about Kathleen for, miss?" His face alight with curiosity, he tagged along behind them.

"I merely wondered if—"

"Daisy, come *on*."

"Never mind." She fished in her reticule and gave him a penny, as promised. It did not seem like much compared to a fifty-cent piece, which would buy a serving of quail on toast at the Hotel de Paris. She hoped he'd had the opportunity to eat something nourishing, at least. "Good evening to you."

Kathleen might be a "decent sort," but to Daisy's mind, she had lost a respectable man and good prospects, even if it had been all her own doing. Silver or not, might the sight of someone else taking the life she had wanted drive a woman to a desperate rage?

And even if it had, how on earth was Daisy going to find out such a thing? For she could not very well go down to Brownell Street herself, knock on the door of the oxblood-colored house, and call upon her. There would be no invitations to quilting bees and the Ladies' Aid *then*.

But there was no time to puzzle it out. For as they turned in at the gate, here was Hugh Meriwether-Astor, strolling down the path from their front door, to meet them.

*8:20 p.m.*

Perhaps it was not quite the done thing to invite a gentleman in for a cup of tea at this time of the evening, but Daisy's scruples about such things were beginning to choke among the weeds of necessity. As they settled at the small round dining table that had clearly been lovingly made by the house's owner, she debated whether or not to close the simple linen drapes.

No. If anyone were to look in, better for everything and everyone to be visible—the equivalent of keeping the parlor doors at Aunt Jane's standing open when a gentleman came to call.

Not that many came voluntarily. But still.

"Did you and the doctor enjoy your dinner, Mr. Meriwether-Astor?" Freddie asked, passing him the jar of milk since Mr. Hansen did not seem to possess a pitcher. "We saw you coming out just now."

"We did." He settled back with his cup as though quite pleased with his company. "We had a discussion over our beef Wellington about the defense of Mr. Hansen. And a number of other things."

"And what did you conclude?" Daisy asked. The tea was hot, and since she did not take milk to cool it, she blew upon it gently.

"Firstly, I have a bit of news, courtesy of Dr. Pascoe. It seems the circuit magistrate will moor in Georgetown on the twelfth."

Daisy gazed at him expectantly, unease prickling in her chest. Did that mean—

He went on, "Here in the Wild West, Dr. Pascoe tells me, the magistrates keep a schedule, sailing from town to town to hear cases and hand down judgment."

"That is Monday!" Daisy exclaimed as his meaning became clear. "Do you mean that Mr. Hansen's fate will be decided on Monday? Seven days from now?" How were they ever to find the miscreant who was really responsible when they had been trying for three days and got nowhere?

"It could be decided on Tuesday, or Wednesday," he said in a maddeningly pedantic manner. "The circuit magistrate stays until all the pending cases are heard, then flies to the next town on the circuit. But Dr. Pascoe tells me that since Magistrate Bismarck is the elder brother of Mrs. Ross, the lieutenant's wife, he will likely stay the full week as their guest."

"*That* magistrate," Daisy breathed, remembering Mary Pascoe's satisfaction as she told the tale of Mr. Hansen's affair with Frances Ross. "Since he is related by marriage to the Texican Ranger in charge here, Mr. Hansen will hardly receive a fair hearing. We must appeal to a higher authority so that someone else may hear his case."

Hugh's eyebrows rose as he gazed at her in astonishment. "What do his relations have to do with it?"

Nothing on earth would induce Daisy to reveal the sordid

details if he did not know them. "Did the doctor not tell you that there may be some … prejudice against Mr. Hansen from both the lieutenant and the magistrate?"

"He hinted at some such, but I did not press the matter."

She hoped he would not press her, either. "To whom ought I to appeal, then?"

"I do not believe you can, Miss Linden. Nor can I. You and I are merely visitors here, not citizens of the Territory or members of Mr. Hansen's family. I imagine there is some governing body in the capital, Santa Fe, but how one would prevail upon that body to prevent a circuit magistrate from carrying out his duty to Georgetown is beyond my knowledge."

Quite unjustly, Daisy glared at him, doing her best not to allow the lump in her throat to become full-fledged tears of frustration.

Freddie, who could see the storm building in Daisy's heart, put a comforting hand on hers. "What other matters did you discuss with the doctor, sir?" she asked gently. "The ones you might share with us, I mean."

He sat back, and the tension broke. "Some good news, I hope. Perhaps I ought to have begun with that."

"Perhaps you ought," Daisy said, her throat tight.

"The doctor and I have decided to hire one of the Rocky Mountain Detectives." He gazed at them as though expecting an outburst of joy.

"Detectives?" Daisy repeated, feeling no joy at all, merely confusion. "Are they like the Pinkerton men?" The Pinkertons specialized in finding missing persons. Did that include missing murderers?

"No, no." After setting his cup and saucer aside, Hugh rested his elbows on the table and clasped his hands. "They are a closed society of intelligence men who investigate matters that the Texican Rangers do not. The Rangers, you see, focus on crimes such as kidnapping or grand theft or treason—serious crimes that affect many people. But here in the mining towns of the Wild West, one may call upon a Rocky Mountain Detective when one needs the facts, such as in Mr. Hansen's case."

Why had the good doctor not told her about this before, when she had gone to see him? They might have had such a man on the case for three days already. Was it because she and Freddie were women, and a man must manage these things? Why must men be so slow to act?

"Murder is not considered a serious crime here?" Freddie said in disbelief, recalling her to the present.

"It is, but it is usually a personal one, affecting only a few. Murders perpetrated in the commission of a bank robbery or a train heist or by air pirates, of course, are different. Those are the particular bailiwick of the Texican Rangers, as are declarations of war."

"I had never thought of murder being a personal crime before," Freddie said faintly. "How educated we are becoming."

"You are more than tourists now," Hugh said, clearly missing the irony. "The point is, the doctor is sending a pigeon this evening to someone who acts as a go-between. The detectives' actual location is a closely guarded secret, as you may imagine. We could see a Detective as early as Wednesday, if we are lucky."

"But in the meantime, we will have lost two days," Daisy

protested. "Mr. Meriwether-Astor, our own inquiries have eliminated several possibili—" She stopped.

Really, despite his kind eyes, those raised eyebrows could become quite annoying.

"Did you not make me a promise that you would cease your inquiries and allow wiser heads to prevail?" he asked in a tone of such fatherliness that it set her teeth on edge. He could not be more than five years older than herself, and had no right to pretend to such a role.

"We promised no such thing."

"I recollect clearly that you did, Miss Linden. Do you have any idea how dangerous your inquiries can be? The murderer is still out there somewhere."

"A fact of which I am perfectly aware," she said.

"We promised to stay out of trouble," Freddie put in. "Not to cease our inquiries. And we have kept our promise."

"That is disingenuous in the extreme." He pushed away from the table and paced about the room. "Allow me to be explicit, then, since the two of you can parse a phrase like a Philadelphia lawyer. Promise me that you will cease your inquiries in support of freeing Mr. Hansen immediately, and allow the Rocky Mountain Detective to handle this case."

"And if we do not?" Daisy asked.

"Then for your own safety, I will—I will—"

What? Lock them up? Force them to board a train back to Denver? Daisy flung herself into the breach.

"Mr. Meriwether-Astor, your concern for our wellbeing does you credit. But the fact remains that you are neither father nor brother, nor are you closely attached to either of us —the only relationships which might give you the right to require any promises at all. You are not connected with us, and therefore cannot exercise such control over our actions as you seem to wish."

His jaw sagged with affront at such bluntness, and then slowly, he forced himself to relax. His face softened with humor and humility. "And the simple claims of friendship and concern—these are not enough?"

Daisy hardened her heart against both humor and concern, and stood too. He had offended her deeply, and a winsome smile could not make up for the presumption that surely still lay under it. A rock might be covered by a limpid stream, but it could still cause a boat to founder.

"The claims of friendship and concern are most welcome and to be respected, as you know very well. But control of our affairs, our thoughts, our activities—these are not."

For the first time, she understood the phrase *getting one's back up*. For her spine was as straight as his, aligning itself by instinct for fight or flight.

"I must thank you for one thing, however," she went on in a quieter tone. "Your very words have recalled me to the true purpose of our inquiries. You may certainly hire your detective and seek to free Mr. Hansen. We will support you in any way we can. But the claims of friendship on our side demand that we seek justice for Miss Makepeace. We will pursue our inquiries without let or hindrance in that regard, and hope that they bear fruit that will exonerate Mr. Hansen."

Mr. Meriwether-Astor adjusted the fine velvet lapels of his coat in the manner of one preparing to leave. "You are determined to put yourselves in danger, then? To disregard advice that is offered with the best of intentions?"

"We are determined to do neither. We will proceed with

the utmost caution and discretion in the hope that justice will be served by the efforts of us all."

"Before Monday," Freddie added.

"I wish you luck, then." He took his bowler from its peg by the door and settled it on his head. "Would you like to meet with the Detective when he arrives?"

"Certainly. Thank you."

Mr. Meriwether-Astor bowed and let himself out. They heard his boot heels on the three stairs, then the click of the gate as it closed behind him.

"I hope we have not lost a friend because you lost your temper," Freddie said quietly.

Sometimes she could be so discerning it brought Daisy up short. Her sister was indeed no longer a child. She was a young woman of intelligence, who often saw things that others did not—the otherworldly not included.

"I hope not, too," Daisy replied. Now that he was gone, she no longer felt brave and indignant, but shaky and anxious. Bravery and indignation had their place, but not, perhaps, when one was in foreign parts and needed the goodwill of others to survive. She could not begin to mend those fences now, unless she wanted to chase Mr. Meriwether-Astor down the street.

But there was one thing she could do to make herself feel better. "Are you going to have another cup of tea, Freddie?"

"No, dear."

"Good. Because I should very much like to paint these blue and white teacups."

# CHAPTER 16

## TUESDAY, AUGUST 6, 1895

*9:30 a.m.*
*Georgetown*

*B*arney was thankful that the sky had cleared and for a while, at least, he would be spared the pounding downpour that had penned him and Lin inside the vehicle for some hours yesterday. The only good thing that could be said about it was that he had been able to finish the story he had begun the other night, and this morning he had written out a fair copy and sent it off to his editor.

On his return from the post office, looking forward to his breakfast, it took a moment to realize that he was being followed with some stealth and no finesse. He turned and smiled. "Hullo, Davey. I trust you are well this morning?"

The boy sidled out from behind a steam dray puffing by the side of the boardwalk. "I am, sir, thank'ee."

What were the odds the child had had anything to eat yet

today? Or yesterday, for that matter? Somehow he knew the answer as well as he had known that hollow feeling in his own stomach. "Would you care to join me for some bread and honey and mush at the tavern?"

"Oh no, sir. I et already."

"Davey," he said gently, "a man can honorably accept an offer given in friendship when he won't accept one given in charity."

Davey's scruples lost the fight with a speed that told Barney just how hungry he was. "I'd like that very much, then, sir. But I can pay you."

With a flourish, he produced a penny. Barney wondered at the honor of a child who would reimburse a man for his offer but would rather go hungry than spend it outright on the same meal.

"You keep it, my friend, for when your need is greater than it is now."

"Miss Linden gave it to me for tellin' her about Kathleen."

Those two names did not belong together in the same sentence at all. "Did she, now?"

Thus encouraged, Davey told him all about their conversation as they consumed their breakfast at the tavern, and took a third portion out to the vehicle for Lin.

"And they're staying at Mr. Hansen's place while they make inquiries," Davey concluded as Lin devoured bread and honey at the same rate he had fifteen minutes before, washing down the mush and blueberries with a bottle of creamy milk Barney had brought for her.

The fact that there were now three people crammed into a space made for one gave Barney a very good idea.

"Davey, I'll give you another penny if you'll go and ask

Miss Linden to call upon us here, and then go across the creek to ask if Miss Kathleen is up to paying us a visit, too."

Both Davey and Lin gazed at him with reproachful eyes. "That would not be proper," Davey said at last. "I got nothing against Kathleen, but it ent fitting for her to be seen in company with Miss Daisy, even if she does want to talk to 'er."

"I realize that, which is why the meeting will take place inside this trusty vehicle, with Lin for chaperone. You and I will comb the field outside for useful herbs while Miss Daisy conducts her business, and provide a diversion in the unlikely event any of the ladies of the town should pass the tavern and enter the meadow."

"And what will I do?" Lin asked. "I am too young to chaperone."

"You will continue to recover, then, and make polite remarks at intervals," Barney told her. "Off with you now, Davey. I will be at home to company in an hour."

If he had had any regrets about his rash arrangements, they were washed away an hour later by the light in Daisy's eyes as she waded through the grass to the back of his conveyance. "I do not know whether to scold you for your impertinence or shake your hand in thanks for your brilliance," she said by way of greeting.

"Good morning, Miss Linden."

"Good morning, Mr. Barnicott. I will scold that rascal of a Davey for betraying my confidence, however."

"Do not be too hard on him. Information is his stock in trade, and he has brought us together for a greater purpose."

Interest fought with caution in her gaze. "Do you refer to information that might secure justice for Miss Makepeace?"

That wasn't what he had in mind, but it would do to be

going on with. "Please, be seated." He indicated the steps that led up into the vehicle, which were all he had to offer. At least he had thought to sweep them. "I have a bargain to strike with you."

She seated herself gracefully upon the topmost step, tucking her skirts very properly around her ladylike half-boots. "I was not aware we were well enough acquainted for bargains."

"But we are in support of greater purposes, as I said. In exchange for brokering this meeting with Kathleen on neutral ground, I would like you to take in a house guest."

A squeak issued from the depths of the sleeping cabinet and through the open door of the conveyance, and Daisy looked about her as though suspecting small animals.

"That was the aforesaid guest," he explained. "I have a young patient, a girl of thirteen years, whom I would like to see more comfortably and appropriately settled while she recovers."

"A patient?"

"A young laundress who was assaulted the other night at the flower house. A customer was mistaken as to her line of work, and beat her with an ebony cane for not accommodating him, bruising her quite severely. It will be two or three days before she can move comfortably, let alone perform any labor. Madam Ophelia would not let her stay, and I cannot help but think Lin would be more comfortable in a proper house, where she can be cared for."

Daisy, it seemed, had been stricken silent.

But Lin had not. "You are not palming me off on a stranger!" she shouted. "I will go now if that is what you want, and you will be shed of me."

"You will not!" He leaped past Daisy up the steps and caught his patient in the act of attempting to swing her legs out of the cupboard. "Lin, this will be for the best, you'll see."

"Why did you not say I was inconvenient? I would not have stayed to trouble you." Tears glittered in her dark eyes. "I thought you were my friend."

"I am your friend. That is why I am asking Miss Linden to give you a place where you can heal."

"I am healing right here!"

The light dimmed as Daisy moved into the doorway. She and Lin regarded each other with animosity.

"I cannot say I am overcome with enthusiasm to have a mannerless child in the house when my sister and I are occupied in matters of life and death."

"Only a mannerless person would call another mannerless," Lin snapped.

"However, if the price of my speaking with Kathleen is the recuperation of this child, I suppose I must give in with as much grace as I can muster."

"Spare yourself the effort," Lin said with poisonous enunciation. "I am not coming. Your misbegotten bargain may stand without me."

"Certainly not," Barney managed to get in. "My terms are fixed."

"I can only offer my acceptance," Daisy said. "If your patient is not willing, then I have fulfilled my part and expect you to fulfill yours."

"That is not how this works!" Barney exclaimed, feeling his excellent plan evaporating in the heat of two stubborn tempers.

"Good morning," called a feminine voice from outside, and

Daisy turned on the step, lost her footing, and jumped rather ungracefully to the ground. "Barney, Davey did not say you were entertaining." Kathleen's voice was rich with amusement.

"Oh, he is highly entertaining," grumbled Daisy, then seemed to remember herself. After giving her jacket a tug and smoothing her skirts, she held out a hand. "I am Daisy Linden. You must be Kathleen Shanahan."

Seeing the two of them together, he realized the girl wasn't much older than Daisy herself. Despite muddy skin and the roseate effect of alcohol about the eyes, she carried herself with a cheerful air. The ruffled skirts and red brocade corset were the same as on her previous visit, but she had added a necklace that combined a lavaliere of black lace with an arrangement of jet beads that suited her coloring admirably.

"I am," she said. "Nice to meet you, though you might keep it quiet that we have." She did not shake Daisy's hand, and Daisy withdrew it rather awkwardly.

"Your necklace is very beautiful," she said, just as awkwardly.

The girl looked pleased. "Thanks. I made it myself. Would you like to know what else I made?"

With a sly glance at Barney, she tapped an ornate bead of the sort that went on the ends of hatpins, and pulled it out of her corset. A blade about the length of her middle finger depended from it on a short haft.

Barney had never seen one before, and came down the steps to examine it. "Busk knife," Kathleen confided. "For when the gentlemen get out of hand. You have to line the busk of your corset with a bit of buckskin, mind you, but there's nothing like a weapon close to when the situation warrants."

"My ... goodness," Daisy managed, clearly torn between interest and the propriety of discussing underclothes in mixed company. Interest won. "I wish my sister were here. She loves all manner of contrivances, especially those related to fashion." Then she turned to Barney. "What a difference such a thing might have made to Emma that night. It might have meant her survival."

There was no way to know now.

"If you ladies would like to go in, Davey and I will guard the gates," he said instead.

"Go in ... with her?" Davey had clearly not told Kathleen the reason for her walk across the meadow. Barney hoped that she was not expecting ... private commerce.

"Washie is inside. Perhaps you would like to say hello, and after that, Miss Daisy has a question or two for you. I believe we might even be able to offer you some breakfast."

"Oh." He had the uncomfortable feeling he had been right, as she seemed to be revising her expectations. No wonder she had sounded so amused earlier. "All right." She mounted the stairs with a swish of brassy, multicolored ruffles, and her voice softened as she greeted the child within.

"Washie?" Daisy said, eyebrows raised in inquiry under the brim of her straw hat.

"Every Canton laundress in these parts, it seems, is addressed so. But this one is to be addressed henceforth as Lin, her given name."

He could see a hundred questions trembling on the tip of her tongue, and possibly a dressing-down at his high-handed presumption as well. He inclined his head politely. "I leave you to your inquiries."

There at last was Davey, bounding through the grass, and

Barney made every effort to appear relaxed as he strolled out to join him.

# CHAPTER 17

## TUESDAY, AUGUST 6, 1895

*10:35 a.m.*

*D*aisy climbed into Mr. Barnicott's extraordinary conveyance and looked about her for somewhere to sit. Kathleen appeared to be perched on the only stool.

"Here," Kathleen said with her mouth full. "Slides out, like this." She pulled a similar seat out of the wall opposite the sleeping cupboard, and swung a slender turned post attached to its underside to the floor for support.

Daisy did not like to speculate how she knew about the amenities of Mr. Barnicott's traveling house, but there was no getting around the fact that the seats were cleverly constructed.

"Thank you for coming to speak to me," she said.

"I didn't know I was, but you're welcome." She swallowed and licked honey off her fingers.

Ignoring the child in the cupboard, who had rolled with

some effort to one elbow so she could watch the goings-on, Daisy cast about for a way to begin. "I will not take much of your time, and I apologize if my questions seem intrusive, but a man's life is at stake. A man I believe you know."

"You're speaking of Bjorn Hansen? He's the only man with a life at stake lately. Everyone's talking about it."

"He is accused of murdering his fiancée, my friend Emma Makepeace. On Thursday night. Or rather, Friday morning, at about half past twelve."

"So I hear. But I don't know what I have to do with it. I was working at that hour, and there are half a dozen men who can attest to it."

Daisy felt the blood drain from her cheeks, and if it were not for the muffled giggle from the cupboard, she might have given up and fled. Instead, she glared at the Canton girl, who glared back. But at least the little wretch subsided.

"It never entered my head to think you might have done the deed yourself," she fibbed.

For surely Kathleen was not so good an actress that she could speak with such a degree of calm—of disinterest, even. By not even the flick of an eyelash did she betray any unease or guilt. She merely wiped her fingers on one of her ruffles and waited for Daisy to go on.

There was no getting around her ironclad alibi, either.

"But with your acquaintance with Mr. Hansen, I wondered if you or some of the—the other young ladies might speculate on who could have done it?"

"I haven't spoken to Bjorn Hansen in months," Kathleen said matter-of-factly. "After I left my employ at the hotel and wound up at Ophelia's, I was too busy to visit. Not that he would have received me anyway. I might have harbored feelings for him once, but I wasn't the only one." She shrugged. "Expects too much, does Bjorn. We wouldn't have suited even if I was still able to stroll the sidewalks of town without jumping down and back up like a rabbit."

"What do you mean, you weren't the only one?"

Kathleen's lips curved in a smile. "The name Frances Ross familiar to you?"

"Oh, yes. I've been well informed on that point."

"It's an open secret that poor Bjorn is in gaol for that crime, not the murder of his fiancée."

"Yes, I had come to that conclusion myself," Daisy said sadly. "And I'm very much afraid I do not know how to prevent his hanging. The magistrate comes on Monday, and if I cannot find the perpetrator and convince the Rangers of his guilt, then Mr. Hansen will hang and my friend will never receive justice." Her lips trembled at the hopeless magnitude of the task she had set herself and her sister.

And yet, how could they walk away?

Kathleen leaned over and patted Daisy's knee. "You are good to care so much."

"I hope you do not think I am planning to step into a dead woman's shoes, too." Daisy wiped her nose and fished in her sleeve for a handkerchief. "Dr. Pascoe certainly does, and said so to my face."

"The nerve of him!" Kathleen straightened with affront. "He's a fine one to talk, when he's no stranger to Brownell Street himself."

This revelation did not surprise Daisy in the least. "But much as I dislike him, I cannot see him as the guilty party. He is a friend to Mr. Hansen."

"Yes, he is." Kathleen seemed to be turning over possibilities.

"It could have been a miner," the little laundress suggested.

"Then we have hundreds of suspects, and no way to winnow them down short of questioning them in the street," Daisy said. "That was the first thing we thought of."

Her suggestion thus dismissed, the girl flopped back on her pillow in a huff.

"No, accosting people wouldn't get you far," Kathleen mused. "Like as not you'd be murdered too, just for causing offense—but at least Bjorn wouldn't be accused of it."

"What about, er, customers at the flower houses?" Daisy forced the words past her embarrassment. What would Aunt Jane have to say about her company and conversation this morning?

"The regulars live here in town, and have no bone to pick with Bjorn," Kathleen said thoughtfully. "Why, he built houses for many of them, and furniture for their wives, besides."

"There are many who are not regulars," came the sulky voice from the cupboard. "The man who beat me, for one. I have not seen him before. Or since."

"Men come in on every train, and seem to find their way to the flower houses sooner or later," Kathleen said, nodding. "But that just gives you the same problem you have with the miners."

"Too many suspects," Daisy said. It was becoming more and more difficult to be positive when the prospects only became more numerous.

"That is not true." The girl rolled to her elbow again, no doubt risking pain in favor of the chance to argue. "A suspect may only be someone with a reason to kill that lady."

"And how does that help, Washie?" Kathleen lifted her hands, palm up. "Just like you, plenty of girls have been beaten for saying no, or for no reason at all. I imagine a man who wants to kill doesn't need a reason, either. Just someone handy, a weapon, and a dark corner."

"Not even a dark corner. She was killed right off Ninth Street not a hundred feet from a church," Daisy said. "He seems to have walked right up to her, stabbed her two or three times through the heart without being observed, and kicked her in the stomach once she had fallen. It's entirely possible she never even had a chance to cry out for help."

"Brute," whispered the girl.

"I didn't know that." Kathleen's face had paled, and now crumpled with distress. "Poor lady, and a bride-to-be too."

"*Jealous* brute," persisted the girl.

"We thought of that." The image of poor Emma's last moments had taken away any urge to bait the cheeky laundress. "Mr. Hansen was prepared to bring up the child she was carrying as his own, so it could not have been him."

"Child?" both her companions exclaimed at once.

At least *that* was not common knowledge on the far side of the creek, even if it was among the ladies on this side.

"So Bjorn was willing to marry her anyway," Kathleen said. "Making up to Heaven for Lieutenant Ross bringing up his boy in full view, perhaps?"

"I do not know," Daisy confessed. "But as for a motive of jealousy, we soon ran out of people to consider. The only person who might have cared that she was carrying his child and marrying another is on the other side of the world."

"And you know this for a fact?"

"I have the word of his brother that he is in Egypt. I have

no idea if the child was actually his. The brother is here in town for the summer, attached to the Pelican Mine."

"Which the parents of Frances own."

"That may not be relevant."

"Perhaps not, but it's another string leading back to Lieutenant Ross."

"Oh, goodness," Daisy exclaimed. "Surely you do not think the man in charge of the Texican Rangers could be guilty?"

"Can you rule him out?" Kathleen asked.

"I could march up to his office and ask him outright, and be tossed in a cell for my trouble."

"Asking questions isn't a crime. Do you want me to do it?"

Daisy paused. *"You* mean to march up there and ask him—"

"Of course not," Kathleen dismissed this silly notion with an airy wave of the hand. "He's a regular at our place. Men married to fine ladies they don't trust tend to be, don't you know."

*Oh. Oh, my.* Daisy pulled herself together. "Why, yes. Do ask him, then, where he was Thursday night at half past twelve. Though ... perhaps in a more roundabout way. I am sure he's perfectly aware of the facts of the case, however much he chooses to disregard them. It would not do to put him on his guard. And ... perhaps ..."

"Yes?" Kathleen leaned in to look under Daisy's hat brim, and Daisy straightened to meet her gaze. "Don't be afraid. It's in all our best interests to catch whoever did this. It could be one of us next, you know."

"I know." Only too painfully. "Perhaps you might put out the word to the other young ladies in Brownell Street. A word could slip during sleep—"

"Or after business and before sleep," came from the cupboard.

Daisy did not want to think what the girl meant, so she pressed on. "Or if someone shows a particular degree of violence—"

"Someone already has. That wicked gentleman with the ebony cane," the girl said.

"Has he returned to Ophelia's?" Daisy asked, conceding the point.

"Not yet," Kathleen said. "Haven't seen hide nor hair of him since Thursday. But from what I saw before the bully-boys pulled him off Washie, a temper like that could easily tip over into greater violence. He is one of many strangers, though, and no way to find a connection between him and your friend."

"Not that you'd want to ask him," the girl said. "Nasty fat Colonial."

"True enough." Kathleen nodded. "He's probably left town. But if he hasn't, do you want me to ask if I see him again?"

Now it was Daisy's turn to put a cautioning hand on the other girl's knee. "Do not put yourself in danger. Even speaking to such a man could get you the same treatment as Lin received."

"Who?" Kathleen looked puzzled.

Daisy nodded toward the cupboard.

"Washie?"

"My proper name is Yang Lin-Bai," the laundress said proudly. "Barney calls me Lin."

"You don't say." Kathleen smiled at her. "I never knew you had a proper name, Miss Yang Lin-Bai."

"You never asked, Miss Kathleen Shanahan."

Kathleen laughed, a sound full of humor and music. "That's the truth, and I won't make that mistake again." She rose. "How shall I let you know the results of my inquiries?"

"If you give a note to Davey, he can run it over to us at Rose Street." Daisy rose, too, and slid her seat back into its hiding place. "Mr. Hansen has given my sister and me leave to stay in his home."

Kathleen's eyebrow lifted. "Has he, now? Be sure you take good care of his chickens. He sets great store by them."

"My sister has already devoted herself to their care." She offered her hand again to Kathleen, and this time the girl took it, giving it a hearty squeeze. "Thank you for your help. You'll be careful, won't you?"

The desert flower was still smiling. "Nothing will happen to me that hasn't happened already," she said. "Good-bye, Daisy. I hope you will be better soon, Wa—I mean, Lin."

She ran down the steps and into the meadow, the sun glinting on her bare shoulders and raven curls as she made her way back to her side of the richest square mile on earth.

AFTER DAVEY and Mr. Barnicott had seen Kathleen safely over the bridge to the rear of the oxblood-colored house, Daisy met them at the steps of the conveyance.

"Were your inquiries a success?" Mr. Barnicott looked her over as though she might have suffered some damage during the course of the conversation. "I confess we did overhear a little. The walls of my conveyance were not designed to be impermeable."

Damage, no. Illumination, perhaps.

"Yes, they were. As you may have heard, we were able to

find some clarity of mind. Kathleen is to close one line of inquiry, and I ... well, I should like to take back what I said earlier, and offer Yang Lin-Bai—" She said the syllables carefully. "—as much hospitality and care as it is in our power to give."

"Oh, I am glad to hear that," he said, his eyes crinkling in a smile of warmth and delight that rather transfixed her for a moment. "It is a great relief to me. If it is convenient, I—"

"I will not go!" came a shout from within. "I cannot be moved."

Daisy blinked and looked away, recalling herself to more important matters than a man's smile. She was not certain if Lin meant being moved in a physical or a moral sense, but it did not matter. One could not care for someone who did not want care, short of tying them to the bedposts.

As smoothly as she could, in a tone pitched to reach the depths of the cupboard, she went on, "I observed a logical and clear mind in the young lady. She asked the right questions, and though we had already discounted many of the answers in the course of our own inquiries, the fact remains that for the next few days, three heads might be better than two."

"I don't care about your silly heads!"

"Lin, do not be rude to my guest," Mr. Barnicott said sternly.

"I am your guest, and she was rude to me. Will you beat me, too?"

"You know the answer to that." He climbed the steps and took the seat that Kathleen had vacated. Both elbows on his knees, his hands dangling, he leaned toward his patient and said, "Please, dear. You will be much more comfortable, and it appears that Miss Linden and Miss Frederica could use your help."

"She was careful to tell me she'd already thought of everything I said. If you take me over there, I shall only run away."

"Come on, Washie." Davey craned around Daisy's skirts to see into the conveyance. "It's for your own good."

"My own good is right here." And the cupboard door slid shut with a bang.

With a sigh, Daisy met Mr. Barnicott's chagrined gaze. "If she should change her mind, please let us know. Mr. Hansen's sofa is quite comfortable and my sister enjoys company."

"Thank you. I suppose there is nothing more to be done but to accept that in some cases, best intentions are not enough. Davey, will you see Miss Linden home?"

The boy's impish grin went some way toward ameliorating the sting of having her hospitality rejected. But why should she care what a Canton laundress thought? Once they were able to leave Georgetown, it was not likely she would ever see her again.

Somehow these practical thoughts did not help. Neither did the prospect of painting teacups, much to Freddie's astonishment. When she told her sister about the interview, and the reasons for her blue mood, her response was bracing.

"Goodness, Daisy, do not let it affect you so. The foolish child does not know what is good for her." Freddie squeezed her shoulders. "You have done your best, and there is nothing more you can do."

Which would make a good epitaph for their entire unfortunate stay in Georgetown.

When she and Frederica returned from dinner that evening, it was to find a note had been slipped under the front door. The smell of rose water wafted up from it as Daisy unfolded the thin paper, and something black slid into her hand.

*Dear Miss Linden,*

*In connection with our conversation earlier, it turns out I didn't need to resort to pillow talk to find out what you wanted to know. It seems the gentleman in question was with our Sallie Thursday after the cancan, and paid for the whole night to boot. She, being a light sleeper, says he didn't move after they were done, and left about five.*

*I may have more news for you tomorrow. It is possible the other gentleman we discussed has left town on business, but is due to return.*

*I hope my information is satisfactory. I am enclosing my lace necklace, which you admired. I can always make another, and I appreciated your behaving civilly to me.*

*Yours ever,*

*Kathleen Shanahan*

Every moral fiber in Daisy's body resisted showing the note to Frederica, but the truth was that there could be no secrets or concealments between them if they were to see this through. It was small comfort to have confirmed what Lin had meant about a word slipping out "after business." She still refused to contemplate how a child would know such a thing, however.

Frederica read through the scented note, the color rising in her face. "The gentleman in question, then, is Lieutenant Ross, as you speculated at dinner?"

"Yes."

"Ah. It was kind of her to give you such a beautiful gift. I see what you mean now, about using this cut-out Alençon lace rather than ribbon or a string of beads to form a lavaliere. It is lovely. Distinctive."

"Which is why I cannot wear it. A pity."

Freddie lifted her gaze from her admiration of the lace and jet. "Why ever not? It would go nicely with your blue dinner dress. Goodness knows we have few enough adornments to enjoy."

"Freddie, one cannot wear the property of a desert flower," she said with some exasperation. "Certainly not here. What if someone should recognize it? What would they think?"

Her sister crossed to the mirror hanging over the wash-stand, and held the necklace to her own throat, turning this way and that. "If it is the ladies of the town you're worried about, it's unlikely they'll have seen it. And no gentleman would say a word if he had, for fear of incriminating himself." She handed it back. "It was given honestly in thanks. That alone makes it special, no matter how the giver makes her living. Do not be a prig, dearest. We are in the Wild West now, not in Bath."

Daisy's estimation of herself had been deflated twice today —first by a Canton laundress, and now by her own sister. Was she really a prig who drove blindly ahead on her own course, concerned only with what was important to her, disregarding people's feelings willy-nilly in the process?

Was that why she had so few friends? Because she could not discern the feelings of others well enough to be a friend herself? Had Emma only associated with her—asked her to be her bridesmaid—because there was no one else to hand and Mrs. Davis was out of the question?

Daisy bit her lower lip in an attempt to stop its trembling, and carefully folded the necklace away in Kathleen's letter. And when, as they prepared for bed, Freddie took it from the dresser and tucked it into the inner pocket of Daisy's valise, she did not stop her or protest.

## CHAPTER 18

## WEDNESDAY, AUGUST 7, 1895

*2:10 a.m.*
*Georgetown*

Since his precipitate departure from Harvard, Barney had not really had a solid night's sleep. Sometimes this was simply the result of a white night and too much thinking. Sometimes, before coming into ownership of the conveyance, it was from the discomfort of sleeping on the ground or the floor of a boxcar. In any case, he had become a much lighter sleeper than he had been in his family's Boston mansion, a fact that had saved his life more than once.

Which was why it was quite a shock to be so deep in slumber that it took a severe bump to bring him awake on the leather seat of the front compartment. It took another moment to realize that *the conveyance was moving*.

And had been for some time.

He sat up, flinching as his head missed the acceleration bar by a hair. To his disoriented mind, it seemed as though the streets of Georgetown were flashing past on either side like the scenery in the flickers.

And immediately ahead—rumps and tossing manes. Neighing. A maelstrom of hooves.

*A pair of runaway horses.*

"Great Caesar's ghost!" Dressed in nothing but his union suit, Barney flung aside the wool blanket and hauled back on the acceleration bar for dear life, but of course nothing happened. The steam engine had been banked and without it even the pressure brakes on the wheels were useless. Not against two horses tearing down the street—two horses who must have been tied to the mooring loops in the front, for there was no other way to secure them.

He poked his head out the window to see his newly repaired fuselage trailing them at a raked angle as the conveyance thundered down the road at the speed of a panicked horse. The horses had no reins—no bits—they had simply been frightened into an uncontrolled gallop and he and Lin were at their mercy.

*Bang!* He jumped at the sound of a shot.

*Bang!* A flash of light.

There were incendiaries tied to the front of the conveyance, exploding at intervals and spooking the poor animals into terror again and again!

He could not control the horses. But he could control the conveyance.

He squeezed through the aperture behind the seat and into the boiler closet, where he began the ignition sequence with rubbery fingers in the pitch dark. Once that process was complete, he set the boiler on full and shoved open the door to the rear.

His heart nearly stopped at the sight of a ghostly figure swaying in the narrow aisle outside the open door of the sleeping cupboard.

"Barney! What is happening?"

Lin. On her feet. Was she mad? "Someone has tied us to a pair of runaway horses! Get in the cupboard and brace yourself!"

But instead of obeying, she staggered to the rear door and pulled it open to look out at the street reeling away under them. Her body tensed. Surely she wouldn't jump—

"Barney—why are we on Alexander Street?"

"I don't know! Get back in the cupboard before you get hurt!"

"But Barney—"

"Now!"

She planted her feet and shrieked, "Alexander Street has no bridge! They have not finished the new one—we will go over!"

A horrible vision assaulted him as surely as the hooves and wheels and explosive bangs assaulted his ears. A vision of a roiling ball of horseflesh and wood and glass and human limbs tumbling over the precipice to certain death. It was not a deep precipice, but two dozen feet would kill them as easily as two hundred.

He lit the lantern and snatched it up. The boiler whistled and he grabbed her hand. "You have to help me. It's going to hurt your ribs. But it's better than dying."

Without a word, she pressed into the boiler compartment with him, gasping in pain at the awkward movement. He pointed. "This is the pressure release for the boiler. If the needle goes into the red, back off some of the steam. Otherwise, wait for my call and keep it on full. The hot air will fill the fuselage and heat the gas. I'm going topside to reel it in."

He scrambled up the ladder, through the hatch, and hauled on the ropes like a madman. Despite his desperation, the wind of their going was against him. The gasbags in their protective fuselage took their sweet time centering themselves over the stack. Normally he would do this alone, while stopped and at leisure, not while being dragged along at a panicked gallop on an increasingly rough road as it approached the bridge construction. But there was no time. He had three choices.

Leap clear, break a few bones, and lose Lin and his living.

Fill the balloon.

Or die.

"Now!" he shouted, and even as he rolled clear of the stack, a gout of steam billowed up and into the fuselage. "Keep it coming!"

Puffing like a train, the stack whumped and exhaled and heated the air in the fuselage that surrounded the inner envelope of precious gas. The gas heated at once—expanded—and the balloon took glorious, sturdy, lifesaving form above the roof.

"Barney!" Lin screeched in warning.

Ahead, the unfinished iron trestle of the bridge glinted in the moonlight.

"Hold her steady!" he shouted back. "Don't slack off the pressure or—"

The steam whistle screamed—or maybe it was he—the horses plunged over the brink—

The conveyance tilted and everything inside that was not secured smashed into the boiler closet door—

Lin shrieked in terror—

—and the ropes to which Barney clung thrummed as they took up the slack of the conveyance's weight.

The balloon dipped so much he nearly screamed himself, expecting to be snatched into the roaring current below.

Every line securing the horses snapped and they tumbled into the river, landing in the deep water in midstream. Eyes rolling, forelegs thrashing, they began to swim.

At the release of their weight, the conveyance bobbed up out of the canyon. Barney shouted, "Starboard propeller, Lin. The switch above your right hand."

While he tied off ropes with a speed he wouldn't have believed himself capable of, securing the fuselage to as many mooring hooks as he could reach while flat on his stomach forty feet in the air, the conveyance leveled out and the entire equipage made an ungainly but gentle turn to the left, bringing them around to face the direction from which they had just come.

"Port propeller!" he called. "They must both turn to carry us on a straight course."

The other propeller chugged into life and at last Barney deemed the airborne vessel secure enough for him to climb down and relieve the poor child of her unexpected duty.

She gibbered with relief at the sight of him, her face shiny with tears and snot, and flung herself into his arms before he was fairly off the ladder.

"I thought we would die—I thought—oh, those poor horses—"

"The horses are unharmed. I saw them swimming for the bank." He patted her back, taking as much comfort from the blessed living warmth of her shuddering form as he was giving. "Do not worry for them. They will return to their stable wet and frightened, but unhurt."

She bawled something unintelligible into his chest.

"Come, Lin, we are not yet safe. Buck up. One must pilot this vessel or run into something—and much as I'd like to knock the chimney off Dr. Pascoe's house, it would hurt *us* more than it would him."

Alaia's son Tobin had made some adjustments to the front compartment that allowed one to turn a set of gears and adjust the propellers' direction enough to provide rudimentary steering. So they floated over the rooftops of Georgetown and its sleeping inhabitants from the relative comfort of the leather seat.

"I suppose it is too much to ask that the person who did this to us might be walking back to wherever he came from, so that we might see him." Lin clung to the door frame, gazing down at a sight few but aeronauts ever saw. She wiped her nose on her sleeve.

"Unlikely," he agreed. "But I do think it unsafe to return to the field behind the tavern just now. They might be thinking more clearly on a second attempt, and cut the ropes to the fuselage."

"I am very glad you woke in time," she said. "I did not know what to do except jump."

"You did very well, Lin. In fact, I believe you have a natural aptitude for aeronautics, though this contraption is no airship." He patted the acceleration bar with affection and leaned out the open window. His hair fluttered on his forehead in the cool wind of their going. A familiar cottage was coming into view. "I hope Mr. Hansen's chickens will not object if we land next to them."

"If they do, I shall boil them for soup."

"That would be poor thanks for their hospitality. Come. Now that we are no longer in danger of our lives, I will show you the landing procedure."

She obeyed his every instruction, opening the release valve to lower the pressure in the boiler. The heated air in the fuselage cooled and, when she stopped the port propeller, he guided the equipage down in a tight spiral past two spindly young fruit trees and into the garden.

The vehicle settled onto its wheels with a sigh, and Barney nodded at her to release the rest of the steam. "Just in case," he said in a voice pitched low so as not to wake the cottage's occupants, "we will not shut down the boiler or bank it. Instead, we will allow it to bubble on low. It might cost a few extra pieces of coal, but I will gladly pay that price."

And then he would find out who had done this, and make that person pay a great deal more.

*7:40 a.m.*

Barney woke with a start to find two pairs of feminine eyes gazing down upon him through the open window of the conveyance. Sunshine streamed through the wind screen, the fact that it had just cleared the peaks to the east telling him that it was not yet eight o'clock.

A shock of embarrassment made him snatch at the wool blanket to cover his union suit, and as he sat up, he clocked his head smartly on the acceleration bar. "Ow!"

"Oh, dear," Frederica said. "We didn't mean to startle you. Are you all right?"

"I will be," he groaned, slewing around on the seat so that

he could wrap the blanket around his shoulders like a cloak, and converse like a civilized person. "I apologize for not asking permission to land in your garden."

"It is not our garden, and you must have an exceedingly good reason for having done so," Daisy said. "No apologies necessary. We will have breakfast ready in half an hour. There is a wash house just there." She indicated the lean-to off the back of the kitchen, where the front of the boiler made cooking possible, and the rear provided hot water for laundry and bathing. "There is a washtub if you would like to bathe."

A flash of slender ankles in the grass told him that he might as well take his time if Lin was going first. He could not blame her—the ointment he had been applying to her bruises, while effective, was also very pungent.

Half an hour later, bathed, brushed, and feeling distinctly thankful to be alive, he joined his patient and his hostesses at the round dining table to enjoy a simple but filling breakfast of melted cheese between two slices of fried bread, a quantity of blackberries and cream, and tea so perfectly brewed his Brahmin grandmother might have supervised it personally.

"That was a meal fit for a king." He sighed happily, pushing his teacup toward Daisy for a refill. "Our most grateful thanks."

"You are very welcome. But you know the price you must pay, do you not?"

"Price?" Lin repeated, sitting up in immediate offense and then wincing.

"I do." He put a calming hand upon the girl's arm. "Allow me to tell you the story of how we came to be planted in the garden."

He did so, glad that he had waited until after breakfast, for there might have been a dropped spoon or perhaps even a broken teacup from sheer shock at some of the details, had he done it any sooner.

"But who on earth would do such a thing?" Daisy managed when he had concluded his tale. Her eyes were wide, her fingers white on the delicate handle of the blue and white teacup. "I can hardly imagine such cruelty."

"Whoever it was must be very good with horses," Lin said, wiping her blackberry-stained mouth with her sleeve since there did not appear to be any napkins. "To hitch a pair to the vehicle, lead them out to the street, then frighten them into a gallop with those incendiaries, all without waking us—it hardly seems possible."

"I did give you a sleeping draught, and I had a glass of whiskey in the tavern with some of the gentlemen of the town," Barney pointed out. "But I have done so before, and it did not cause me to sleep so heavily."

"It might if it were drugged," Lin said bluntly. "But why? Why not simply shoot us as we slept?"

"Because it might be heard, so close to the tavern?" Daisy wondered aloud. "Because whoever it was wanted it to look like an accident?"

"But that does not tell us *why* anyone would want to harm you at all." Frederica's eyes filled with tears. "Such evil!"

"Perhaps someone heard that we were asking questions of Miss Kathleen, and wished to send us a message," he suggested quietly.

"One does not attempt to kill people simply for asking questions," Daisy said.

"In your world, maybe not," Lin told her. "But in the Wild

West, a man can kill simply because he does not like the cut of your coat."

"Remember Ed Bainbridge," Frederica said softly. "Killing a man over a tin of oysters."

"Freddie!" Daisy exclaimed. "Do not speak of it."

"So you heard that story, too?" Barney smiled. "Whether it's true or not, it does prove a point. Kathleen comes to talk to us, and mere hours later, I am drugged—if indeed I was— and rather a lot of effort is made to take our lives. It cannot be coincidence. The two events must be connected."

"But she did not come to talk to you," Daisy objected. "She came to talk to me."

"Unseen," Lin put in. "Barney and she have talked outside in full view more than once since he took me in."

"Maybe it is not Barney who was their target, then, but you, Lin," Frederica said, and then pressed a hand to her lips. "Oh dear," she said a moment later. "I am sorry. That was dreadfully inconsiderate."

"Attempted murder is, rather," Barney said dryly. "But Lin knows nothing worth being murdered for. Nor do I—unless you count my recipe for liniment, which is very good. I confess I am mystified."

"Maybe you have hit upon it," Daisy said slowly. "Maybe someone wants you out of town. Someone who views you as competition."

"Someone like Dr. Pascoe," Frederica said. "He has already been violent with you, hasn't he?"

Barney could hardly believe they had taken his little joke and turned it into something so serious. "You cannot mean it. Why, he is a gentleman."

"So was the man who beat me," Lin snapped. "Nice clothes

and a gold chain do not make a gentleman. That must come from the inside, and can go around in rags."

Like Davey. He had to concede that she was right.

"The point is, someone *thinks* you are a threat of some kind," Daisy said. "And is convinced enough of it to take drastic measures."

"We must take measures ourselves, then," Freddie said, rising to clear the table. "Where did the horses come from? There is only one livery in town, is there not? One of the poor things could have been the horse we hired ourselves, to visit the paupers' field on Saturday." Her hands full, she turned in the kitchen doorway. "A lovely spotted creature of a breed I have never seen before."

"They call those paints here." Barney pushed back his chair. "I could not determine their coloring in the dark, with the flashes from the incendiaries, but they will bear signs of their landing in the river, I am sure. We must ask who hired them—or whether they were stolen, tack and all."

"Not all," Lin pointed out. "No collars, no shafts. Just tied to the mooring rings, reined together and set to running."

"Horrible." Daisy shuddered. "The poor creatures. I am very glad they survived."

"I ought to tell Kathleen what has happened," Barney said, "and advise her to be very discreet in future. In fact, we must not speak with her again. And Lin, I am afraid that I must insist on your accepting the Miss Lindens' hospitality. At least no one can hitch a pair of horses to a cottage and run away with it."

To his enormous surprise, she did not rear and paw the air in protest. Instead, she merely hugged herself about the middle, as though trying to hold her sore body upright. "If the ladies still want me, I would be honored to accept," she said in a small voice.

"I think your exertions of the night have increased your pain," Freddie said gently, bending down to her. "Come. It won't take a moment to make up the sofa, and you may lie down for a nap. The sun will travel around to the front window before long, and you will be lovely and warm."

Freddie helped her into the parlor, and before Barney could open his mouth to express his thanks, a knock came at the kitchen door.

"Why, Davey," Daisy said, letting him in. "I was wondering where you'd gone. Will you take a message to Kathleen?"

He shook his head violently. "Ent no one can do that now."

"But—why not? Has she left town?"

Fear stood stark in the boy's eyes, and Barney's stomach plunged with a sudden terrible knowledge. "Davey, has something happened to her?"

"Aye, sir. They found her this morning on the outside staircase. Doc Pascoe is delivering a baby, so Madame Ophelia says will you come right away."

# CHAPTER 19

## WEDNESDAY, AUGUST 7, 1895

*8:10 a.m.*

*D*aisy solved the difficulty of Mr. Barnicott's resistance to her accompanying him by the simple expedient of putting on her hat, slipping her sketchbook into her reticule, and walking off toward the nearest bridge without him.

"I have shown great forbearance and even generosity in the matter of vehicles landing in the garden," she informed him down her nose when he caught up with her. "You, sir, owe me one."

"The dead body of a girl you spoke to only yesterday is hardly a fit sight for a lady!"

"She is not the first deceased person I have seen. Leaving funerals out of it, I saw poor Emma twice before she was buried. In fact, let us stop a moment. I have something to show you."

Pausing in the middle of the bridge, she was thankful their

conversation would be masked by the rushing of the water below. Daisy let the boy run on ahead and pulled out her sketchbook.

"You sketched your friend?" She could not tell whether his wondering tone came from the depiction of Emma's injuries, or his disgust that she had drawn them at all. "When?"

The latter, then. "We stopped the burial and had them open the coffin."

He gave an exclamation that would have horrified Aunt Jane and caused her to rush Daisy away with both hands over her ears. "What on earth possessed you to do such a thing? Why, that is—that is unnatural!"

She glared at him. "Go ahead. You want to call me a ghoul. Say it."

"I shall not."

"You are thinking it."

"My thoughts are my business."

"And my friends are mine. Dr. Pascoe has not mentioned these wounds except to one person, and did not show them to Mr. Hansen and myself." She tapped the page. "I suspect it was so he could trap Mr. Hansen in his testimony before the magistrate."

"He could have wanted to spare the poor man."

"Perhaps," Daisy said, unwillingly. "When we spoke before, you implied that an individual blade could leave a unique impression. I wanted to record that impression. Now I am glad I did, in case we see it again."

"It is not likely *we* will. Poor Kathleen could be the victim of any number of men—miscreants or customers."

Daisy put the sketchbook back into her reticule. "We shall see."

But he prevented her setting off again with a hand upon her arm. "Please, Miss Linden. I must beg you again—do not risk everything by accompanying me."

"I doubt I am in any danger by daylight."

"That is not the risk I mean. Your reputation in Georgetown will be reduced to mud under the wheels of a steam dray if you are seen on Brownell Street. That, I suspect, is the real reason Dr. Pascoe does not practice here. I beg you, allow me to go on alone, and I will tell you everything when I return."

"I do not care what the people in this town think," she said in exasperation. "What matters is finding out who killed Emma and Kathleen."

"You will care when you and your sister are no longer received. If a further line of inquiry presents itself, no door will be open to you. How will you serve Emma's memory then, as a woman known to be her friend?"

No argument he could have presented could have affected her save that one. All that remained of Emma Makepeace now after a burial in the pauper's field and the general blackening of her name was the reputation of her friends. She could not tarnish Emma's memory further by her own headstrong, headlong behavior—could not have Emma's name associated with Brownell Street even once removed, for fear that the likes of the doctor's wife would take their nasty speculations even farther.

Mr. Barnicott had the grace to stand silently while she recovered from her chagrin.

"Very well," she said at last. "I will visit the greengrocer's and then return to Rose Street. Please bring Davey back with you, if he will come. He will be in need of a meal."

He took a long breath. "Thank you. Both for seeing the truth, and for your kindness to Davey and Lin."

"And Mr. Barnicott—forgive me my indelicacy, since I know the subject offends you ... but if it is possible to examine Kathleen in order to discover the nature of her death, I beg you will do so."

He struggled with himself for a moment—a moment in which Daisy had no doubt the word *ghoul* again crossed his mind. But she was not a ghoul. Kathleen's final act of generosity might be to tell him something, if he would only listen!

"I imagine that is the other reason Ophelia sent for me," he finally said. "To see if it can be proved that no one in her house is responsible, before someone sends for the Rangers. I am no doctor—I am a chemist—but I am a gentleman. She knows my word will carry weight despite Dr. Pascoe's feelings about me and my line of work. I will do what I can."

He bowed, and strode across the bridge in one direction, while she returned to town in the other.

As she chose vegetables and meat and arranged for them to be delivered to the cottage, a hundred images of what might have befallen Kathleen played like flickers across her mind. Her imagination became increasingly troubled, to the point that when she returned, she removed herself to the garden to let the chickens out, hoping to sketch them a second time. But so alarmed were they at the menacing behavior of Mr. Barnicott's fuselage in the breeze that they would not set foot outside the door of their safe enclosure.

As a last resort, she sought employment in cooking. While the scent of a beef cassoulet was comforting, it did nothing to distract her mind. Not until the gate banged shut behind Mr. Barnicott and Davey did she find any relief.

In order to disturb Lin's recovery as little as possible, she and Freddie served a late lunch in the parlor, with their guests balancing their plates upon their knees. With a heroic effort, she managed to give Mr. Barnicott time to consume his first plate of cassoulet and fresh bread, but when he filled it a second time, her patience ran out.

"Mr. Barnicott, you must tell us what you learned at Madame Ophelia's."

"It ent a subject to be discussin' over a meal," Davey said with his mouth full. "Believe me."

"I have no doubt of that, but you will find the three of us are made of sterner stuff," she said. "I do not imagine Lin is a stranger to the darker side of life and experience, and it is certain Frederica and I are not."

Mr. Barnicott looked as though he might be more interested in this line of conversation than in relating what had happened, but she shook her head at his inquiring gaze. "Please. I can bear it no longer."

He swallowed and seemed to resign himself to the inevitable. "I will proceed in order of my discoveries, then. Consider yourselves warned."

Nothing could be worse than having to examine the remains of one's friend, no matter how gently and lovingly. The mere account of a similar experience could certainly be borne. Daisy glanced at Freddie, who nodded in encouragement.

"As you know, Davey went on ahead to let them know he had found me. When I arrived at the house, he guided me around to the side, where there is a steep set of steps up to the second floor."

"The girls' private entrance," Lin put in. "So they don't have to pass the gentlemen in the parlor if they're not available."

"Thank you, Lin," Mr. Barnicott said, looking pained, but not shushing her, either, for which Daisy was grateful. "Kathleen was lying on her back upon the steps, about two-thirds of the way down, her feet uppermost. It seemed she had tripped and fallen in the dark."

"Seemed?" Freddie repeated.

"That's what I said," Davey remarked to his plate.

"You are both of a skeptical turn of mind." Mr. Barnicott smiled at the boy, who straightened and smiled back.

"She could have been pushed," Lin suggested.

"She could, indeed. Madame Ophelia would have been only too happy to tell the Rangers she had lost her balance from too much drink and broken her neck. She was not impressed when we moved Kathleen to flat ground and I unfastened her corset. I had noticed it was torn, you see."

Daisy took a deep breath and released it. "In what way?"

"Two slits explained the presence of a quantity of blood. While Davey held up a shawl to offer the deceased a little privacy, and witnessed by Madame alone, I moved her shift aside and found two blade wounds near the heart, with tight circles of bruising around each one."

Daisy gasped. "Just like Emma!"

"I am glad that you showed me your sketchbook, Miss Linden. Otherwise I might not have been alerted to the slits in the corset, and would certainly not have gone so far as to examine the—Kathleen herself. Goodness knows what the

Rangers will make of it—if they even bother to look. One desert flower more or less is nothing to them."

"So the same person could have killed both Emma and Kathleen?" Frederica asked after a moment.

"It is safe to say the same kind of weapon might have been used," Mr. Barnicott said. "But I cannot imagine what that would be, or how many men might carry such a thing—neither knife nor rifle, but a combination of both, from all appearances."

"And she was not seen with anyone?" Daisy asked. "Surely two people on a set of steps would be clearly visible, even at night."

"Two shadows, maybe," Davey said. "It's dark on that side of the house because of the pines. Easy to come and go quietly, though. The needles make soft treading, and there's the noise of the river."

"Madame Ophelia was equally puzzled." Mr. Barnicott nodded to acknowledge Davey's observations. "Kathleen was working that night, and Madame seemed angry that the girl might have taken some time to herself outside on the landing. When I suggested she might have been talking with someone, that seemed even more offensive."

"Talking doesn't bring in money," Lin pointed out.

"If she was talking, it must have been to one of her ... customers," Daisy said. "Does Madame know whom each girl, er, sees of an evening?"

"She keeps a list," Lin said. "But it's under lock and key, and you're not going to get to see it. Even the men whose names are on it don't know about it. She says it's worth all the silver in Silver Plume."

"No doubt," said Mr. Barnicott wryly. "But that is the place to start. Anyone who was with Kathleen after two o'clock in the morning, which is the last time she was seen downstairs, could be the person we seek."

"Davey, when was she found?" Daisy asked.

"Just at daylight," the boy said. "One of the girls came out to get the milk and found her."

Milk was delivered to a flower house, just like it would be to any household in England? Daisy swallowed down the ingenuous question. Then something else occurred to her. She excused herself and fetched Kathleen's letter from her valise.

"She sent this to me yesterday while we were out. Listen: *I may have more news for you tomorrow. It is possible the other gentleman we discussed has left town on business, but is due to return.*"

"What other gentleman?" Frederica asked.

"The wicked brute who beat me," Lin said. "But that has nothing to do with Emma or Kathleen or who killed them."

"She was encouraging you to be cautious, which makes me more glad than ever that you are staying here," Mr. Barnicott told her. "In fact, I have something for you."

He slipped a hand into his coat and drew out something wrapped in a handkerchief. It was a slender object about the length of a woman's palm, topped by a large bead encrusted in paste jewels.

"Why, that is Kathleen's busk knife," Daisy said. Then another thought occurred to her. "She was still wearing it when you examined her?"

Mr. Barnicott nodded. "I set it aside to open her corset. But it does bring up an interesting question."

"She wore it for protection," Lin said. "So why didn't she use it?"

"Because she didn't think she needed it?" Davey asked. "Just talking to someone on the stairs?"

But who? Someone she knew? A friend? Or someone else who merely appeared trustworthy?

There was no way now to answer those questions.

"Freddie, you will appreciate the skill of its construction," Daisy said at last. "One fashions a sheath behind the corset busk to conceal it."

Interested, Freddie leaned in as Mr. Barnicott handed the knife to Lin. "Madame Ophelia asked me to give this to you. She says—and I quote—if that misbegotten blighter comes back, you may need this, compliments of Kathleen."

Lin took it, careful not to touch the sharp blade. "But I do not wear a corset."

"Then fashion a sheath and tie it round your ankle, concealed by your boot," Frederica said promptly, much to Daisy's astonishment.

Lin looked delighted by the suggestion. Daisy could not help but wonder again about the company Freddie had been keeping in London. Who but Maggie Polgarth and the Carrick House set would know about such things?

# CHAPTER 20

## WEDNESDAY, AUGUST 7, 1895

*1:30 p.m.*

When a knock came at the front door, Davey lost no time vanishing out the back. Daisy did not know whether he was prescient, but when the caller turned out to be Ranger Willets, she wondered if perhaps the boy's activities might not be entirely on the up-and-up. Frederica's blush when the young Texican Ranger stepped into view was enough to make her forget all about Davey, however, and brace herself for this new complication.

The young man tore his gaze from Freddie's rosy face and settled instead on Mr. Barnicott. "If you'd like to come with me, sir, I understand you have some information about an incident that occurred this morning."

"Do you mean Kathleen Shanahan's death, or the kidnapping of my vehicle and the attempt on my life?"

The Ranger's eyes widened and he blushed furiously at the same time, no doubt at the mention of the desert flower's name in mixed company. "The former, sir, though we would certainly like to hear about the latter as well."

"How did you find me?" Mr. Barnicott asked curiously. "I did not think my whereabouts were currently known."

"The balloon, sir," the young man said. "It shows above the rooftops."

"Of course it does," Mr. Barnicott said with a slap of his palm to his forehead. "I must remove from here as quickly as may be."

"Or simply deflate it a little," Freddie suggested.

"It is hardly proper for him to be here in any case," Daisy said when the two men went out. "An unmarried man camping in the garden?"

"It may be too late now for propriety." But Freddie did not seem unduly disturbed by the prospect. "Daisy, I should like to visit the stable, since Mr. Barnicott is otherwise occupied this afternoon and someone must stay with Lin. We must not delay, or the horses will no longer show signs of their ordeal. I will merely say I am planning a drive to the lake later in the week."

"Very well." Daisy nodded and began to clear the remains of their lunch. "But be careful. If you see Davey, ask if he might go with you."

"I will."

The house seemed very quiet after everyone had gone. But it was not a restful quiet in which a woman might read or paint. For one thing, the only English books in the glass-fronted bookcase in the parlor were limited in subject to carpentry and a biography of Mr. Tesla, and the remainder were written in the Norse tongue. She would have liked to paint, but she had already done the teacups, the chickens would not cooperate, and the milk jar was rather uninspiring.

That left only her guest.

She perched on the edge of a glossy pine slat-back chair facing the child, who lay with the spare pillow behind her shoulders. "Lin, would you mind very much if I painted your portrait?"

The girl ceased her contemplation of the front garden and street, which were just visible over the back of the sofa, and turned her surprised gaze on Daisy. "Why?"

"Because I have exhausted my usual subjects, and painting calms me. I can think better when my hands and mind are occupied."

"What are you thinking about?"

"What we are *all* thinking about ... the death of my friend, and of yours. At least, I believe I am not mistaken in calling Kathleen your friend. You seemed on familiar terms."

"Just because someone calls me Washie does not make them my friend."

"I should think just the opposite," Daisy agreed. "But she did call you by your proper name when she learned what it was."

"That is true." The girl gazed at her. "Are you my friend?"

Daisy blinked at the unexpected question. Was she? What constituted a friend here in the Wild West? And how did one claim friendship with a Canton laundress who until recently had lived in a flower house?

But that was horrid of her.

Lin was only a child, and could not be held responsible for what others had made of her life so far. She was prickly and proud, but she had a good mind. If Daisy had learned her lesson at all on the subject of friendship, maybe she ought to overcome her propriety—priggishness, Freddie called it—and diffidence, and be the first to extend a hand.

"I hope so. I hope we will become friends, despite our rough beginning."

"But you are a lady, and I am a laundress from Brownell Street."

Behind her pointed defiance, could the child read minds, as Freddie sometimes complained Daisy herself did? Daisy called it deduction and logic, but Freddie never seemed to believe her. Perhaps Lin's good mind employed similar skills.

"You are a child who cannot be blamed for making her way in the world after losing her family," she said gently, feeling her way along the thread of her own thoughts. "One must put food in one's mouth, and if washing clothes is the only work available, then I cannot blame you for taking it. I should likely do the same."

"I never worked upstairs," Lin said, her chin lifting.

"I never imagined you did."

"It wasn't easy to refuse. The madams don't take kindly to my taking up space by the stove if I don't earn my keep."

"But you did. A laundress's task is not easy."

"They could get much more for me upstairs. A virgin, and young."

Daisy's skin went cold and she felt again the prickle of tears. "Oh, Lin, do not speak of it. It breaks my heart to think of your enduring such a thing, and of others, too, who are not able to refuse. It hurts even to hear you say those words—that you have been forced into such knowledge at only thirteen."

Lin lifted a shoulder, making Daisy feel like the inexperienced child here. "Knowledge can keep you alive."

"I know. I am afraid I do not know one hundredth the things you do. Nor have I experienced nearly what you have." A dam seemed to break inside her, and words spilled out through the breach. "How are you not curled up in a closet, terrified of this strange new world? How do you go on, knowing that the people you love are gone, that there is no one to care for you, no one to protect you, and at any moment—"

She choked, and the telltale torrent stopped.

"Where are *your* parents?" Lin said at last, when Daisy had had a moment to compose herself.

"My mother passed away last year, and my father is missing somewhere in the Wild West. That is why Freddie and I are here. We are looking for him. He was last seen in Reno, but we believe he will have made for Santa Fe, so Freddie and I are going there as soon as—"

What? As soon as they unmasked a killer? As soon as they found that all their efforts were for nothing? As soon as they became so frightened that there was no option but to flee?

"As soon as we finish here," she concluded lamely. "We had reliable information that he was headed to Santa Fe in April. We hope to pick up his trail."

Lin gazed at her, with a light of recognition in her eyes. "We are a little alike, then. My only relative is missing, too. My aunt Yang Jiao-Lan—my father's sister."

"What happened to her?"

"I do not know. My father died before he could discover her. All I know is that she came to Gold Mountain—that is San Francisco—to marry a man of good family. But the man deceived her and took her dowry and turned her out. Rather than working on the railroad or going to a flower house, she ran away. And that is all I know."

"Good heavens," Daisy said weakly. "On a day like today, when I am tempted to feel sorry for myself, I must think of the travails of other women here in the Wild West, and remember my blessings."

A little silence fell in which Daisy did remember them ... Freddie, her dearest sister. Her Aunt Jane, who really did care about them, and meant well. Mr. Hansen, whose kindness had given them a place to stay despite his own extremity. Even Mr. Barnicott, who could have floated away in his peculiar conveyance and resumed his own life, but who instead seemed interested in helping them.

Lin shifted, as though she were uncomfortable. "Very well," she said. "You may paint my picture. How long will it take?"

Daisy's heart squeezed with happiness, which she endeavored not to show in case the contrary child changed her mind. "Emma's portrait took several hours, but hers was a more complex composition. Between her masses of hair and the lace of her bridal bodice, the detail that required my rigger brush seemed to take a very long time. But it was worth every moment. Would you like to see it?"

Lin nodded, her eyes bright with the prospect of something new after several days of confinement and inactivity.

Daisy fetched the parcel, still wrapped in its tissue paper and ribbon from the portrait studio. She unwrapped it carefully. "Mr. Hansen said he did not want to think of what he had lost, but when he has his freedom again, he might want to be reminded of his blessings, too," she said. "This was Emma Makepeace, my friend."

Lin took the portrait and gazed at it with wondering appreciation. "You are a very good painter."

What could this child know of portraiture? But perhaps simple appreciation was best of all. Freddie had used to gaze raptly upon the pretty balls on the Christmas tree in their childhood home. Was her appreciation of beauty of any less value than that of some art critic in a famous museum?

"I had a lovely subject," she said with as much truth as modesty.

"Will I look like this?" Lin handed the portrait back and Daisy wrapped it up again with care, then laid it upon the mantel.

"You will look like ... you, with glossy blue-black hair, dark eyes full of life and intelligence, and smooth skin."

"Madame says I'm bony and ugly. I suppose she is right. The girls let me look in their mirror and that was pretty much what I saw."

What a thing to say to a child who had little but her dignity left to her! "Madame was in error. That is not what I see at all." For one thing, the girl had had a few regular meals lately. And for another, her cheekbones had the stark beauty of the curve of a new moon, her brows the arch of a butterfly's feelers.

"What do you see, then?"

Daisy smiled at her. "You will see for yourself. Now, make yourself comfortable."

"I wish I had something to do while I sit," Lin said fretfully. "At least lunch was interesting, because I could talk and use my mind."

Daisy went into the bedroom to fetch her sketchbook and palette, and to fill a canning jar with water to mix her colors.

"There is nothing here that either of us can read, sadly," she called. "Oh, wait."

There was Emma's scrapbook. It wasn't much, but at least it would occupy the child for long enough that Daisy could get the main outlines of her face and hair on paper. Once she had those, even if Lin fidgeted or refused to sit still, she could manage.

She brought the book, full of the cheerful, colorful debris of another woman's life, and settled into the pine chair to draw.

Silence fell—a silence whose nature had been changed, now punctuated by the turn of a page, the scratch of the pencil, the occasional rub as Daisy created a smudge of shadow with a finger. It was her favorite kind of silence, filled with creativity and contemplation.

In it, her thoughts freed themselves to return to her conversation with Kathleen yesterday. For the first time, she marveled at the girl's generosity in taking an hour to talk, and to think through the possibilities at hand with her. Kathleen was in a business where time was money. Perhaps she'd given up a gentleman for that hour. She had certainly given them a tremendous gift in eliminating Lieutenant Ross. For if she had not, who would have the nerve to question him?

Certainly not herself or Freddie.

Daisy concentrated on capturing Lin's eyes, the most important part of the face, and the place where the viewer's own gaze instinctively went first.

So Lieutenant Ross was stricken from the list of murderers, though his motive for keeping Mr. Hansen in gaol was still deeply suspect.

Mr. Barnicott could be eliminated, because he had been

treating Lin that night, and besides, he had no reason to wish Emma ill, having never met her.

Mr. Meriwether-Astor had none, either, and had been at the mine with Mr. Davis. His brother Sydney, while he might have had a motive, had no opportunity, being in the deserts of Egypt.

Reluctantly, as she drew the graceful lines that would become Lin's brows, she concluded that Dr. Pascoe could also be removed from the list. He and Mr. Meriwether-Astor had engaged the Rocky Mountain Detective, after all, so it was not likely he would risk that clever individual's following a trail straight back to himself.

It seemed that Freddie had been right in the beginning. Emma knew no one but Mr. Hansen and the Davises in Georgetown. The guilty party was more likely to be one of two things: Someone from her past life—in which case they could not investigate, situated as they were on the other side of the country from New York, never mind London. Or secondly, a complete stranger.

In both cases they were helpless to act. Daisy frowned as Lin's cheek took shape beneath her pencil.

Perhaps this Rocky Mountain Detective had resources to which two sheltered young ladies had no access.

Perhaps that was their best and only option—to hand over their list of crossed-out names and wish him well in sending telegrams to Sir Robert Peel's constabulary in London, and questioning every last miner in Georgetown.

Perhaps she and Freddie would—

Lin gasped and flung the scrapbook from her so violently that it landed upside-down on the glossy planks of the floor.

She pushed herself up against the arm of the sofa, breathing fast, her eyes wide with panic.

Daisy's heart pounded with fright and annoyance. "Lin, for heaven's sake! Look what you've made me do." Carefully, she took a bit of India-rubber and erased the jagged line she had made.

"Why is he in there?"

"My dear child, calm yourself. Why is who in where?"

"Do not tell me to calm myself! If you had been beaten with his cane, you would not calm yourself! Tell me now—why is he in this book?"

At last, Daisy's brain caught up with her heartbeat. She laid her sketchbook down and gave the girl her full attention. Lin breathed as though she had been running—or wished she could.

"Show me," Daisy said simply, and picked up the scrap-book. A paper flower had been crushed as it fell, and lay on the floor. As she moved to sit next to the girl, she scooped it up, cupped in her palm.

Lin paged through the chaos of colorful memories, and two-thirds of the way back, allowed it to fall open. Theater tickets, a swatch of lace that Daisy realized with a tingle of recognition was from Emma's wedding bodice, and a pressed rose. The three daguerreotypes that Daisy remembered from the other day—the blond child, the literary club ladies, and the heavy-set man she had been so sure she had recognized.

Lin pushed the scrapbook back into Daisy's lap, her hands trembling. Daisy pressed the flower in among its fellows absently as she gazed at the daguerreotype. There was no inscription, no name, only the name of the studio in New York inked along the bottom.

"Lin ... are you saying ... you recognize this man?"

"Are you deaf? I am saying that it is he. That is the man who beat me at Madame Ophelia's when I would not go upstairs with him, the same night your friend was murdered."

Daisy stared at the image while thoughts darted this way and that in her mind like frightened fish.

*The man from breakfast on Friday morning. I did recognize him.*

*He is real, and he is here.*

*And he is violent. So violent that he would beat a child because he did not get what he wanted.*

*What else is a man like that capable of?*

"But—but—who is he?" she finally said. "And what was he to Emma that she would keep the portrait of such a brute in her scrapbook?"

# CHAPTER 21

*3:10 p.m.*

"He must be a relative—perhaps even her father." Freddie had returned just in time to see the shocked tableau that Daisy and Lin made upon the sofa, the scrapbook open on Daisy's lap. She wasted no time in extracting the details from them. Then she said, "Where is the portrait you painted of Emma?"

Daisy pointed toward the mantel. "Be careful of the wrapping. We are going to leave it for Mr. Hansen in hopes of better days to come."

Frederica brought over the portrait and held it and the daguerreotype side by side. "He is not an attractive man, but there is a distinct similarity in the eyes, isn't there?"

Daisy examined the two. The size and clarity of the eyes were the same, as was the depth of the lid and its distance beneath the brow. "I think you may be right. Her mother must have been exceedingly beautiful to make up for his ugliness.

But his portrait in her scrapbook—I did not think she cared so much for her father as that."

"One must observe the proprieties, mustn't one?" Freddie said. "Family portraits are expected in a memory book. And perhaps she wanted to show Mr. Hansen a likeness of his father-in-law, though they might never meet."

"I wish she had burned it," Lin said, now curled up so tightly that she gazed at them over her knees, the blanket tucked around her feet. "Who is the child, then?"

"I have no idea, but ..." Freddie moved the child's picture to join the other two. "The eyes are the same. It cannot be Emma, for this is a boy in short pants."

"A younger brother?" Daisy guessed.

"No matter," Lin said, losing interest in the child, her gaze flinching away as it passed over the older man. "I never wish to see picture or real man again. Put it away."

"No, give it to me," Daisy said. "If this is her father, then wealthy and consequential as he is, he will be known at the Hotel de Paris. I have only to show it to the desk clerk and we will have a name to put to Lin's tormentor."

"For all the good that will do," the girl mumbled into her knees. "Kathleen said he was away on business."

"She also said he might be coming back. We do not know why he was in Georgetown on Friday, when Emma went to such trouble to keep her destination secret," Daisy said. "It cannot be coincidence when from all accounts he is supposed to be in London. But the fact remains that if he is a member of her family, he must be informed of her decease."

"How can he not know?" Freddie asked. "Everyone in town does."

"Not if he has not been here. If he was, surely someone

would have seen him. It is only right that someone tell him and express their condolences, as distressing as the details might be."

"Oh, dear," said Freddie. "Are you sure? If he can beat a defenseless child, who knows what he is capable of? Murder? Emma's murder?"

That was a chilling thought. Had they been looking in the wrong places all this time? But her own father—! Daisy's mind shied away from it like a frightened horse. "I suppose we can leave no possibility unexamined. But to be safe, perhaps one had better not see him alone, even to condole."

"Perhaps one had better not see him at all," Lin said. "He doesn't deserve any courtesy. And if he did kill that lady, he will laugh at your condolences."

Lin really had a gift for pointing out uncomfortable truths.

"We might ask Mr. Meriwether-Astor to go with us, perhaps?" Freddie suggested.

And risk another lecture, though a condolence visit was the last thing likely to get them into trouble? No, she would ask Mr. Barnicott, who at least gave her credit for intelligence even as he deplored her methods.

"Perhaps," she said mildly. "Meanwhile, let us turn our thoughts to other lines of inquiry. Freddie, what did you discover at the stables?"

"Quite a lot," Freddie said, settling into the pine chair and noticing Daisy's sketch of Lin with interest. "Oh, are you drawing Lin? It's going to be lovely."

"I am. But the horses?"

"When I inquired about hiring the pony and trap again, the smith told me that both their horses were unavailable. The nice stable boy let me in to visit them. The paint had a large bruise upon its leg that he was rubbing with liniment, and had lost the shoes on both forefeet. The bay that we did not hire was in such a state of nerves that it could not even be approached, but backed into the rear of the stall and pawed the straw at the sight of us. Poor things. I felt dreadful for them, to have been treated in such a manner."

"At least they are alive," Lin observed.

"That is true," Daisy said. "Did you find out who hired them last night?"

"That is the problem." Freddie leaned toward them. "They were not hired. They were stolen. The stable boy says they woke him when they returned to the stableyard, soaked and frantic. It was all he and the smith could do to get the bay into its stall without injury."

Daisy could not help her disappointment. "We thought as much."

"I suppose it was too much to expect that we would find a signed receipt with a name on it," Freddie agreed, sitting back. "What shall we do now?"

Daisy picked up her sketchbook and despite Lin's interested craning to see the initial stages of her portrait, turned past it to the scrap of paper tucked into the rearmost pages. "I have an idea. Do you remember saying that Emma's murderer had to be someone from her past, or a perfect stranger from here, since she knew no one but Mr. Hansen?"

"She knew Mrs. Davis," Freddie pointed out.

"I think we can agree that Mrs. Davis did not kill her friend. We both saw their good humor together. I cannot believe that was forced. And what reason would she have?"

"None that I can see," Freddie agreed readily. "She couldn't very well be jealous of Emma when she was the one who deserted Mr. Hansen—the man she had promised to marry."

"Quite so. Where was I?"

"Someone from her past or a miner," Lin said.

"This man, father or not, is from her past—and it is fairly clear she wanted him to stay that way. But do you remember in her letters that her father was always wanting her to mix with the Dunsmuir set?"

"Yes," Freddie replied. "I hope you are not implying they had something to do with it. The Queen would have a few words to say on that head."

"Of course not," Daisy said impatiently. "But Sir Ian and Lady Hollys move in that set." She held up the slip of paper bearing the code for *Swan*. "I am going to write to Lady Hollys this very day. And I am going to include a sketch of this man. If there is anything they can tell us, it will come to us much faster than a reply from London ever could."

*4:05 p.m.*

Barney emerged from a rather grueling two hours in a windowless office being interviewed by the Texican Rangers as to the circumstances of Kathleen Shanahan's death and also his own misadventure by runaway horse. Blinking in the afternoon sunshine, he realized that a straight-backed female figure was waiting at the bottom of the detachment's steps.

"Why, Miss Linden. Has something happened?"

When he joined her, he offered his arm, and after a moment's hesitation, she took it. Her ever-present reticule seemed even bulkier this afternoon as it swung from her other wrist.

"I require your assistance, and since you had not returned, I hoped to find you still here. Did your interview go well? You do not seem to have been arrested."

He was rather glad about that. "They weren't very happy about my conclusions, and I'm not even sure they believed my report about the attempt on Lin's and my lives. But I have done my duty, and now it is up to them to do theirs." He attempted to see her face, shaded under the straw hat brim with its navy and yellow cockade and ribbons. "How may I be of assistance?"

She told him, first what her sister had discovered about the horses, and then about a scrapbook and Lin and a horrid man from breakfast on Friday and the longer she spoke, the more his astonishment slowed his pace, until finally they stopped altogether opposite the Hotel de Paris.

"I say, that is quite a leap—that a society man moving in the highest circles in London should suddenly appear in a town many have never heard of and take up violence and murder. What possible reason would he have?"

"If what we suspect is true, Emma kept her destination a secret from her father. Could he have followed her here, to try to change her mind perhaps, or to force her to go back to London with him? Could he have vented his rage and frustration on someone who was not in a position to protest?"

Barney shook his head. "This is speculation, and far-fetched at that. I think you are arranging the facts to suit yourselves."

Her generous lips thinned, and too late he realized he ought to have been less blunt.

"Thank you, Mr. Barnicott. Perhaps I will not trouble you after all. Good day."

And before he could say another word, she had stepped down from the boardwalk and crossed Sixth Street, weaving between a wagon and a steam dray to emerge on the other side.

"Daisy, wait—!"

He plunged into the street and pushed through the door into the elegant lobby of the hotel just as she smiled at the owner and he kissed her gloved hand.

"*Bonjour,* Monsieur Dupuy," she said with a flawless accent. "I wonder if I might ask you a question?" She removed something flat from her reticule as Barney hung back near the door, panting and wishing he had put on a cravat before he had left his conveyance hours ago.

"*Certainement,* Mademoiselle Linden. I am at your service."

"I wonder if you recognize this man?" She slid the picture she had shown Barney earlier across the counter.

"*Mais oui.* This is 'orace Makepeace. 'E 'as just returned from inspecting 'is investments in Leadville and has booked the Grand Suite. May I ask what is your business with 'im?"

"Would you be so kind as to leave him my card? I have something to tell him regarding a ... family matter. He may reply to me, if he chooses, by a message sent with the boy Davey, who knows where we are staying."

"And may I not know?" Mr. Dupuy looked puzzled and not a little worried. "'Ave you left us for another 'otel, mademoiselle? Was the 'Otel de Paris not suitable?"

"Oh, no, no, sir." She laid a reassuring hand upon his sleeve. "We are simply staying with friends, and I should like to respect their privacy."

"Ah." The man was all smiles once again. "I shall give 'im your card the instant 'e returns."

*"Merci beaucoup, monsieur. Au revoir."*

He bent over her hand once again and Daisy sailed past Barney as though he were not even there.

"Daisy—Miss Linden—deuce take it—"

At least she allowed him to open the door for her. And to walk by her side, apologizing, halfway to the post office. At which point she relented.

"You observe that several of our speculations have been proven true. The man in the portrait is confirmed to be Emma's father. He is not a gentleman, and in fact is capable of violence."

"Yes, but—"

"Will you go with me to inform him of Emma's death? I do not wish to be alone with the man who injured Lin."

He noticed she did not speak aloud her last speculation— that the man might be a murderer—while several people passed them on the public street. "Of course, but—"

"Thank you, Mr. Barnicott. I hope you will join us for supper. Now, if you will excuse me, I must buy paper and send a pigeon."

> *Captain Lady Alice Hollys*
>    *HMAS Swan*

> *Dear Captain Hollys,*
>
> *I hope you and Sir Ian and your crew are well, and that the celebration of your mother's marriage was everything you hoped it would be.*
>
> *I am writing to you today to request any information you may have about the man whose portrait in pencil I enclose. It was taken from a daguerreotype found in a scrapbook belonging to Miss*

*Emma Makepeace, whom you will remember from our voyage to Denver from New York. I deeply regret to inform you that Emma was murdered in the early hours of what was to have been her wedding day. Instead of performing the happy duty of bridesmaids for her, Frederica and I are still in Georgetown, attempting to discover who could have done this awful thing.*

*The man in this sketch was guilty of violence upon the person of a young woman here. We have identified him as Horace Makepeace, Emma's father, who was until recently a resident of London. If you or someone among your connections there has any information about him or Emma, about their relationship, or about their friends and pursuits, I beg that you will vouchsafe it to us. Even the smallest detail might assist us in our inquiries.*

*Yours in friendship,*
*Margrethe (Daisy) Linden*

# CHAPTER 22

## THURSDAY, AUGUST 8, 1895

*2:05 p.m.*
*Georgetown*

By the next day, as Mr. Barnicott and Davey busied themselves—much to the hens' consternation—in letting enough air out of the contraption's fuselage to sink it from view behind trees and rooftops, Daisy's temper had long returned to its usual equilibrium. To her relief, the small roast and vegetables turned out well, and the trifle was a positive triumph, so the midday meal was a congenial affair and Mr. Barnicott took care to keep any lingering skepticism out of his remarks.

When dessert was cleared away and the dishes done (he'd even volunteered to wipe them), Daisy fetched the little pile of Emma's letters to Mr. Hansen from their place in the lower drawer of the wardrobe in the bedroom.

"We know that Mr. Makepeace is a man of violent temper," she said, untying the ribbon and spreading them upon the dining table, "but we do not know more than that. I have a proposal. Let us all read these letters again, this time with an eye to clues as to whether his temper was ever directed at his daughter. Or if not he, perhaps another suspect might have been in the company that Emma was keeping."

"But you already read them," Freddie objected. "We found the reference to Mr. Meriwether-Astor, and look how that turned out."

"How did it turn out?" Lin asked.

"We accused the wrong man of being the father of her child," Daisy said unhappily.

"To his face?" Mr. Barnicott wiped the amusement from his own when Daisy shot him a sharp look.

"How were we to know that Hugh Meriwether-Astor had a brother?" Freddie shrugged. "Anyone might have made the same mistake."

"Hugh Meriwether-Astor?" Davey repeated. "Him what's renting the house on Taos Street and goes into the mine every day even though he's a gentleman?"

"Yes, the very one." Freddie reached for several letters and opened the first. "He says he wishes to learn mining from the ground up."

"Ground below, more like. You wouldn't catch me going down the shafts, even if they let me put great hunks of silver in me pockets." The boy shivered. "No dark little holes for me, no sir."

"They will bury you in one, you know," Lin informed him, most unnecessarily, Daisy thought.

Mr. Barnicott forestalled what was surely about to become fisticuffs with a return to the subject at hand. "I agree that the letters could be most illuminating. It would be good for us to be prepared, now that Davey has brought us Makepeace's note."

For the gentleman had written this morning to say he would be at home to visitors in the parlor of the hotel at ten o'clock the next day.

"An excellent idea," she said. "Set aside any that might be helpful."

They had left off reading the top letter at Mr. Sydney Meriwether-Astor's name, but there were at least a dozen others. Now and again a phrase leapt to Daisy's eye that had less to do with suspects for their list than with the hollow strangeness of Emma's life. Had Mr. Hansen remarked on its peculiarity, too, as he read?

*Papa insists on my going to these affairs, though I cannot imagine why when the likelihood of my marrying anyone there is nil.*

*You will think me very deceitful, dearest, when I tell you that I managed to escape Mrs. Hartwell's watchful eye this afternoon by the simple expedient of going out the study window, having thrown down my hat and gloves beforehand. I must see my literary club and read my letters there.*

*No callers today, except for Mr. Lewis Protheroe. Papa practically ran him off the property, poor boy. He might enjoy the regard of the Dunsmuir set (and rumor has it he has been acknowledged by the Queen herself) but he hasn't any money. Consequently, though his Persian roses were very fine, they fell victim to Papa's new cane. At one stroke, all their poor heads lay about the lawn like those of Anne Boleyn's lovers on Tower Green. Did you ever study English history in the Norse Kingdom, dearest? There are some very dark periods, I must say. Matrimony was hazardous at best when it came to kings. I much prefer a more humble man, with whom a cottage can become a veritable castle.*

"Lewis wanted to court Emma?" Freddie exclaimed. "Isn't he a dark horse—I wonder if Maggie and Lizzie know?"

"You know that gentleman?" Mr. Barnicott said, looking up from the sheets in his hand in some surprise. "I must say that reading these letters is like reading a novel. One has the sense that such things are not a part of real life."

"Mr. Protheroe is very real. He is secretary to Lady Claire Malvern, who is a member of the Royal Society of Engineers and an intimate of Lady Dunsmuir. I have spoken with him myself," Freddie said. "How strange and small this world is."

*Sir Warren Weatherley called this morning, but was told that I was not at home to visitors. I am not at home to anyone, it seems, other than Lady Dunsmuir or young Lady Selwyn, both of whom I rather like. It is ridiculous that Papa insists I go to these events when he forbids me to receive the subsequent callers. Not that it matters to me, but I do feel for them. They are sincere, poor chaps, so I do my best to see that the collection of their flowers in the sitting room is not neglected. At least the ones that make it through the door do not have their heads lopped off.*

In the end, the collection of letters containing telling lines numbered more than those that did not, and a chilling and distressing picture had formed.

"Poor lady." Davey could not read, but he listened as intently as the others while line after line was read aloud. "Seems he kept her a right prisoner, innit?"

"But why?" Daisy could not understand it. "Why insist on balls and parties, on having your daughter accepted as being out and available for courtship, and deny every caller but married and titled ladies? It does not make sense."

"The only reason she went along with it is because it provided a veil for her true activities," Freddie said. "Imagine the torture if she had not had Mr. Hansen's promise to sustain her."

*Torture.* The word sank in around the little table.

"You may have hit on it, Miss Frederica," Mr. Barnicott said slowly. "It does seem like torture. To a woman of her looks and accomplishments—" He nodded to the portrait propped on the mantel. "—whom no one could blame for wishing to be married and freed from such a suffocating existence, it *would* be torture."

"He was taunting her," Lin said. "Showing her what she couldn't have. Showing all those fancy people what they couldn't have, either."

"But *why?*" Daisy asked again. "Surely any reasonable man would not keep a young woman to himself—spoil her life for his own convenience. It is not as if he needs a nursemaid."

"It happens in Mr. Charles Dickens's serials all the time," Mr. Barnicott said, most unexpectedly.

"You read Mr. Dickens?" Daisy said in surprise. "He is banned in England, you know, for criticism of the government. I believe he was asked to leave the country, for his readings were stirring up not only crowds, but riots."

"He is doing very well here," Mr. Barnicott said. "As is the gentleman who writes the *Tales of a Medicine Man*, which share some similarities. I saw Mr. Dickens on one of his lecture tours in Boston. His stories can be harrowing, but he insists they all have a basis in truth, as all good stories ought."

But Davey was not to be put off by talk of people he had never heard of and couldn't read anyway. "So are you still going to meet with that man in the morning, miss?"

"I fear I must, now that he has agreed to receive me." Daisy's glance took in both him and Mr. Barnicott. "We have a great deal to think about. But I fear I do not have the courage to ask him outright why he was keeping his daughter a virtual prisoner in their house. Nor whether he might have killed her on Thursday night. He might take his cane to me."

"Best stick to condolences, miss," Davey advised. "And me and Barney, we'll be with you."

"Thank you, Davey. Without your company, I am sure I could not bring myself to go at all."

*Friday, August 9, 1895*
*10:00 a.m.*

The next morning, Daisy dressed as carefully as her limited wardrobe would allow. Her navy walking suit and hat were an appropriate color for a condolence call, despite the yellow in the hat's ribbons, and in her reticule she carried a handkerchief and her sketchbook and pencil. The latter seemed to have become necessary wherever she went. Likewise, Mr. Barnicott had unearthed a coat that might once have been black, but which had rusted along the seams to a sort of violet blue. And he wore a cravat, which made him look much more formal and ... older.

Perhaps this was how he would have looked all the time had he remained in the Fifteen Colonies in his previous life. A life about which he had never spoken, except in asides such as that regarding Mr. Dickens. A life about which she would probably never know.

Wasn't it strange how quickly one could become used to another after such a short acquaintance? She was quite sure it had something to do with his living in the garden, where he seemed to be agreeably more than a neighbor but less than a lodger.

After leaving Davey on watch at his usual post between the hotel and the opera house, they were shown into one of the private parlors used by the commercial travelers, which was set for tea. Daisy recognized their quarry at once. Mr. Makepeace occupied a table in the middle window, a choice location from which he could see nearly all of Sixth Street, and had no doubt observed their approach.

He rose. "Miss Linden?"

There were Emma's eyes, yet ... not. Hers had brimmed with warmth and humor. These were somehow hard, and he looked them over carefully. Though not, thank heaven, with the lascivious contempt he had used on Friday last. There was no recognition of that occasion in them, either. She supposed she could be thankful for that.

"Yes." This call would be one of the shortest of its kind, if she had anything to say about it. "Thank you for seeing us, Mr. Makepeace. This is my ... neighbor, Mr. William Barnicott."

The gentlemen shook hands, and then Mr. Makepeace waved them into a pair of chairs opposite and invited Daisy to pour the tea. While she did so, Daisy observed him—the broad shoulders, the taffy-colored hair that had not shown to much advantage in the sepia daguerreotype. And here again was the plum brocade waistcoat, a little too showy for a gentleman. It had probably cost as much as her entire suit. The breadth of it, she realized now, did not come from fat, but from a muscled, stocky build. As he passed a plate of biscuits, she saw his hands were those of a workman, thick-knuckled and having no elegance, but possessing instead a sense of quick and final competence.

Had he been living closer to the land, every rooster within half a mile would have given him a wide and leery berth.

"To what do I owe the pleasure of this call?" He sat back in the gilt chair and made it creak. His accents were those of the Fifteen Colonies seaboard, which she could only recognize because she had been hearing them in Mr. Barnicott's speech all week.

"I am very sorry to be the bearer of sad news, sir," she said in an appropriately somber tone. "I do not know if you have heard already, but I very much regret to inform you that your daughter Emma passed away during the early hours of last Friday morning."

He choked on his tea and dropped the cup in the saucer. Snatching up a damask napkin, he pressed it to his mouth while he got himself under control. "I do beg your pardon," he managed, dabbing at his mouth and chin. "Excuse me. I just heard of it yesterday, but from the lips of strangers, it is quite a shock."

"Please accept our condolences, sir," Mr. Barnicott said with a glance at Daisy.

"I am so sorry you have heard through talk in the town," she said. "But we did not know you were visiting. If we had, we would have waited upon you much sooner. Such news should never be given but by a friend."

"Thank you for that." He laid the napkin in his lap, his color high as he controlled his breathing. "Clearly you were acquainted with my daughter. How do—did—you know my darling girl? I thought there was to be a wedding, but she said not a word about friends. Why have I never met you before?"

Somehow Daisy had the feeling that this was meant to make them feel small, beneath his notice. Was this how all Emma's friends had been made to feel? And how could he know about the wedding when Emma had gone out of her way to keep it a secret? Had she told him, there on the street at midnight? Had she flung it in his face that he had failed in keeping her a prisoner, and he had killed her for it? What game was the man playing, this abuser of children, this gaoler of young ladies, this possible murderer?

Her spine straightened into the kind of hauteur she had seen demonstrated in the Pump Room at Bath on the rare occasions she had accompanied her aunt and uncle there. "I am from England, as you may have observed, and am acquainted with Lord and Lady Dunsmuir and their set, as was Emma. I am sure we must have met at some time or another."

In the spindly chair next to her, Mr. Barnicott shifted, as though accommodating the size of this falsehood.

But across the table, Mr. Makepeace seemed to transform into an altogether different sort. Gone was the direct, suspicious gaze of a man sizing up his opponent, and suddenly appeared an urbane gentleman who could not do enough to see to her comfort.

More hot water was called for, and a three-tiered caddy containing iced teacakes, and a cushion for her back. All this took place as though it were expected for a woman of her station to be cosseted, as though no wish of hers was too small to be immediately granted.

Daisy was quite breathless at the speed of the change. He had shown her two faces in the space of ten minutes. Another face, it seemed, was reserved for the daughter he kept the next thing to a prisoner. What would come next?

"I am all at sea," he said when the waiters had departed. "I had no idea that Emma had friends from *London* here who could tell me of her last days. What a blessing to have made this discovery!" He beamed at them—an expression that resembled real appreciation about as much as the old-fashioned electricks in Bath resembled sunlight.

"Oh yes, she has a number of friends here," Daisy said, helping herself to a teacake with a pair of delicate silver tongs. "Mrs. Davis, the wife of a mine manager, for one. Ourselves. And the man she was to marry, of course."

His mouth worked. "I did hear something of him," he said at last, "though we have not met. Hensen ... Jensen ... some Norse name. The beast who did this."

A pang of apprehension struck Daisy, the way a rod strikes a tuning fork. "Hansen. And he is not a beast. He did not do it."

"It's a shame you did not arrive in time for the wedding," Mr. Barnicott said, laying a rather clever trap, Daisy thought.

"She married him?" The words came with the speed of a whiplash as he fell right into it. "When?"

"No," Daisy said after a moment. "She was killed in the early hours of their wedding day. Before the ceremony."

"Ah." Mr. Makepeace sat back, his fingers laced over the silver buttons of his waistcoat. "If she had, he would have come into a significant portion, you understand. Her mother's money."

"I am sure he would rather have Emma alive and well than a portion of any size," Daisy said with significantly more tartness than the lemon curd in the cakes.

"So you know the gentleman?" Makepeace asked Mr. Barnicott, but Daisy answered instead.

"Yes. He is a kind and honorable man, and is devastated by his loss." *Unlike yourself. You say the right words, but the marks of sorrow are nowhere to be seen in your face. You seem to be more concerned with your daughter's portion than her death. Is it because you caused it, sir?* "It is nothing short of tragic what has happened to him."

"We do not understand how he can be accused of the very deed that has ruined his every hope of happiness," Mr. Barnicott said. "I wish to assure you, sir, that he is innocent of the crime. We are doing everything we can to see that the real perpetrator is brought to justice."

"Well ... that is very good of you," Makepeace said from behind his cup.

"I am sure you are doing the same," Daisy said. Would that flat gaze perceive that she was acting? "Have you been able to make inquiries yourself?"

"I?" He put his cup down in the saucer with slightly more control than previously.

The china was Sèvres porcelain, with a red rim whose color would be rather challenging to mix, halfway between scarlet and oxblood. Imported from France, naturally. Only the best for Monsieur Dupuy.

"I have no intention of sullying my hands with such a sordid task while I am in mourning," Makepeace said. "Or of calling into question the competence of the Texican Rangers. I have already spoken with the lieutenant at Mad—" He harrumphed. "And expressed my satisfaction with the speed and correctness of the investigation."

Daisy couldn't keep the consternation out of her expression or her voice. "Clearly, you cannot have met Mr. Hansen if you could believe him capable of murdering his fiancée. He was very much attached to her—as was she to him."

"I doubt that," he said with the dismissive tone of utter ignorance of the matter. "Thank you for coming to condole with me at this sad time." He rose. "I have an appointment, so I hope you will excuse me. Feel free to remain for as long as you like to enjoy your tea. I reserved this parlor until noon."

And to Daisy's helpless astonishment, he bowed and walked out. A few minutes later, their excellent vantage point revealed him in top hat and coat, cane swinging in his hand, walking up the hill toward the district where several of the mines had their offices.

Mr. Barnicott's gaze moved from his receding form to the sparkling silver caddy with its sweet burden. "If I had not seen these teacakes arrive with my own eyes, I would have thought I had dreamed the past half hour. Did he really say he has known of his daughter's death all week, has been serenely conducting business in Leadville, and is perfectly happy for the man she cared for to go to the gallows?"

"He did, he has, and he is." Daisy could not eat another of the cakes. They were far too sweet, and the thought of enjoying any more of Mr. Makepeace's largesse was abhorrent.

Mr. Barnicott rose. "Come. Let me see you home. I think both of us could use some fresh air."

*Saturday, August 10, 1895*
*Noon*

*Miss Margrethe Linden*
  *804 Rose Street*
  *Georgetown, the Texican Territories*


*Dear Miss Linden,*

*Alice Hollys gave me your letter at dinner last night—how fortuitous that his lordship and I should be moored in the Northern Light also, for a little shooting with his two brothers. And of course one must enjoy a ball or two when they are given for one, do you not agree?*

*But I am being flippant, when your message was sent in all solemnity. Yes, his lordship and I, as well as Lady Claire and Dr. Malvern, have lately become acquainted with Horace Makepeace and his daughter. Emma is a jewel, and I am devastated to learn of her passing. Such a loss for us all!*

*Alice assures me that despite your youth, you are the sort of woman to appreciate frankness, so I will indulge my tendency to be blunt. There was something both peculiar and repellent about the relationship that man had with his daughter. I do not know how much Emma was able to tell you of her time in London, but one example shall serve to illustrate the whole.*

*After finagling an invitation to a ball at Hatley House, HM put forward his daughter to every eligible bachelor there, requesting introductions on the slimmest of acquaintance so that she would have a surfeit of partners. Only when her card was full and her crowning as the belle of the ball was assured was the poor girl given any respite. She was not allowed to choose her partners, and* whether tall or short, fat or thin, a rake or a gentleman, had to dance with them all.

Word came to me by Lady Claire that her own secretary, Lewis Protheroe, was denied entry to the house following one such ball—that in fact no male caller was ever permitted to see her. HM's rage at Lewis's call knew no bounds—I was told that he came within inches of striking the young man with an ebony cane. I can hardly credit it, but both Lady Claire and Lewis are the sort one must believe. When word spread about London and the invitations were consequently reduced to a trickle, poor Emma became little more than a prisoner in her own home.

I am of the opinion—shared by his lordship—that after his wife's death several years ago, HM developed a suffocating kind of love for his girl child. The boy, on the other hand, is nearly completely neglected by his father. Emma had become a mother to him.

Oh, how grieved I am that she is gone! I shall take comfort in remembering the lovely light in her eyes at the sight of a perfect rose, or her grace as she spun about the floor in the arms of someone like Lewis. He is one of the richest self-made Wits in London and would have been entirely capable of appreciating her warmth and intelligence. I am glad at least that she had friends with her at the end.

If my husband or I may be of further assistance to you, I pray you will let us know at once. I am enclosing the code for our airship, Lady Lucy, should you wish to send a pigeon directly.

In friendship, I am

Davina Dunsmuir

# CHAPTER 23

## SATURDAY, AUGUST 10, 1895

*12:10 p.m.*
*Georgetown*

To Barney's eye, the contents of Lady Dunsmuir's letter had depressed Daisy's spirits. She handed it to her sister, who read it ... nodded sadly ... and offered it to Barney. He scanned the lines written in the lady's elegant hand once—twice.

He laid the letter on the table and crossed into the kitchen, where the kettle was whistling on top of the steam boiler. He removed it, welcoming the boiler's homely warmth. The day had become chilly. The clouds were moving in; they were in for a storm before long. Almost without conscious thought, he made tea according to his grandmother's training, though it was not his house and there were two capable women present.

The simple actions comforted him, somehow.

"So," Daisy said, "we have a third party's confirmation of

what we already knew—that she was virtually a prisoner in her own home. But we still do not know what was in her father's mind to prompt such behavior."

"He is a monster, and that is the end of it," Lin put in. She had begun to walk about a little in the house and garden, which made him revise his initial diagnosis. The rib did not appear to be broken, merely severely bruised. After eight days of rest and his herbal salve, the worst of the bruises about her shoulders and back had faded, and her natural grace had returned.

It was clear, though, that the memory of that night would take much longer to fade.

Frederica laid a tray, and he brought the teapot to the little round table while she set out cups as though it were perfectly normal for a man to insinuate himself into their domestic routine. Davey had not yet come back, but she set out a cup for him anyway.

"It might explain one thing, at least," Daisy said.

"What do you mean, Miss Linden?" Barney sipped the hot tea with a sense of relief at its normalcy. "Explain what?"

"Her body," Daisy whispered. "Her stomach was bruised. She had been kicked. Why would someone stab her and then risk discovery by taking those moments to kick her as she lay dying?"

"Why indeed?" he asked.

"It was a very personal act, not the act of a random stranger," she said, her voice becoming hoarse, as though she were about to cry. "Almost as if her attacker knew she was in a delicate condition. An attacker who knew practically every move she made."

Barney had heard of a case or two at Harvard that had

ended in social disaster and the disappearance for some months of the young ladies in question. But no one had been murdered, for goodness sake.

"That is a leap I am not yet prepared to make," Barney said slowly. "We have no way to connect the two acts to a single person. We have no proof at all that the man who beat Lin is the man who killed his own daughter that same night—a daughter, moreover, who was carrying a child."

"But there is a connection ... isn't there, Daisy?" Frederica's gaze upon her sister was intense, as though she was willing her to understand something. "A single word spoken that night. *Father.*"

Daisy stared at her, then all at once seemed to comprehend her meaning. She made a violent motion with both hands, as though pushing an idea away with all her might. "Freddie, no. Do not do this."

"Not ours," Freddie said, her tone rising. "Hers. She was not telling us to be about our business. She was telling us *who did this to her.*"

"No!"

Barney was doing his best to understand, but he could not. "Are you saying that you saw Emma that night after she was attacked? Why in heaven's name didn't you say so before? This could change everything!"

"We did not." Daisy was nearly in tears. "My sister is speaking of something else. Please, let us change the subject."

Freddie lifted her chin and plowed on in spite of her sister's distress. "I saw her fetch. Emma's. She woke me at about half past twelve, bending over me. She said, 'Father,' and disappeared."

Daisy pulled her handkerchief out of her sleeve and blew

her nose, her eyes wet with distress. "You must say nothing," she whispered fiercely. "You and Lin. Not a word of this to anyone."

He had been thinking they had meant something much worse. He was no stranger to apparitions on those long nights with his rifle by his side and his knife strapped to his leg while he tried to sleep. One of them had even saved his life.

"Certainly not," he told Daisy, who looked as though she was about to fall to pieces. "One cannot use a fetch as a witness, sadly, so, as much as this casts an even deeper shadow on Makepeace, we must recall ourselves to this earthly plane. Suspects. Fathers. Children."

Having dropped her bombshell and had it acknowledged, Frederica seemed willing enough to go along with him. "If Mr. Makepeace was showing Emma off to every eligible gentleman in London at considerable expense, would he not fly into a murderous rage if he suspected she had lost her virtue to one of them?"

"I cannot believe that of Emma, Freddie," Daisy objected, clearly trying to control her emotions and return to practical matters. "One does not simply go from dancing with someone to having his child. Once again, it is too great a leap." A final dab with the handkerchief, and she returned it to her sleeve. "Besides, by the time we read of her dancing with Sydney, for instance, we know she was already writing to Mr. Hansen."

"She could have been seduced and deserted," Barney suggested.

"Or attacked, like I was, with no bully-boys to pull the man off," added Lin.

Frederica subsided, acknowledging these possibilities with

a sad nod. Daisy had lost color again, but bore up under her emotion. He had to admire that kind of strength.

"We must look at what we know, and apply our intellect," she finally said. "We know Mr. Makepeace arrived in Georgetown at most a day after we three did, because he attacked Lin Thursday night. We know that for certain, though we do not know where he was staying. Perhaps, like Lieutenant Ross, he bought a night with a girl, only at another flower house. Perhaps he was staying at the Hotel de Paris under an assumed name. Who knows? But let us say he left Madame Ophelia's and followed us to the Davises' when we went for the groom's supper. Could he have concealed himself, waiting for an opportunity to waylay her?"

"A gentleman in a top hat and cane, hiding in the bushes?" Lin's voice held the same doubt as Barney felt at this scenario. "He could not have known she would be alone on her way home. It was only chance that the rest of you left before she did."

"I think much may be laid at Mr. Davis's door for not escorting her back to the hotel." Barney couldn't help himself. "Disgraceful."

"He could not help being called away to the mine. So she was alone when she met the man—oh, for heaven's sake, let us just say it was Mr. Makepeace—on the boardwalk near the church," Daisy said. "But there my imagination fails me. One does not meet one's daughter by chance on the boardwalk and stab her."

"Maybe he was not waylaying her there on purpose," Barney suggested. "Maybe he was on his way from the flower house to the hotel by a circuitous route, so as not to be suspected of patronizing the houses across the river. And there he met her, quite by chance. Was overcome with rage that she had escaped him, and beat her."

"Are you saying that someone else came along and stabbed her?" Frederica's brows knit with her objection.

"No," Barney admitted. "The stabbing is what I do not understand. Kill his daughter for being in a family way? Why not simply have her admitted to a sanatorium or private home for unwed mothers?"

"I wish you could just ask him," Lin said crossly. "All this guessing and going round is wearing me out."

"It is a pity we cannot convict a man on revulsion alone." Daisy gazed at the teacups in a way that somehow found them wanting. "One person has the opportunity to harm her, but not a reason to. Another has a reason, but nothing with which to commit the crime. I wish the Rocky Mountain Detective would—"

A knock came at the door and she stopped. With a glance at each of them, Daisy rose to answer it.

Four Texican Rangers stood there, and though Frederica rose in anticipation, it was evident that none was the person she sought. She seated herself again in flustered disappointment.

"May I help you, gentlemen?" Daisy asked politely, though it was clear their number made her uneasy.

Four men were usually sent to make an arrest. That made *Barney* uneasy.

The gaze of the tallest one went straight past her and fixed upon Barney. A lance of cold fear darted through his stomach. What did they want with him now that they couldn't have asked him the other day in their offices?

"We're here to apprehend Mr. William Barnicott," he one said. "Come with us, if you please, sir."

"For what reason?" Daisy cried, holding on to the door as if to deny them entry. "He has done nothing wrong since the day before yesterday, when he was in your detachment helping you with your inquiries!"

"It's those very inquiries that have led us here," the one in charge said. "Mr. Barnicott, you are accused of the murder of Kathleen Shanahan, attempted escape, horse theft, and criminal concealment of a weapon."

It took a lot to render Barney completely speechless. But as his mouth hung open in disbelief and dismay, the Rangers pushed past Daisy. Two flanked him on either side, grabbed his arms, and duck-walked him out the door of the cottage while the remaining two walked ahead and behind, rifles at the ready.

His tongue loosened as his feet were forced over the threshold. "The Rocky Mountain Detective!" he shouted over his shoulder to the stunned occupants within. "Find him, quick as you can!"

And then the Ranger behind him cuffed him on the head with the butt of his rifle and, dazed, he could no longer speak.

*3:45 p.m.*

Daisy and Freddie had no more pinned on their hats so that they might dash over and collar Mr. Meriwether-Astor, demanding the detective's immediate presence, when another knock came at the door.

"They've realized their mistake," Freddie said, and practically ran to answer it.

Daisy thought it more likely that one of the ladies of the town had seen poor Mr. Barnicott's apprehension and had come to indulge her curiosity about it, so she hurried out after her sister. Lin watched from the parlor, her body partially concealed behind the door frame.

"Ranger Willets." Freddie's voice held surprise and no warmth at all. Not so eager to see him now, was she, after the arrest of their friend? "Are you here to arrest us, too?"

"Forgive me, Miss Frederica," he said, glancing over his epaulets as though he expected someone to catch him on the porch. After all, not one man but two from this house had been dragged away in the last week. Heaven forbid he should be seen to associate with the criminal element. "I must speak with you."

"Let him in, Freddie," Daisy said. "As long as he does not want to forcibly remove young ladies, he is welcome."

He stepped into the little entry and Freddie closed the door behind him. He removed his hat but did not come into the parlor, as though he realized his welcome had its limits. "I saw them taking Barney to the detachment and came through the neighbor's back garden."

"Perhaps you can tell us who Mr. Barnicott's accuser is, sir?" Daisy said. "For you know as well as we do that he is guilty of none of those charges."

"I could be dismissed if I were seen here—or if I said a word about it, miss." He stood awkwardly, turning the brim of his hat around and around in his hands.

"You will be dismissed from here if you don't," Freddie snapped in a tone that brooked no compromise.

Poor Ranger Willets looked as though she had just broken his heart. "I came to help you, Miss Frederica," he said, his fingers tightening on the grey hat brim in a way that would surely leave marks. "You must depart Georgetown and continue on your journey as soon as may be. The next train goes at six."

As though to punctuate his urgency, the wail of the departing four o'clock pierced the air in a faraway farewell.

"Why should we do any such thing, sir?" Freddie said, stiffening even more, if that were possible.

"Because I believe you to be in danger."

"From whom?" Daisy demanded. "Certainly not from Mr. Barnicott. He has been nothing but kind and helpful."

"It's Mr. Makepeace, miss. He's a very powerful man, and if he finds out you've been associating with Barney, I can't answer for what might happen."

"Oh, what nonsense," Daisy said. "The two of us took tea with him just this morning, and he was perfectly civil."

"Oh. So that's why I heard your names mentioned." Ranger Willets let out a long breath of understanding. "He was fit to be tied, miss, he was so angry when he came to make his complaint. He demanded to know who the two of you were. The lieutenant took him into his office and was telling him about Barney and his snake oil and the horses and everything, and the next thing you know, the whiskey has come out and they've both concluded that Barney must have killed Kathleen and stole the horses to hitch to his conveyance because the balloon was being repaired. The only thing that prevented his escaping justice was that the bridge was out."

"And he waited about town for three days before he brought himself to your attention?" Lin asked in disbelief while Daisy tried to untangle this wild interpretation of the facts. "That story has holes in it a buzzard could fly through."

"He was injured in the horses' wild flight, they think, and could not flee." The young man's gaze was pinned on Freddie's face as though he were pleading for his life before a bench on which she alone presided. "But regardless, your names came up too often for comfort. Breaking and entering this house. Squatting. Creating a public nuisance."

"We have permission to be here!" Daisy's breath could hardly escape her lungs at this fresh insult.

"That's why I've broken every regulation in the book to come over and warn you. Before they decide to put you in gaol as well."

What nightmare had they stepped into? "What is wrong with them? Have they no idea how to investigate anything?"

"We don't, either," Freddie said.

"At least we possess a thimble full of logic. At least we do not go around arresting innocent people on the basis of a story made up in our heads! Are the Rangers really so incompetent?"

"Most of 'em are good men and true, miss," poor Willets said, bravely coming to his comrades' defense. "We have a reputation far and wide for keeping the peace and upholding the law in a lawless land. But the lieutenant, he—" Willets stopped himself, his honest face flushing. "I may as well just say it. He's eyeballing his brother-in-law's position on the circuit, you see. With enough successful cases, he'll be in a fair way to take up the gavel when the magistrate steps down. They serve for ten years, and that time is almost up."

"Now *both* Barney and Mr. Hansen are in gaol because of politics and ambition. Not because anyone cares about upholding the law." How demoralizing. Clearly a sensible woman needed to be in charge, not these nincompoops. "Present company excepted."

Ranger Willets could not reply, only ducked his head and chewed on his lower lip.

Freddie's hand moved convulsively, as though she wanted to lay it on his sleeve to give him comfort. But before she could give herself away by completing the motion, a knock sounded on the door for the third time in an hour.

"For heaven's sake," Daisy said in exasperation. "It never rains but it pours."

A crack of thunder deafened them all, and as though it had been waiting for its cue, the rain came down in a torrent, pounding on the roof. She wrenched the door open with such force that the two gentlemen on the porch took a step back in surprise.

"Miss Linden?" Hugh Meriwether-Astor took in Ranger Willets's lanky form behind her. "Is everything all right?"

"Certainly not." She threw up her hands and turned away. He could decide for himself whether he wanted to come in. "Mr. Barnicott has just been arrested. We, apparently, are not far behind. The magistrate arrives on Monday, and—" She swung around as they closed the door behind themselves. "And *where*, pray tell, is the Rocky Mountain Detective you promised us?"

"Right here," Mr. Meriwether-Astor said.

"Good afternoon, miss." The accents of the young man beside him had been grown in the Avon River valley, right in their own county of Somerset. He lifted a battered black fedora that looked as though it had been trampled by stolen horses itself. "I am Detective Barnaby Hayes, at your service."

## CHAPTER 24

SATURDAY, AUGUST 10, 1895

*4:25 p.m.*

*T*here followed one of the most aggravating, frustrating hours of Daisy's life. Beginning with their arrival last Wednesday afternoon, she and Freddie laid out the facts and events as they had occurred—omitting only any mention of the fetch. On a piece of precious watercolor paper from the back of her sketchbook, she carefully listed the people whom they had already considered and dismissed, with the reasons they had been considered and the facts that had caused them to be crossed off.

And with every fact, every suspect, every logical point, the detective asked questions. Some they could answer. Some no human being on earth could answer, so why did he ask? And through it all, there was Mr. Meriwether-Astor, inserting himself into the narrative, contradicting her now and again, and having to be corrected or informed or finally, put in his place with a curt, "For heaven's sake, sir, do be quiet. You were not even there."

Let this be a lesson to Freddie the next time she made calf's eyes at a gentleman simply because he had velvet lapels and a nice smile!

At least Mr. Hayes listened to her answers. He read Emma's letters, the missive from Lady Dunsmuir, and studied intently her sketch of Emma's wounds. He became even more intent at the account of the similar wounds on Kathleen's body. When Daisy closed her dissertation with the news that not an hour ago, Mr. Barnicott had been arrested for that crime for no other reason than ...

"Well, I have no idea why he was arrested, because none of the charges make any sense at all, and there are plenty of witnesses to say so. So there you have it, sir. Everything we have seen and done and thought for the past week."

Lin had taken the tea tray away and washed the pot and cups, and Freddie had made a fresh pot of tea. Now Mr. Hayes sat back with his cup and sipped thoughtfully. After a moment, he met Daisy's expectant and increasingly impatient gaze. "I must say, if I were ever facing the gallows, I would want you to be in the witness box on my behalf. Seldom have I ever heard such a cogent, well-reasoned account."

Since she considered it both disjointed and maddeningly incomplete, this was a surprise indeed. "Thank you, Mr. Hayes." She took a sip of her own tea. "But two questions remain. One, however much we might suspect the father of killing the daughter, how are we to prove it? And two, how can we prove the innocence of Mr. Barnicott and Mr. Hansen without answering the first?"

The rain thundered on the roof, the sound pushing its way

into the discussion with the rudeness of a bully. "Does it always rain like this here?" Mr. Hayes asked no one in particular, glancing at the ceiling as though expecting it to spring a leak.

"As a Rocky Mountain Detective, I thought you would have plenty of experience with the weather in these parts." Mr. Meriwether-Astor was clearly still miffed at being elbowed out of the conversation.

"I am but lately come from the Royal Kingdom of Spain and the Californias," Mr. Hayes said mildly. "It does not rain like this there. I say, are you related to Gloria Meriwether-Astor, by chance?"

"Why does everyone ask me that?" Hugh huffed out an irritated breath. "Cannot a man make his way on his own merits, and not those of his relatives?"

"When his relatives are like Gloria, I suspect not." Mr. Hayes's tanned face relaxed into a smile. "I proposed to her once, you know, in what seems like another life."

"Good heavens." Daisy could not muster another word, and Freddie seemed stricken dumb with astonishment. Proposed to the woman who had prevented a war—who had entertained the affections of a prince—who had changed history—really?

"I take it she refused you." Hugh was not about to ease the way for him.

"She fled away into the sky in the dead of night." He smiled at the memory, so he must not bear any ill will toward the lady. "I suppose you could call that a refusal. But she was meant for greater things than being mistress of a country manor given to—" He stopped. "Well, back to the business at hand, and the two questions we must answer."

"We have been trying to answer them for a week, even without Mr. Makepeace in the picture," Freddie ventured. "Perhaps you can spot something we have missed."

"I do not see that you and your sister—and Mr. Meriwether-Astor, of course—have missed a thing," he said, much to Daisy's gratification. "We have the facts. We simply lack a way to connect them to find the proof we seek."

"Isn't that tantamount to arranging the facts to suit the outcome you want—the arrest of a man you do not like?" Hugh was trying to sound sober and logical, but Daisy could still hear the displeasure in his tone. He was not over his temper yet. "Mr. Makepeace is known on both sides of the Atlantic for his business acumen and his clever investments. My brother and I have sat with him at the tables of society hostesses and been dazzled at his knowledge of economics and natural resources, though he does not possess an advanced education. I will advise you now that you cannot make a mistake in finding your proof. For if he is wrongly accused, his retribution will be swift and final."

With self-control as heroic as Aunt Jane's, Daisy held back her remarks on the retribution that had already fallen upon Emma for the sin she had committed in escaping him. It had been both swift and final. Whether he was the man responsible or not, he would reap his reward for his treatment of her.

"If there is a link, we will find it," Mr. Hayes assured them. "If more facts must be flushed from the grass, we will find those, too."

"But quickly," Daisy said. "The magistrate arrives the day after tomorrow."

"So Hugh tells me." The detective nodded. "Here is what I think we should do."

But before he could enlighten them, footsteps pounded on the back steps. Davey burst into the kitchen and proceeded to track rainwater and quantities of mud all across the spotless floor.

"Davey!" Freddie cried. "Your feet!"

He halted in the kitchen doorway, panting. "You won't care about my feet, miss, when you hear what I got to say," he said, clinging to the doorframe. Then he hauled in a breath as he caught sight of the gentlemen at the round table. "Who's this, then?"

"You know Mr. Hugh Meriwether-Astor," Daisy said.

"I know of 'im," Davey said cautiously.

"You may speak freely in front of him, Davey. We have just explained all the facts of Emma's death to both our guests. This is Mr. Barnaby Hayes. The Rocky Mountain Detective. He has come to help us."

"Finally!" Davey said, then dismissed the detective to turn to Daisy, his news trembling on his tongue.

"If it is about Mr. Barnicott's arrest, we already know," she said.

"It ent that—at least, that's part of it, but not the important part. Ent you wondered where I been all afternoon?"

She had, rather. "I assumed you must have had business of your own."

"I did, and today it was following that Mr. Makepeace away from the hotel after you and Barney took tea with 'im this morning. And you'll never guess what I saw."

"I am done with guessing, Davey," she told him rather bleakly. "I am in dire need of more facts."

"Then I got a whopper for you. Remember Miss Emma said in 'er letters about 'er dad lopping the 'eads off the flowers what young gentlemen brought her?"

"I do." It was an image that lodged in the memory, especially when that same cane had been used on poor Lin.

"Well, I tried it wiv a stick while I was waiting for 'im to come out of the Rangers' office." His Cockney accent was becoming more pronounced, the flat vowels of the Territories regaining their original shape in his excitement. "You can't really do it, not like she said. Not with the heads of flowers laying all about. All you get is a bunch of petals flying, and the heads mostly stay on the stems."

"What is the boy on about?" Hugh demanded in exasperation.

"Quiet," Freddie commanded.

Hugh's mouth dropped open, so great was his affront, but no words came out.

"And then I saw 'im, miss, on 'is way back to the 'otel. He was grinning like a skull and 'e pressed a button on 'is cane and out come a ruddy great knife! And he lopped off a lady's whole 'erbacious border—delphiniums—bam!—just like that, right even with the top of her fence."

Daisy's own jaw became slightly unhinged.

"A knife. In his cane." With Lin following, Mr. Hayes left the dining room and joined Daisy and Freddie in the kitchen. "Think carefully, young man. Did it fold out of a slot in the side of the cane, or shoot from the tip?"

"Out from the tip," the boy said promptly. "Slick as you please, the bottom tipped back on a 'inge when he pressed the button at the top, and out it come—*whsshht!*"

Daisy saw the image as vividly as though she, too, had

been there. "That's it. That's what he did. He saw Emma alone by some terrible mischance and marched up to her. She did not even have time to turn and run before he prodded her hard with his cane and out shot the knife."

"Those wounds you drew." Mr. Hayes nodded, seeming to see in his own mind the scene she had painted, both with her words and in her sketchbook. "They would be produced by such a device. A circle of bruises around a deep, fatal cut. I have heard them called stiletto canes. They are manufactured in the Duchy of Venice, supposedly for a gentleman's defense against footpads. But how often are they used for much darker purposes?"

"Such as killing your daughter for the cardinal sin of caring for another man," Daisy breathed. Heedless of his mud, she fell to her knees and pulled Davey into a tight hug. "You have done it, Davey! You have brought us the one physical thing that connects Mr. Makepeace with his daughter's murder, and Kathleen's, too. The weapon he used to do it has been in plain sight all this time."

His face red with embarrassment, Davey wriggled out of her grasp. "But what are we going to do now, miss? He'll never admit to it, never."

"Not now the Rangers are his new best friends," Lin observed. She was pale, and Daisy had no doubt that they were thinking the same thing: The girl had had a very narrow escape from the business end of that cane.

"He will not admit to it, no," Detective Hayes said thoughtfully. "Not consciously. In order to get a confession, we will have to trick him into doing it unconsciously."

"How d'you mean to do that, sir?" Davey asked, still a little suspicious of the stranger in their midst. "Are you going to mesmerize 'im, like I seen once from the rafters in the opera house?"

"No, he will be awake and very aware of what he is doing," the detective assured him. "He may even take pleasure in it. All we need is one thing."

"And what is that?" Daisy demanded. She had had quite enough of mystery and incomplete ideas and people not saying what they meant. She would shake the rest of that speech out of him if he didn't get on with it, just see if she didn't!

"It is quite simple. I will lay a trap for him and lead him to confess."

"That don't sound very simple," Davey said doubtfully. "He ent a man to be led down the garden path, seems to me."

"I agree," Freddie said. "Why would he speak to a perfect stranger on such a dangerous topic?"

"You would be surprised what men do when they are drunk," Hugh said, finally deigning to enter the conversation. "We will simply ply him with drink until we have a confession."

But Daisy shook her head. "It is too risky. We have only one chance. To trap him into speaking recklessly, we must have bait that he cannot resist."

"And what would that be?" Hugh demanded. "Surely you don't mean to lure him in with promises of this poor child."

Lin gasped and would have fled had not Davey grabbed her arm and stopped her. "Wait. Miss, what do you mean? What bait can't the man resist?"

"Someone he already knows. Someone with a reason to speak to him alone. Someone he cannot imagine could be a threat to him. In a word ... me."

# CHAPTER 25

## SUNDAY, AUGUST 11, 1895

*2:15 p.m.*
*Georgetown*

The previous evening, the details of the plan had at last been worked out. It would never have taken so long, however, had not Hugh Meriwether-Astor put up such a fuss over Daisy being the primary means of drawing Mr. Makepeace in.

Ridiculous man. It had added at least an hour to the proceedings.

Davey had been dispatched with a note to the Hotel de Paris advising Mr. Makepeace that Miss Linden would be at home on Sunday afternoon should he wish to come to a decision about Emma's trunk and belongings. Daisy added a postscript that it would be a particularly good time, since her sister would be at the hymn service at church, and he would have privacy for his sad errand.

So here she was, humming tunelessly and picking flowers

in Mr. Hansen's sunny front garden as she watched Make-peace turn the corner onto Rose Street and stroll the two blocks in her direction, swinging that wretched cane. Fluffy clouds moved across a sky of intense blue like a river between the mountain ranges. Two finches played hide and seek in the laurel hedge.

Everyone was in place.

The detective had concealed himself in the wash house with the peculiar contraption he had assured her would produce the evidence they needed to take to the Rangers. Lin took refuge in Mr. Barnicott's conveyance, where she had shut herself in the sleeping cupboard with the wool blanket over her head. Hugh was in the pantry, his pistol in his hand, and Freddie was hiding behind the bedroom door, watching anxiously through the crack, her task to slip out the open window to fetch Ranger Willets the moment he was needed.

As for Daisy, the only thing to be happy about at this moment was that the fly making its way to their trap was male, for a woman would certainly have wondered why she was picking flowers in a walking suit. Snug against her chest, strapped to her body over her corset but under the blouse and jacket, was a clockwork device of a kind she had never seen before, with wires running down the sleeves to small speaking trumpets strapped to her forearms. It was somehow a cross between the Babbage computing engine and Mr. Tesla's invisible wave experiments, what Mr. Hayes referred to proudly as his Surreptitious Speech Transcriptor. It would transmit their voices to his contraption in the wash house, which would type out their words on a paper tape. It was not a telegraph. It did not use Morse code. She could not explain how it worked—she only hoped it would.

She had been this thoroughly frightened only once before in her life—on that dreadful day when she had awakened flat on her back in the red desert soil, her father gone and her mother half demented with fear and grief, screaming up at the sun.

Now she faced a man who had killed his own daughter and even worse—his own grandchild. Her mind shuddered away from the thought of those innocent lives ended so callously. And even though she was surrounded by allies, she could not help feeling that they would be too far away to help her should he brandish that cane and press the button.

"Good afternoon, Mr. Makepeace," she said as pleasantly as her pounding heart and liquefying insides would allow. "Do come in."

"Good afternoon, Miss Linden," he said as pleasantly as if he had not been plotting her arrest only yesterday. He closed the gate behind him and followed her into the house, making the very flesh creep on her back. "Thank you for your considerate offer. It had not even occurred to me to think where Emma's things might be."

She took his beaver hat and gloves, but when she reached for the cane, he leaned on it with a smile. "Old injury," he said. "It crops up most inconveniently, so I have become used to having a little support by me."

So much for stuffing the horrid thing in the boiler.

They had rolled Emma's travel trunk next to the round dining table, where her scrapbook and diary lay. The pretty leather valise sat on a chair. Emma's letters to Mr. Hansen were still safely concealed in the wardrobe, from which they would not emerge again unless Mr. Hansen wished it. Makepeace paged through the books with a semblance of interest, then unlatched the trunk and riffled through the waists, skirts, and dresses inside.

"What is this?" A finger flicked the linen bag hanging on the end.

"That was to be her wedding suit," Daisy said as steadily as she could. She must not protest the sight of his thick fingers on the fine fabrics Emma had chosen so lovingly for her trousseau. "My sister and I were to have been her brides-maids, so she showed it to us. It is beautiful."

He glanced at her. "You and my daughter are of a size?"

Taken aback, she said, "Emma was an inch or two taller, but I suppose we were fairly similar."

"Then you should have her clothes." He let fall a tailored jacket sleeve with leather knot buttons. "Goodness knows they're of better quality than you're probably used to, and I'd rather they went to you than be wasted on charity."

Wasted? A charitable act was never wasted. "But—but do you not wish to take her things home as a keepsake?"

He shrugged and pulled out a chair, seating himself while she was still standing. "She is dead. Since her mother's death when she was ten, I have had no use for women's frippery. Perhaps I might keep the scrapbook." He opened it again. "She was quite the belle, you know. I took her to all the best affairs this spring, including to your friends at Hatley House. Everyone agreed that she was the most sought-after woman in London."

Here was her opening. She seated herself and rested her chin on the backs of the fingers of her left hand so that the speaking trumpet concealed in the sleeve pointed at her lips. She lay her right forearm along the table so that the other was pointed in his direction.

Taking a breath, she plunged in. "It is strange, though, that you did not allow her partners to call upon her afterward. A number of our circle remarked upon it."

He was the fly no longer. Suddenly he was the snake, tongue flicking as he sought to scent her meaning. "Did they, now?"

"Did you not intend for her to find a husband during her season? For that is the usual purpose of making a woman the toast of the town, is it not?" Oh, how bland and civil she sounded. She hoped her face held the same polite inquiry.

"Her heart wasn't in it," he said carelessly. "She was going to stay and keep house for me, her father, whom she loved devotedly."

Daisy gave a pointed glance at the wedding suit, and his face flushed.

"She was mistress of a house at one of the best addresses in London, to say nothing of New York. What husband could offer her that? Certainly not that bounder Meriwether-Astor."

"Sydney?" His name popped out of her mouth in her surprise.

"Oh, you know him? He was sniffing around her, but I ran him off. Once it became clear he would never inherit the Meriwether-Astor Manufacturing Works, there was no point in the connection."

So there had been more than just a dance at a ball.

"From her actions, it seems the desire of her heart was for something a little less … ostentatious … in any case. And more conducive to affection and a family of her own."

"Family!" His snort held derision. "Her responsibility was to her own family—myself and her brother. I still cannot fathom how the selfish chit could get this far away. If Hansen wasn't in gaol already, I'd demand satisfaction from him. In blood."

"But he is in gaol, and likely to stay there until he is hanged. But returning to Emma, it seems you were not far behind in your pursuit. What made you suspect she planned to esc—to travel?"

"I had her followed, of course. Things weren't adding up. This book club of hers was a sham from start to finish. It didn't take long to get the information out of one of the other girls."

Daisy felt the blood draining from her cheeks as she imagined just how, with so much at stake, a young lady might be persuaded to betray a friend.

"I had business in New York, anyway, so I merely hired a private airship and made good time."

"And once you arrived here? Did you also have the information in hand as to whom she was to marry?"

"The girl gave me the man's name, and a simple request of the ninny behind the desk at the hotel provided an address. I had planned our reunion a little differently, but a chance meeting made it unnecessary."

"She must have been happy to see her father," Daisy suggested. "I have never been married, but I can only imagine my own happiness at the prospect of his being able to give me away at the altar."

"Give her away!" He had been investigating the contents of the valise, and now snapped it closed. "Hardly. I came to rescue her from her own appalling judgment. I demanded that she pack up her things and return with me to New York."

"And?"

"And the stupid cow refused. She said she would rather be

a carpenter's wife than a rich man's prisoner. You can imagine how I felt. She had every advantage that money and education could offer. Prisoner, indeed."

"Strong language to use to one's father, I must agree."

"My feelings exactly. And when she turned to run, I grabbed her shoulder to prevent her, and she opened her mouth to scream. As though I, her father, were some common miner or drunk stumbling home and looking to accost her."

"Shocking," Daisy murmured.

"Of course I couldn't allow it. She began to struggle, and she even managed to get a shout out before I—"

"Before you...?"

"Before I stopped her once and for all. Ungrateful hussy. Tramp. Whore. Breeding and disgraced, after all I did for her."

"Mr. Hansen's child?"

His glance showered disdain and loathing on her for even suggesting such a thing. "Don't be disgusting. Her body was a temple sacred to the Makepeace name."

She could see his amusement at her discomfort.

"Such a conversation to be having with an old maid! But you've brought it on yourself, Miss Linden. As did my daughter. Despite my vigilance in London, it was clear she had eluded me long enough to fall for that boy's promises. Stupid female."

Which boy? "Do you mean Sydney?"

His lip curled in a silent snarl. "To think all my efforts to bring her to the attention of an earl or a duke's son were utterly wasted. She flung his name in my face, there on the street, as though to prove my authority meant nothing. Like thousands of fools before her, she had believed him and succumbed. When he fled like thousands of men before him, it was no more than she deserved."

"But—but she did find happiness. Afterward." It must be said. One good thing must come of the ruin of a life. "She and Mr. Hansen learned to care for one another. She did have that."

His face contorted in revulsion. "What nonsense. The point is, she was of no use to me any longer."

*No use! As though she were a horse or a landau, her only value what he chose to make of it. Oh, Emma, how did you survive living with this man for so long, before you tried to make your own life?*

She must not break down. She must hold to her purpose and conclude this dreadful interview.

"So she was no longer a ... a temple, was she?" Hang the speaking trumpet—she could not manage more than a whisper. "She ran away. To marry a carpenter, of all things. After you ... pierced her disloyal heart, what did you do?"

"That's a good way of putting it." He swung the cane up and Daisy flinched.

It took every ounce of courage she possessed to remain motionless when he pushed the button at the silver head of the cane, and the wicked blade flashed out of the hinged bottom.

"She wasn't worthy of anything but a good kick. I've had dogs I wanted to treat better. Ungrateful wretch. She might have been beautiful, but deceit and disloyalty make women ugly, just like her mother. The world is better off without women like that."

Had Emma's mother died at this man's hands, too?

"Ah," Daisy breathed past her hammering heart. "This is the blade you used, then?"

"It is." The snake's gaze held her immobile, every nerve thrilling with the desperate need to flee. "You seem awfully well informed about the events of that night, Miss Linden. One might almost think you were a witness."

"No indeed," she said, her voice pitched a little high. "Would you mind sheathing that blade, sir? It is not quite proper to draw a weapon indoors."

"This isn't your house."

"No, but we have permission to stay here."

"From Hansen."

"Yes."

"Because you're on his side. Because you're trying to prove he didn't kill my daughter."

"It is clear he didn't. You have just said that you did."

Daisy had seen more convincing expressions of regret on the villains in the flickers. "I am glad you were such a good friend to Emma. It makes all this rather fitting, somehow."

"All what, sir?"

"Your death." Fear finally goosed her to her feet, watching the snake coil, about to strike.

*Take a step away. One step. Move.*

She forced her leg backward, and put her weight on it.

*One more step. Why doesn't anyone come? Where is Hugh? Detective Hayes?*

"You know far too much about events I would rather keep private. I don't know how you ferreted out the facts, but your transparent attempts to draw me into conversation have only confirmed my decision to remove you from danger."

"Danger?"

"To me, you simpleton."

"How will you do that?" Her lips were so dry they could hardly form words.

*Another step. The kitchen door is right there.*

"I have made an acquaintance who is fairly handy with the implements of manual labor. I heard from the good doctor that he has been used to steal horses, for instance, and hitch them to the vehicles of undesirables. Whereas I, the owner of a Bentley six-piston steam landau, would not know a rein from a rhubarb plant. Some things, like chatty whores, are easier dealt with in person. My friend can dig up a grave, though, and make enough room in a coffin for a second body. It's a lucky thing you girls are of a size, isn't it? Most considerate."

He lunged, and Daisy's shriek of fear escalated into a scream of sheer panic as the blade plunged into her chest.

Or rather, into the clockwork compendium of machinery that she desperately hoped had been transcribing each word they said. The blade shrieked, too, when the brass plate in the back stopped its progress to her heart and the gears and cogs ground on around it, twisting it to match their path before they, too, screeched in protest and juddered to a halt. Makepeace wrenched on the cane to haul it out for a second attempt, but the blade stuck fast, bent and mangled beyond repair.

The force of his yank, however, hauled Daisy over the table and when she landed on the floor, he lost his grip on the cane.

Pain was a brilliant flash of red and blue as her head bounced off the oak planks.

With a roar of rage, he fell upon her, his hands closing

about her throat and squeezing with all the force of which those blunt, ugly fingers were capable.

"Unhand that lady in the governor's name!" came a voice from far away as Daisy's vision spiraled into darkness punctuated by stars, moving and dancing.

"Daisy!" someone screamed.

With an explosion, the world went silent.

Was this death?

Was she a fetch? She must give her message and then she would die. Yes. Something important she must tell Freddie ... *I love you, dearest ...*

And then the flashing white stars went out.

# CHAPTER 26

## TUESDAY, AUGUST 13, 1895

*11:15 a.m.*
*Georgetown*

*I*t was the pain in her throat that eventually woke her, after an eternity spent floating in a nightmare where voices came and went between flashes of pain in heart and lungs.

Is this what the afterlife was like? For if so, no wonder the spirits were such an unhappy lot.

"Daisy? Dearest, can you hear me?"

She dragged her eyes open. Her lashes were crusty and stuck together, as though she had been ill, or crying in her sleep.

Freddie's anxious, drawn face hovered close to hers, and in a moment, joy suffused it. "Lin!" she called over her shoulder. "Run and tell Barney she is awake!"

"Water," Daisy croaked.

"Do not try to speak, dearest. Your poor throat has been horribly abused and Barney says it will take some time to heal. Here. He has left some sweet meadow tea for you that he says will help. A Navapai shaman told him how to make it. Isn't that thrilling?"

The tea, scented with summer and honey, was better than water. Thrilling indeed.

"Ba ...?" was all she could manage.

"Yes, he has been released. So has Mr. Hansen. All is well thanks to your bravery, dearest, but oh, my goodness, we've been so worried. You have been ill for two days."

Two days! "Make...?"

"Do not speak," Freddie chided. "I have strict instructions to do all the talking if you were to wake. When you fell, you see, it appears you hit your head. As though being choked practically to death by a murderer was not enough. Anyway, the floors in this house, while lovely, are also very hard. And then when Hugh burst in, he shot Mr. Makepeace, but a ball in the behind, fortunately, is not enough to kill anybody, so he was perfectly able to stand trial when the magistrate arrived yesterday morning. His was the most urgent case on the docket, as you may well imagine."

"Make ...?"

"Hush. No talking. He made a terrible fuss, saying that you had tried to blackmail him and then kill him—I have no idea how, since you were unarmed except for Mr. Hayes' Surreptitious Speech Transcriptor, which saved your life."

Daisy remembered *that.*

"Needless to say, my alarm was such that I had gone out the window some minutes before, and Ranger Willets and I returned just in time to see that blackguard stab you right in the chest, just the way he stabbed poor Emma and Kathleen. With the combined testimony of Ranger Willets, Mr. Meriwether-Astor, who of course heard everything, and the corroboration of the Transcriptor—such an amazing device, Daisy, what a pity it is destroyed!—the horrid wretch was condemned. They do not waste time here in the Texican Territories, and there are so many wealthy men in silver country that one commands no special treatment over another. He was hanged from the tree in the town square at dawn this morning."

A long breath of relief and thanksgiving rushed from Daisy's lungs, so deep that it hurt like the very devil to draw in the next one. Tears leaked from the corners of her eyes, both from the pain and from sheer gratitude that the nightmare was truly over.

Mr. Barnicott and Mr. Hansen were free.

Emma had her justice at last.

And the world was rid of a monster.

"Mind you, the magistrate wasn't best pleased with his dear brother-in-law the lieutenant's sloppy investigation of the case," Freddie went on, sounding like quite the journalist. "It became quite clear that the lieutenant's grudge against Mr. Hansen had clouded his judgment, and an innocent man had nearly paid for it with his life. A report, apparently, has gone to Santa Fe, along with any hopes the lieutenant might have cherished about succeeding to the gavel."

That was good news, to be sure, but at what a price!

They heard a commotion in the doorway, as both Mr. Barnicott and Mr. Hansen attempted to enter at the same time. Finally the latter stepped back so that the former could gently check Daisy's bruises and look down her abused throat.

"We ought to send for Dr. Pascoe," Mr. Hansen said, watching her anxiously from the foot of the bed.

"No, thank you," Freddie replied briskly. "She is awake and cogent, and all she needs is rest."

"And another cup of this tea," Mr. Barnicott said firmly. "Freddie has brought you up to date, I assume?"

Daisy nodded, then attempted a smile. "Happy," she whispered.

"I am, too." He glanced over his shoulder. "Bjorn and I are grateful to you. Without your persistence, bravery, and powers of observation, I shudder to think who would have been hanging from that tree in the square this morning."

"Do not speak of it," Mr. Hansen said. He came around the bed and took Daisy's hand, his fingers rough and yet gentle. "You must rest and recover, and be my honored guests for as long as you like. I can never repay you, Miss Linden. Never."

Her eyes filled with tears once more, and she squeezed his hand. "Daisy."

"Daisy. For if this is how you treat your friends," he said gently, "then your friendship is to be valued indeed. I only wish—" He choked and could say no more.

But Daisy knew. She wished the same thing.

When the two men had gone out, Freddie sank into the cane chair next to the bed and took Daisy's hand between both of hers. When she did not speak right away, but bit her lip, her lashes lying on her cheeks as though she was gathering her courage, Daisy squeezed her fingers. Questioning. Comforting. Giving permission.

Freddie looked into Daisy's eyes. "I saw her again, you know. Emma."

*When?* Daisy's lips moved soundlessly.

"This morning, when they hanged him. She was standing in the crowd, watching. She turned and looked at me."

*How?*

"With ... forgiveness. And love. And gratitude." Freddie's lips trembled. "And then she walked away into the mist, until I could see her no longer."

Daisy tugged on her sister's hands, and Freddie laid her head on her shoulder. Together, they wept for Emma, and for Mr. Hansen ... for the loving life that might have been ... and for the lives that could now go on, richer for having known her.

*Wednesday, August 21, 1895*
*7:50 a.m.*

"And you are certain that it will fly?" Daisy shielded her eyes against the sun as she gazed down the long hill above Georgetown, where in the distance she could see the very top of the striped fuselage of Barney's trusty conveyance. It still sat in Mr. Hansen's garden, but for how much longer Bjorn and the hens would put up with it, Barney did not know.

"It has done, most reliably, since I came into possession of it. Are you sure you want to get on this train?"

"We must. We have been here far too long, and I am anxious to begin the search for Papa."

Barney couldn't help a wry grin. "I am glad you have been here far too long. If you had not, I might have joined Bjorn in dancing the gallows gavotte."

"Mr. Barnicott, please do not be so crude. That is no joking matter." She frowned, and he was almost sorry to have displeased her. Almost.

"It's the truth," Freddie put in. "Daisy, come on. The valises are in our compartment, and the porter is wheeling up Emma's traveling trunk now." As if to emphasize her urgency, the train's whistle blew the five-minute warning.

"Miss Linden, wait—" Barney pulled off his disgrace of a hat and crushed it in his hands. He had to say it, no matter whether he displeased her again. But he hoped he wouldn't. "I should like to accompany you."

"What?" Both young ladies stared at him in astonishment. "Now?"

"Well, not on this train, but today. I should like to know that if I were to float my way south to Santa Fe, you would not object to my being there upon your arrival."

"Why—why—" Daisy seemed to gather herself. "Of course you are free to go wherever you please. Neither Freddie nor I have a hold of any kind on you."

She was so reliably proper, and at the same time so bull-headedly wrong.

"I know that. But I should like to help. In your inquiries after your father. We make quite a good team, you know, when we're not being arrested or stabbed or ... or anything." He stumbled to a stop as her spine straightened in a way he was coming to know all too well.

"Mr. Barnicott, are you saying that you do not believe us to be competent enough to search for our father? I had enough of that from Detective Hayes, thank you very much."

"Of course not. You know I have the highest regard for your competence. I shouldn't be standing here without it."

"Then what on earth would prompt such a suggestion? Of course we will part on the best of terms, and I thank you again from the bottom of my heart for your care of me when I was recovering. But really ... it will not do, you know."

He didn't see why not.

He also couldn't articulate why he didn't want to say good-bye just yet. Why the thought of floating off and finding another town that needed cures and probably never seeing her and Freddie again made him ache inside.

That spine, those erect shoulders, that direct, speedwell-blue gaze, though, all served to stopper up those words like a cork in a bottle.

"All right, then," he said at last, with his best attempt at a smile. "I wish you a safe journey. Perhaps our paths may cross again in some completely unplanned fashion."

"Perhaps," she said. "Good-bye. And thank you." Without a backward look, she boarded the train.

"I hope they do cross again." Freddie flung herself against him in a fierce hug. "Don't listen to her," she whispered, and then was gone up the steps, her skirts flicking out of sight behind those of her sister.

Barney stood for a moment, hoping that what he had just heard was ... what he thought he'd just heard.

Then, whistling, he began the long walk back into town. He had gone far enough down the road that when the train passed overhead on the terrifying, rickety trestle he was glad he would never have to cross, he caught a glimpse of two white handkerchiefs fluttering in farewell from the window of the second-class coach.

He waved back, and picked up his pace as the train chugged its way out of sight among the pines. He had already said his good-byes to Davey. Lin was staying with Mr. Hansen as temporary housekeeper while she established herself as a laundress in his wash house. With any luck, he could lift and make his way out of these mountains before the afternoon's storm rolled in.

## EPILOGUE

With both skinny arms, Davey clung like a limpet to the steps at the rear of Barney's vehicle. He had on his jacket, and the raggedy rucksack that contained all his worldly goods, but he'd never suspected that flying on an August morning would be so darned cold. His hair blew in his face as the wind eddied around the vehicle, teasing tears from the corners of his eyes in a most unmanly way.

Next to him, Lin's fingers were equally rigid as she clung to the planks of the step above the one where he sat. She was wearing his winter coat, but since it had big holes in the shoulder seams, it was probably doing her as much good as it had done him last winter, which wasn't much. But it was the last thing his mother had been able to provide for him before the pneumonia took her, and he wasn't ready to give it up yet.

"You hang on, you hear?" he said in a voice just above a whisper. If Barney caught them, there was plenty of time to turn the conveyance around and take them back to George-town. "Barney told me to look after you and I will, but you can't let go even for a second."

She might be two years older than he but she was four inches shorter, and as unpredictable as a cat. She might take it into her head to try and open the door and crawl into the rear, and that would end their trip in discovery for sure.

"I swear, if I fall, I will come back and hant you," she promised through chattering teeth. "And you know there is nothing worse than a Canton hant."

Davey did know that, in fact. He gritted his teeth, deter-mined not to let them chatter and show his own fear, while his feet betrayed him by scrabbling closer to his body all by themselves. Maybe that wasn't so bad, though. The last thing he needed was to drop a boot.

The ground fell away with sickening speed. They were as high as the ravens flew ... now as high as the eagles. What flew higher than eagles? He dragged his gaze from the terrifying sight of the mountainsides and the hungry peaks waiting to tear at them, and fixed it over his shoulder at Georgetown instead.

Barney wouldn't mind when he found they'd come along. And even if he did, he and Lin would make themselves so useful that he'd be glad in the end. They were friends. They'd make a life together, just the three of them, and leave behind for good the loneliness and hunger and danger of life on the streets.

Barney would be glad to have their company. He would, truly.

Davey watched, hope blooming like a little snowdrop in

his chest as, far below, Mr. Tesla's tower, the rooftops, the hotels, and the flower houses of the richest square mile in the world sailed away behind them into memory.

## THE END

# AFTERWORD

Dear reader,

I hope you have enjoyed *The Bride Wore Constant White*, and our return to the Magnificent Devices world via this new series. If this is your first visit to that world, I hope you will begin your adventure with Magnificent Devices Book One, *Lady of Devices*. You will find many questions answered, such as, "Who are Lady Claire and Maggie Polgarth? Where is Carrick House? Who invented the walking coop, and why are there chickens aboard Her Majesty's Airship *Swan*?"

Daisy and Freddie's adventures will continue in Mysterious Devices Book Two, *The Dancer Wore Opera Rose*.

I invite you to visit shelleyadina.com to subscribe to my newsletter, browse my blog, and learn more about my books. Welcome to the flock!

Warmly,
Shelley

## ABOUT THE AUTHOR

Shelley Adina is the author of 24 novels published by Harlequin, Warner, and Hachette, and more than a dozen more published by Moonshell Books, Inc., her own independent press. She writes steampunk and contemporary romance as Shelley Adina, and as Adina Senft, writes Amish women's fiction. She holds an MFA in Writing Popular Fiction from Seton Hill University in Pennsylvania, where she teaches as adjunct faculty. She is currently working on her PhD in Creative Writing at Lancaster University in the UK. She won RWA's RITA Award® in 2005, and was a finalist in 2006. When she's not writing, Shelley is usually quilting, sewing historical costumes, or hanging out in the garden with her flock of rescued chickens.

*Shelley loves to talk with readers about books, chickens, and costuming!*
www.shelleyadina.com
shelley@shelleyadina.com

**The Mysterious Devices series**

*The Bride Wore Constant White*

*The Dancer Wore Opera Rose*

*The Matchmaker Wore Payne's Gray*

*The Engineer Wore Venetian Red*

*The Judge Wore Lamp Black*

*The Professor Wore Prussian Blue*

## ROMANCE

### Moonshell Bay

*Call For Me*

*Dream of Me*

*Reach For Me*

*Caught You Looking*

*Caught You Hiding*

*Caught You Listening*

### Corsair's Cove

*Kiss on the Beach* (Corsair's Cove Chocolate Shop 3)

*Secret Spring* (Corsair's Cove Orchard 3)

## PARANORMAL

*Immortal Faith*

CPSIA information can be obtained
at www.ICGtesting.com
Printed in the USA
LVHW110834111118
596664LV00001BA/23/P

9 781939 087782